THE **STORY** *That* **WOULDN'T** DIE

Also by Christina Estes

Off the Air

THE STORY That WOULDN'T DIE

A MYSTERY

CHRISTINA ESTES

MINOTAUR BOOKS
NEW YORK

First published in the United States by Minotaur Books, an imprint of St. Martin's Publishing Group

EU Representative: Macmillan Publishers Ireland Ltd, 1st Floor, The Liffey Trust Centre, 117–126 Sheriff Street Upper, Dublin 1, DO1 YC43

THE STORY THAT WOULDN'T DIE. Copyright © 2025 by Christina Estes. All rights reserved. Printed in the United States of America. For information, address St. Martin's Publishing Group, 120 Broadway, New York, NY 10271.

www.minotaurbooks.com

Design by Meryl Sussman Levavi

Library of Congress Cataloging-in-Publication Data

Names: Estes, Christina author
Title: The story that wouldn't die : a mystery / Christina Estes.
Other titles: Story that would not die
Description: First edition. | New York : Minotaur Books, 2025. |
    Series: Jolene Garcia Mysteries; 2
Identifiers: LCCN 2025006133 | ISBN 9781250364135 (hardcover) |
    ISBN 9781250364142 (ebook)
Subjects: LCGFT: Detective and mystery fiction | Novels
Classification: LCC PS3605.S7325 S76 2025 | DDC 813/.6—dc23/
    eng/20250414
LC record available at https://lccn.loc.gov/2025006133

Our books may be purchased in bulk for specialty retail/wholesale, literacy, corporate/premium, educational, and subscription box use. Please contact MacmillanSpecialMarkets@macmillan.com.

First Edition: 2025

10 9 8 7 6 5 4 3 2 1

To Phoenix,
for welcoming me, challenging me,
and cheering me

THE **STORY** *That* **WOULDN'T** DIE

CHAPTER

1

It's a slow news day.

Scratch that.

It's a slow news day, according to David Matthew. There are plenty of stories to tell in a metro area of five million people, but when your executive producer has an inferiority complex about working in Phoenix instead of Los Angeles, it's an argument you often lose. We call David "Sexy" behind his back. Not because he's sexy. Because he's always asking if a story is sexy.

"Hey, it might be silly but at least it's a first." Nate glances at me from the driver's seat of our news truck.

I grunt. "Aren't you a ray of sunshine."

"You're just hangry," he says.

"And tired of chasing stupid stuff."

Nate's worked with me long enough to let it go. He flips the radio to KEZ. Christmas is six weeks away and Mariah Carey, Nat King Cole, and José Feliciano dominate the airwaves. I've never felt as rich as my first holiday season in Phoenix. Lounging coatless in a wicker chair on a slab of concrete patio, I was Oprah on the terrace of my Maui estate. After two years without snowstorms, freezing rain, and below-zero wind chills, I still pinch myself. As Nate hums along to "It's the Most Wonderful Time of the Year," I check my phone, hoping for a new text. But the same words that interrupted our lunch taunt me.

Mayor's stuck in elevator. Get to city hall.

Although Phoenix is the nation's fifth-largest city, we lack the Hollywood A-listers found in the second-largest, so on this day our biggest star is a local politician.

"Wonder how Mayor Ace is doing."

"Don't call him that, Nate. He's not our friend. He's—"

"Yes, Jolene, I know your opinion. He's an elected official and we should refer to him by his last name. But Ace is how he introduces himself and it's what everybody calls him. I'm just being conversational. That's what broadcast news is supposed to be, right?"

This time, I let it go. Not every story can be as big as the murder of Larry Lemmon, a controversial radio talk show host. To be clear, I don't need to come face-to-face with a killer again, but covering legitimate news would be welcome. My reporting on Lemmon's murder landed me on the network's radar a couple months ago, but since then it's been radio silence.

We pass the twenty-story city hall and my eyes are drawn to the sunburst sculpture above the main entrance, its copper center a nod to Arizona's mining industry. Nate takes a right at Third Avenue and pulls into the only available parking space between two oversized SUVs. I open the door and slide out, giving myself a mental pat on the back for wearing sensible shoes.

"I can carry the tripod."

"I got it," Nate says. "We'll use the backpack unit if we have to go live."

"If? C'mon, you know we will."

Nate slips black straps over his shoulders. Through the magic of cellular networks that I'll never understand, the eleven-pound device lets us report live without stringing cables from the truck. It's faster and safer.

"You're probably right." Nate grips the camera in one hand, tripod in the other. "After all, we're dealing with a mayor who is unavoidable for comment."

"And a manager who is unable to recognize real news."

Waiting on the corner for a break in traffic, we watch a woman direct a young girl to stand under the Orpheum Theatre marquee. They probably decided to wear their matching pink shirts as they giggled over homemade pancakes with fresh strawberries. The woman straightens a ribbon in the girl's hair before kneeling and taking a photo.

As we cross the street, the girl squeals, "Now both of us, Mommy!"

Nate offers to take their picture while I extend a courtesy smile and curse my phone. Still no text offering an escape.

Nate holds the woman's phone horizontally. "I'll take a couple this way to get the Orpheum name and building." He flips the camera. "And then this way. Will that work?"

"That's perfect." The mother bends down and wraps an arm around her daughter. "What do you say, Riley?"

"Perfect!"

"No, sweetie, what do you say to the man who's taking our picture?"

"Thank you."

"That's my girl." She kisses her cheek and says, "We're celebrating Riley's last birthday before she starts school. Having photos that aren't selfies will be special. Thank you."

"I understand," Nate says. "My daughter's in kindergarten."

"Don't tell anyone, but I called in sick to work so we could have a mommy-daughter day."

"Family is more important than any job."

I grab the tripod. "Nate, I'll meet you at the entrance."

As I walk by the memorial wall honoring city employees who've died in the line of duty, I realize I've avoided Mr. Unavoidable since last year's ceremony. Of course, I've seen his social media posts. Who hasn't? Somehow, the mayor managed to turn the murder of a local radio talk show host into a springboard for his own talk show. A syndicated TV show, picked up by half the markets across the country.

Nate's smiling when he arrives. "I might have to schedule a daddy-daughter day."

"Ready?" I plunk the tripod on a conveyor belt.

One guard eyes our gear through the X-ray machine and another asks, "Are you here for Mayor Ace?"

Nate smirks at me. "We are here for Mayor Ace. How's he's doing?"

"Oh, probably getting antsy would be my guess. Been in there about half an hour."

"Anyone with him?"

"Yep." He jams thumbs into belt loops and hikes up polyester pants. "PPD. That's personal protective detail."

Near the faulty elevator, a congregation has gathered, heads bowed in devotion to digital devices. Sexy must be psychic because he texts for an update.

I respond with, *We just got here.*

You need to post! Mayor is.

"I'll get a few shots while you figure out what's going on." Nate pops in an earbud. "I'll be listening. Here's the mic."

Holding a microphone with the station's call letters is like walking into a political fundraiser waving a wad of cash.

"Hi, Jolene, nice to see you again."

It takes me a second to recognize Faith Williams, the mayor's chief of staff. Like the mayor, Faith has changed since the radio host's murder. She's traded conservative blazers for trendy dresses. Dropped eyeglasses and added fake lashes. But her focus remains the same: making her boss look good.

"Did you see Mayor Ace's posts? Is that what brought you here?"

"The station texted us to come. That's all I know." I raise the mic so Nate can listen in. "Can you fill in the blanks?"

"Happy to. The mayor was heading to a meeting with the human services team on the eighteenth floor to express his gratitude for their hard work when the elevator got stuck. Inside, the button for eighteen is lit. Outside, seventeen is lit. We're waiting for the technician to arrive." She peeks at her phone. "Are you going live?"

Not if I can help it, I want to say. Instead, I ask who else is in the elevator.

"One officer is with Mayor Ace, a member of his security detail. Once the technician's here, we're told it should take about fifteen minutes to open the door." She inches closer and lowers her voice. "But we can hold off if you need more time to set up a live shot."

I drift back. "No, no. That's unethical. Besides, if you were stuck wouldn't you want to get out as soon as possible?"

"Most definitely. However, we are talking about Mayor Ace. As you know, he has a flair for drama."

And a knack for getting fluff coverage.

"Any idea what went wrong?"

"Not yet," Faith says. "Could be a blown fuse. It's happened before." She gestures to the elevators. "There's been talk of replacing them, but you know Mayor Ace, he's all about fiscal responsibility and making sure taxpayers get their money's worth. With proper maintenance, we should get a few more years out of them."

"Thanks for your help, Faith. I need to check in with my producer and photographer."

"My pleasure. Let me know if I can do anything. You have my number?"

I nod.

"And just so you know, the mayor still has cell reception, so you could even talk to him during your live shot. Or maybe you could be reporting live as the door opens. That would be fun!"

Yikes. Is she related to Sexy?

As I make my getaway, Faith calls out, "I'll keep you posted. I can give you a countdown to the door opening."

To avoid wasting time texting back and forth, I dial the dreaded hotline. Producers from the four, five, and six o'clock newscasts can jump on. It's meant to provide clear communication for everyone at the same time, but people are often multitasking, not listening, or in Sexy's case, hearing only what he wants to hear—accurate or not.

"Why aren't you posting?"

"David, I've been here all of five minutes. First, I gathered information. Then I thought you might be interested in what I learned. But if you'd rather I hang up and post, I can do that."

"How about you skip the sarcasm and tell us what you have?"

After I explain, David suggests I look at the mayor's posts. "He tells a much more interesting story."

"Because he's the one stuck. And he's a politician. I'm a reporter." I watch Nate come down the grand staircase. "Nate's shooting video and we can talk to the mayor after he's out. You'll have stories for the early newscasts."

"Jolene, have you learned nothing from our social media meetings? The story's happening now. You're live on the scene of a big-city mayor trapped in an elevator. Any other stations there?"

"No."

"How about going live on Facebook as he's freed?"

Freed? He's not leaving prison after being wrongfully convicted.

"Oh, looks like the mayor's chief of staff is waving for me. Gotta go."

"Get posting."

I stab the red button to disconnect but David beats me to it.

"What's the word?" Nate asks.

"Technician's on the way," I say. "Then it'll take about fifteen minutes to get the mayor and one officer out. Can you keep an eye on the mayor's chief of staff?" I hand him the mic. "She's by the security desk, in the purple dress. I need to take photos and post."

Nate sticks the mic in his back pocket. "No problem. All I need is video of the door opening."

After snapping a shot of the atrium with the elevators in the background, I circle around the crowd to get a tight shot of the elevator doors.

"Ma'am, I'm going to have to ask you to move back."

A tall woman wearing brown pants, a beige shirt, and a stern expression blocks my view.

I point to the lanyard with my press ID. "I'm a reporter. Just need to get a photo."

"Ma'am, I'm sorry. I'm not authorized to let anyone pass. We have an emergency response team on the way."

"Yes, I know a technician is coming, but I won't be in the way, I promise. It'll take thirty seconds."

"Ma'am, you are not—"

"Need help?"

The mayor's chief of staff can not only spot a microphone from a distance but also smell a reporter in trouble.

"Hi, Faith. I just need to get a little closer for a quick pic."

Faith shows the guard her ID and promises to escort me.

"Ma'am, my orders are to keep the area secure."

"I appreciate that, Officer . . . ?"

"Begay, ma'am. But I'm not a police officer. I'm private security."

"But you provide the first line of defense, Officer Begay, and I can assure you the mayor will be pleased to hear about your diligence. And he'll appreciate learning that this reporter was treated appropriately as she carried out her professional duties in keeping the public informed."

"Yes, ma'am." She steps aside, her face blazing with disdain.

I follow Faith to the elevator and snap photos of the doors and floor number. Walking away, Faith gives the guard a thumbs-up. She responds with a sharp nod.

"Thank you, Faith."

"No worries. Let me know if you want to talk to the mayor during the rescue."

"My orders are to post right now but that could change."

"I'll be around."

I move to the edge of the crowd to compose a post.

"Excuse me, aren't you the reporter who helped catch Larry Lemmon's killer?"

The question comes from a person I see every night before falling asleep.

"I'm Whitney Wright."

No introduction needed. Whitney and her brother Marcus are household names. Thanks to catchy jingles, a unique tagline, and ample advertising budget, more people on the street can name their law firm than can name the mayor. For six months straight, the same commercial has been airing on every station's late newscast. "The Wright team will get you the right results."

The real-life Whitney interrupts my TV version. "Are you interested in a real story?"

I almost say, "You mean the right story?" but her expression stops me.

CHAPTER
2

Like a good lawyer, Whitney Wright plays to my ego.

"Since you solved Larry Lemmon's murder, you'll find what I have to say intriguing."

Before I reported on the controversial talk show host's murder, I was an average reporter. No major social media following, no chance of making the *New Times'* Best of Phoenix list or being featured in *Phoenix* magazine. But when Larry lost his life, I gained a new one, granting interviews to national media and winning my first Emmy.

Whitney pulls her shirt cuffs and clears her throat like she's about to address a jury.

"I have put the city on notice that the Wright Legal Firm, on behalf of our client, is prepared to file a complaint in Superior Court over an unlawful contract."

"What's the contract?"

Scouting for potential eavesdroppers, she motions me away from the elevators. If Whitney really wants to avoid attention, she should skip the band of metal bracelets on her wrists.

"It's a flooring contract," Whitney says. "A two-year deal worth a million dollars with an option to renew."

"Sounds like a lot of flooring," I say while scanning the crowd for Faith. I can't miss the mayor's magnificent exit.

"The city owns a lot of buildings. Police and fire stations, community centers, libraries, public housing, just to name a few."

"What's your client's complaint?"

"The bid system is rigged. Same guy always gets the contracts."

"And you're saying he doesn't offer the best deal?"

"I'm saying something shady is going on." She twists a shoulder, providing a view of thick monogrammed letters on a leather satchel: WOW. "Shady enough to cause the winning bidder to verbally threaten my client's life." Whitney flicks the flap, pulls out a red folder, and rifles through papers. "Here's our letter of intent."

"Thanks." I catch Faith's eye and wave. "I'll look it over."

Whitney's bracelets clink as she clasps my arm. "There's more. Remember Rich Gains?"

I shake my head and disappointment clouds her eyes.

"He's the lobbyist who was shot and killed in his home."

"Oh, yeah. Didn't he surprise a burglar?"

"Allegedly. That was the early word from police, and reporters accepted it as the gospel. No investigation. No follow-up. Nothing."

I bite back a defensive response. With corporate cutbacks and dwindling resources, there's rarely time to report more than what you can gather in a few hours. And then there are stories that go untold because a manager makes you cover the mayor stuck in an elevator.

"What do you think happened to Rich Gains?" I say.

"Personally, I don't know, but rumor is the scene was staged. It certainly warrants a closer look. I mean, what kind of burglar caught in the act manages to fire a single, fatal shot to the chest?"

"This is Arizona. A lot of people like guns and know how to use them."

Whitney gives me the same look I give Sexy when he assigns me a dumb story.

"Okay," I say. "What can you tell me about the lobbyist?"

"In the development world, Rich was a rock star. Need to cut through red tape at city hall? Rich was your guy. Need to keep a project under the radar to avoid angry neighbors? Call Rich. Time is money and he cut it like a butcher."

"And you think his work upset someone enough to kill him?"

Before she can answer, another text from David reminds me why I'm at city hall.

Why aren't you posting?

"Whitney, I've got to go, but I'll follow up."

Her look says she's not convinced.

"I will. Can I call you?"

She hands me a card with her cell number and email. "Listen, I know Rich Gains isn't going to get you on CNN like Larry Lemmon did, but my gut never fails me. People in power count on a shrinking number of journalists to keep doing business how they want—with no one watching and no one questioning."

"I'll call you."

And I mean it. Even though I complain about ridiculous assignments, I'm lucky to be doing what I do. I get to split my week between stories I have to produce in one day and stories I get to spend more time on, stories that matter to the community. Right now, I have to figure out whether the mayor's chief of staff is doing the chicken dance or trying to get my attention.

"Technician's here!" Faith beckons for me to follow.

Nate has set up his camera and tripod near the elevator. The security guard is standing five feet from the doors, feet wide apart, one hand on a thigh, the other on a hip, like a football player ready to block.

"Should be no more than five minutes," Faith says. "I was just telling Nate the elevator car will open on the seventeenth floor. I can take you up so you can get video of Mayor Ace coming out."

"Can we trust the elevator to get us there?"

"No problem. We'll use the freight elevator. It was serviced last month." She leads us past restrooms and down a dark hall. "Please tell me Whitney Wright wasn't grilling you about the elevator."

"No."

"Wouldn't be surprised if she tried to talk the mayor into suing the city for emotional distress."

"She didn't mention anything like that."

We get on an elevator big enough to carry every TV crew in town.

"I'm surprised you guys are the only station to show up," Faith says.

"The others probably figured the mayor would be out by the time they got here," I say.

As the doors close, Faith looks at me. "Mayor Ace is probably expecting a press conference. I should've called them."

Nate's eyes widen, a signal to keep this story to ourselves. "Jolene, didn't you post the mayor was on his way out?"

I mumble something that could have been interpreted as "Mm-hmm" and peck out a line that'll make Sexy proud—or maybe chill a bit.

BREAKING: #Phoenix Mayor trapped in city hall elevator to be freed any minute.

We pass through another dim hallway to the proverbial light: doors that will bring us exclusive video. Behind it, Mayor Ace Logan is likely combing his hair and popping a breath mint. Nate clicks his camera into place and passes the mic as we wait for signs of life. A soft whir comes first, followed by an aggressive ding. The mayor emerges with a smile fit for a presidential campaign and waves at the camera.

"Hello there!"

Ace Logan could be cast as the guy in prescription drug commercials strolling along the beach with his wife, beaming with pride at their kid's wedding, and cheerfully pushing grandchildren on swings.

"Hi, Mayor, I understand you're running behind schedule but can you spare a minute?"

"I always have time for the press." He holds his phone for Faith to take. "After all, you keep the public informed."

A plainclothes officer steps out of the shot while staying close enough to take us down if our questions get too hard. Nate tugs my elbow to move me closer to the camera.

"Mayor, can you start by telling us what happened?"

"I was on my way to a meet and greet. Every week, I visit a different department to say hello and express appreciation for their hard work. It's important that staff understand how much I value their dedication to public service. Detective Martos and I got on the elevator and everything was fine until it wasn't. The elevator jerked three, maybe four times, and then abruptly stopped. We waited a few minutes, punched the button several times, and eventually called for help. Fortunately, we didn't lose cell service."

"You were stuck for more than an hour. What was it like?"

"I'll tell you what, I've been working at city hall close to two decades and ridden these elevators thousands of times. But this time was just . . ." He takes on a thoughtful look perfected by years of asking for votes and money. "I'm not claustrophobic, but when you're trapped in a steel box, you can't help but experience a tad of discomfort. I appreciate Detective Martos remaining professional, as he always does. Luckily, it was just the two of us. Had it been a full elevator, others may not have remained as calm and the wait could have been more challenging."

"How'd you spend the time?"

"As I said, we still had our phones so we were able to get work done. The good news for the public is that Mayor Ace continued doing the city's business even while trapped in an elevator." He grins. "Hey, there's your headline, right there."

You don't want to hear my headline, Mr. Unavoidable.

"Anything else you want to add?"

"I am grateful, truly grateful to my protection detail and the technician and, of course, to God, for keeping me safe so that I can enjoy another day in service to this beautiful city we call home."

"Thanks, Mayor."

Faith hands his phone back. "I posted the part about you still working while being trapped."

"Excellent. It's important our citizens know Mayor Ace is always on the job for them."

Faith offers to send me photos of the interview.

"No, thanks, we have plenty."

The mayor shakes our hands. "I appreciate you sticking around to make sure I made it out safely."

Since the mayor's brush with death ended hours before our newscast, Nate and I head back to the station and face another man with an exaggerated sense of life-and-death situations.

"Hey, Jolene, we're going to run a thirty-second voiceover on the mayor," Sexy says.

"Don't you want sound? We interviewed him."

"Nah, no time. Lots of breaking news. A brush fire off Interstate 17, car ran into a drive-thru restaurant, and I gotta prep for the social media meeting."

SMH again? Shelley Munro Hammett is a consultant the station brings in about once a year. Her specialty was rehashing ideas from the nineties and passing them off as innovative until her last visit. That's when SMH got all TMI about social media.

"She was just here."

David's eyes blink in annoyance. "Jolene, it's been two months. It's called a follow-up."

"Funny you should mention it. I have a tip I need to follow up on."

"Then, today's your lucky day. Go for it—after you write the mayor's story."

I contemplate a lead that's compelling, not cliché or boring. Ah, forget it. Whatever I write, David will change to sound "sexy," so I keep it simple and move on to what I can control: learning more about the lobbyist murdered in his home.

On his law firm's website, Rich Gains's expertise is listed as zoning and real estate development. For twenty-five years, the Chamber of Commerce recognized him as a top attorney. A recent profile from a national business magazine quoted Rich as saying, "Arizona is the best place in the United States to practice real estate law because of its increasing population and decreasing regulations."

The article includes a photo of Rich and his wife, Stacey, posing on a pickleball court named after them. A thank-you from a client, he said, for squashing naysayers who'd been making a racket about the noise a massive pickleball complex would bring to their neighborhood.

An azcentral.com story by reporting legend Scott Yang grabs

my attention. He's covered state lawmakers and governors longer than most Phoenix reporters have been alive. Scott has the tenacity of a terrier and the memory of an elephant. His story challenged the pro-growth cheerleaders by pointing out limited housing options, especially for low- and moderate-income residents. Rich Gains spoke on behalf of a developer planning to bulldoze the Home Sweet Home Mobile Home Park to build luxury apartments.

"My client has been more than understanding and generous," Gains said. "He has gone above and beyond what is required by law to ensure residents have ample time to make other arrangements. And once the project is completed, they are welcome to return as residents."

The last line is absurd, considering rents will be five times what residents of a modest mobile home park pay. The story quotes a community activist who blames city and state leaders for prioritizing developers over families. My desk phone interrupts my reading. It's Alex Klotzman, our assignment editor. He's sort of like an air traffic controller, directing us where to go and when. He can also be a vital mediator between crews in the field and managers in the newsroom.

"Hey, Alex, what's up?"

"Scanner traffic. A 900 at city hall."

"And why do I care about a welfare check?"

"Excuse me, I thought I was talking to a reporter. That's how the mayor's call started. Could be nothing, but if someone else is stuck in an elevator, I gotta tell David."

Across the newsroom, David's pointing at a computer, suggesting the four o'clock producer rearrange the order of stories in her newscast, no doubt to make them sexier.

"Thanks for the heads-up. I'm out of here. If Sexy asks, tell him I'm meeting with a source."

"About what?"

"Keep it vague but make it sound big and exclusive so he leaves me alone."

"Roger that."

CHAPTER

3

Other than escaping the newsroom, I don't have a plan as I pull out of the garage. The mobile home park that Rich Gains's client wants to demolish is nearby and I head east to Arcadia. Specifically, Lower Arcadia. Some people who live in Arcadia Proper are very particular about their boundaries. Originally home to citrus orchards, Arcadia is among Phoenix's most expensive neighborhoods, thanks to large lots, trendy restaurants, and proximity to Camelback Mountain. To the west is Arcadia Lite with smaller lots, retail chains, and indie eateries. In Lower Arcadia, the neighborhood is filled with hammers, nail guns, and concrete mixers as mid-century homes are covered in smooth stucco and stone accents. Pockets of affordable housing still exist around Lower Arcadia. Tiny pockets.

The Home Sweet Home Mobile Home Park is on the edge of Lower Arcadia, located behind a strip mall that hasn't seen business in years. I deduce this based on the 2021 Happy New Year sign and a poster promoting a pandemic special. If history is any indication, the property is owned by someone outside Phoenix with zero interest in the neighborhood. Investors love to play the holding game.

At the park's entrance, I'm welcomed by a sign:

COMING SOON: PRESTIGE MANOR, A LUXURY COMMUNITY FOR DISCERNING TASTES.

A rusted metal gate surrounds what used to be a swimming pool. Weeds and wild grass grip its edges. A ladder and lawn chairs fill the shallow end. My Honda Civic creeps along a narrow path of cracked asphalt. The sound of a telenovela drifts from a home adorned with a white picket fence. If I don't find anyone outdoors to talk with, I may go back. But if the resident only speaks Spanish, it could be challenging because I do not. An orange cat darts across the road and disappears under a home stacked on cinder blocks. To avoid clipping a Kia sticking out of a driveway, I nearly nail a mailbox. Around the corner, a man unloads groceries from a pickup truck. I flip on emergency flashers, hoping they'll prevent someone from rear-ending my car, and call out a greeting. The man's smile is wary but his manners are too good to ignore me.

"Can I help you?"

I introduce myself and explain I'm interested in learning more about the community's future.

"Let me take this stuff inside first."

Snippets of Spanish float out the window. A couple minutes later, the door opens and an older woman steps out, followed by the man. She's wearing a floral dress that hits mid-calf and brown shoes with thick soles. Her white hair is pulled back in a low bun.

"Jolene, I'd like to introduce you to my grandmother, Mrs. Dolores Rios. And I am Carlos Rios. Nana, this is the reporter who wants to know about the project. Por favor, sé buena."

"Mrs. Rios, it's nice to meet you. Lo siento, mi español es muy mal."

"Your Spanish *is* bad." Her smile is gentle. "It is malo, not mal. As you can tell, my English is fine. Come, we can sit over here and talk."

At the front of the driveway, next to a waist-high garden bed, are two chairs and a bench. Mrs. Rios takes the bench and Carlos waits for me to choose a seat. He's about forty-five, with slivers of gray in dark hair. Strong eyebrows frame observant eyes.

"What do you want to know?" he asks.

"I'm trying to understand the developer's plans and what will happen to residents. Do you both live here?"

"I used to. Nana raised me here. This has been your home for what, Nana, fifty years?"

She nods. "Fifty-one years come January. And now they want to kick me out. It's not right. I'm eighty-five years old. Where will I go?"

"Nana, you know we want you to live with us."

She waves a dismissive hand. "I do not want to burden my family. This is my home. I want to stay here. I want to die here."

Carlos's sigh signals it's not the first time he's heard her preference.

"How many people live here?" I ask.

"There are forty-four lots," Carlos says. "But ten, maybe twelve are vacant because people have already moved."

"Everything is so expensive," Mrs. Rios says. "Some had to move far away to find a place they could afford. Far away from their family and friends." Her eyes shift to Carlos. "Remember little Pablo? Qué dulce. He cried and cried when he had to leave his school." She looks at me. "There is nowhere for me to go. Nowhere I can pay five hundred dollars a month."

"You own your home and pay rent for the lot, is that right?"

"Yes. My home is old, like me, but it is all paid for." Her voice takes on an urgency. "Even if I could find somewhere else to live—and it is not possible because the rich people keep buying apartments and trailer parks—my home is too old. Not up to code, they say, and they will not let it in. I cannot afford to buy a new home."

"That's why you will move in with us," Carlos says. "We have a room ready for you."

"A room? Mijo, I do not want to be treated like a child. I am used to my home, my way of life. And what about my garden?"

"We'll plant flowers, Nana."

"It is not the same. Your grandfather and I made this garden together." Her voice returns to its original cadence. "You know, snapdragons were his favorite." She caresses a yellow petal. "I do not want to go. Mijo, you must tell your friend he cannot kick us out."

Carlos tilts forward, resting his forearms on blue jeans. "Nana, he is my employer. I cannot tell him what to do."

I ask Carlos if he works for the developer who owns this property.

"I work for the general contractor. That's who the developer hired to build the apartments."

"What do you know about the developer?"

"Never met him, but he extended the move-out date by six months so people could find other places to live. And he offered a thousand dollars per trailer if they move before the deadline."

Mrs. Rios clucks her tongue.

"I understand, Nana." He squeezes her hand and turns to me. "I also understand the developer's side."

"Did you know an attorney named Rich Gains? He represented the developer."

"Yes. It's very sad what happened."

"Sad," Mrs. Rios murmurs. "But perhaps he was not such a good man."

"Nana," Carlos softly scolds. "Rich was a good man. He helped me compete for city jobs."

"And how many jobs have you received, mijo?"

Carlos says nothing.

"Mijo applies for city jobs, but he never gets them. Tell the

"I agree with your grandmother. It doesn't sound right. Will you give your attorney permission to share information with me?"

Now his look is all skeptical.

"I don't want to do anything to hurt my business."

"It sounds like your business may already be hurting. Don't you want to change that?"

"Like I said, I don't know how far I'm going to push it. I don't want to make things worse."

"I understand. I wouldn't report anything without talking to you and Whitney first. But without access to your information, I don't even know where to start."

He glances at Nana and nods. "Okay. I'll let Whitney know you'll be calling her."

"Thank you. And make sure she knows you're okay with her sharing details."

Carlos's phone chirps. "I have to get this."

I snap a couple pictures of Nana's garden and when I turn to take a photo of her home, she's still at the window. Our eyes meet before she disappears and the curtain falls.

From the Home Sweet Home Mobile Home Park, I head to Regal Palms. There's nothing regal about my apartment complex, but we do have a dozen palm trees dotting the main drive. At eighty feet tall, they look completely out of place towering over patio-style apartments. Someone might say the same thing about a twenty-nine-year-old living in a complex that caters to seniors. When I pull into the entrance, the self-appointed Neighborhood Watch captain is on her regular patrol. Norma is also my next-door neighbor. We share a carport that separates our homes. When I signed the lease, I mistakenly thought it would be adequate buffer. Norma's outside my car before I open my door.

"Hi, Jolene." She's wearing her signature Puma tracksuit

reporter about the lawsuit you are filing." She doesn't wait for Carlos to speak. "The famous TV attorney is handling his case."

My hand goes up like a stumped student. "Wait. Is Whitney Wright your attorney?"

"Yes," Carlos says. "But it's not a lawsuit. It's more like a complaint."

Carlos says Rich Gains explained how to bid on city contracts, helped him fill out paperwork, and introduced him to staff.

"Rich told me the city wanted to spread the opportunities and get more business owners involved. They call it the small and disadvantaged enterprise program." He leans back, crosses his arms. "But it hasn't worked. Same guy who got the contracts before I started applying still gets them."

"Why don't you get the contracts?"

"His bids are lower."

"Shouldn't the city go for the lowest price?"

Carlos untangles his arms and shifts toward the edge of the chair. "The thing is there's no way he could do the work at those prices. Something else is going on."

I wish I'd studied the document Whitney gave me. I don't know enough about flooring or city contracts to know if Carlos has a valid point or if he's a sore loser.

"Mijo, tell her about the bad accountant."

I keep quiet. If Carlos doesn't fill the silence, I'm confident Mrs. Rios will.

"This whole thing has been really hard," Carlos says. "The guy who gets the contracts, Kris Kruger, used to be my boss. I suspected his accountant was fudging the numbers."

Mrs. Rios opens her mouth, ready to jump in, then changes her mind.

"Kris's former accountant submitted the bids and they were too low. There's no way Kris would've approved them. Before my attorney filed a complaint against the city, I tried to tell him."

"He got mad at Carlos," Mrs. Rios says.

"Why?"

She gives a half-hearted shrug, like it's not her place to spread stories.

"Kris felt betrayed because I left his company to start my own. It was nothing against him. It's always been my dream to have my own business."

I tell Carlos I met his attorney at city hall and she mentioned Kris had threatened his life.

"He was upset," Carlos says. "Said some things he shouldn't have, but it wasn't anything serious. Kris is passionate about his business. Just like me."

Mrs. Rios makes a tsk sound. "But you would never threaten someone. He should be thanking you for warning him about the bad accountant. If he doesn't want to listen to you, that's his fault."

Carlos pulls back a sleeve to check his watch. "I gotta get back to work."

"If it's okay, I'd like to take a photo of you both. In case I need it for a future story."

Carlos is reluctant but Mrs. Rios pats the bench for him to sit. "We must do all we can so people know how the rich developers are hurting hardworking families."

I text the photo to Carlos and save his number.

"Mrs. Rios, I'm sorry you're dealing with this."

"You can call me Nana. Please tell people what is happening. We need help. We cannot lose our homes."

Carlos guides his grandmother up three steps, kisses her cheek, and closes the door.

As we walk to his white pickup truck, he says, "I hope you understand my situation."

"Of course. When professional and personal lives collide, it can be difficult."

"Nana is more than my grandmother. She saved m her everything."

His words punch my throat.

"Me and my sisters ended up in foster care, all in c homes. We were separated for years."

I grind a thumbnail into my palm, a trick to keep t away.

"If Nana had not taken us in, I could've ended up i like my father. Or like my mother—dead."

The tendons in my palm are screaming. I push hard

"I'm sorry," Carlos says. "I don't usually talk about sure why I did."

Maybe you have foster care radar.

"After all Nana has done for me, I need to make thin for her."

Tears blur my vision and I struggle to make out the his truck: MIJO'S FLOORING.

"Some guys make fun of my company name but yo what? Nana loves it and her opinion matters more than else's." He opens the door. "It was nice meeting you, Jol

"What about your complaint against the city?"

"Whitney says we wait for their response. She expec to play hardball and thinks we should keep pushing. B yers are expensive and, even if she can prove cheating o thing else, it's not like I automatically get a contract would have to fix the process and probably start all over He looks past my shoulder, smiles, and waves to Nana watching from a window. "I have a family to take care o business to run. Not a lot of extra money or time for a lega you know?"

"What if I look into it?"

I can't tell if his expression is suspicious or confused.

"Why?"

and a new pair of Skechers. Norma waves a paw. "Baby says hello."

Baby is a ten-pound shih tzu named Tuffy. He's not fond of me and the feeling is mutual. What Tuffy doesn't understand is I have valid reasons to stay clear of canines. Being attacked as a child can make you skittish as an adult.

"How was your day?" Norma asks.

"Fine, how about you?" I reach in the back seat to grab my bag as Norma chatters on about something she's looking forward to.

"That's nice," I say. "See you later."

I unlock the door leading into my kitchen. The oak cabinets, ceramic tile countertops, and white refrigerator would make the perfect "before" photo on a makeover show, but it works for me. I've never turned on the stove or dirtied enough plates to miss not having a dishwasher. Neither has Oscar, my roommate.

"How you doing?" No response, as usual. "Oscar, you can't be mad at me. You're getting dinner on time."

As I reach for his goldfish flakes, my eyes drift to a wooden box in the corner. Not long after my grandma took me in, I painted the box and presented her with my first gift ever. It took a few years before I caught the spelling error: I had painted GRANDMA'S RECEIPES. She never pointed out my mistake, but she couldn't hide her frustration when trying to teach me to cook. Gathering ingredients and taking time to prepare a meal never clicked for me. I was a sneaky snacker and frequent hoarder. Side effect of going hungry as a child. Although we didn't connect with cooking, we bonded over *Wheel of Fortune*. Grandma had a crush on Pat Sajak and I dreamed of being as glamorous as Vanna White. I never heard "I love you" from my grandma, but often heard "Good solve" when I figured out puzzles before the contestants.

I grab a half-full bag of Food City chips, an almost empty container of salsa verde, and a bottle of Pepsi.

In the living room, Jim Thornton smiles and welcomes me to America's Game. "Ladies and gentlemen, here are the stars of our show."

Grandma would've been devastated when Pat retired. When he announced his plans, I started recording episodes so I would always have shows with Pat and Vanna together, the way I watched with my grandma.

The bonus round puzzle is a phrase. Keep your eyes on the prize.

CHAPTER

4

The next morning Sexy wants an update on my so-called investigation. Management is betting we'll find cupcakes advertised as gluten-free that contain gluten.

"It's slated to air before Thanksgiving," Sexy says while scrolling social media sites on two computer screens.

I resist the urge to question how it's on the schedule to air when they haven't even been tested. What if they're all gluten-free, as advertised?

"It's news people can use," he says.

More like "News Lou can use." Lou is the station's general manager. His wife has a gluten intolerance and claims she bought gluten-free cupcakes that gave her horrible stomach pains. Her pain led to my pain because Lou suggested an investigation and David, always angling to move up the management food chain, chomped at the opportunity.

"Pamela Worthy is getting samples today," I say.

"That's great experience for our intern," Sexy says. "What about you?"

"On it."

I head to the reporters' pod on the other side of the newsroom.

It's the quietest time of day. Morning show crews are in the field and I'm the first dayside reporter in. By nine thirty, things will be buzzing. Morning crews putting their final stories together, the editorial meeting underway, reporters scheduling interviews, and newscast producers planning their rundowns.

Before I visit any bakeries, I need to talk to a lawyer. On hold, I'm treated to the Wright team's most popular commercial. The image plays in my mind. Standing back-to-back, Whitney points a thumb to her chest and announces, "I'm right." Marcus pokes a thumb to his chest and declares, "I'm right." They spin toward the camera and, in unison, say, "We're both Wright. And we'll make sure you're treated right."

In the middle of reciting their toll-free number, Whitney picks up the phone.

"Carlos told me you visited the mobile home park," she says. "I must say I'm shocked to hear from you so soon."

"I was surprised to learn about his connection to Rich Gains, the lobbyist."

"Hold on. If you presume Carlos had anything to do with Gains's murder, you are way off base. Carlos's issue is with the city."

According to the Wright Legal Firm, the bid process is all wrong because it lacks transparency. Whitney says the document she filed is basically a warning that a lawsuit could be coming unless the city takes immediate action to remedy the problem by awarding the contract to Carlos. While Kris Kruger submitted the lowest bid, Carlos had the second lowest. The letter of intent claims an unnamed city representative provided an unfair advantage to a person or business that ultimately misled and harmed other bidders.

"We're alleging collusion after Carlos twice failed to win the contract," Whitney says.

"You think someone was working with Kris Kruger?"

"We don't know for a fact he has inside help, but it's a logical guess and enough to proceed."

"Carlos mentioned an accountant who used to work for Kris. Do you have her contact information?"

"Yes, Simona Park. Asking my assistant to email you." Over the keyboard's clacking she says, "It's not right for people who work hard and play fair to get screwed by the system. Carlos deserves better. Listen, I've got to run, but I'm available after lunch if you have questions."

I review the document Whitney gave me when we met at city hall. It's light on details, heavy on legalese. Definitely not sexy enough to hook David. But it is real journalism, a textbook case of what we should be doing: holding the powerful accountable. "This is actual news people can use."

"Talking to yourself again?"

The question comes from Elena Ramirez, my desk mate, fellow reporter, and a newsroom favorite. She regularly brings in cakes and cookies and keeps a well-stocked candy jar on her desk.

"What's the news people can use?" Elena asks.

"Questionable business at city hall."

"Look at you, chica. Flexing your J-school creds." She tosses a bite-size Snickers on my desk.

"If only Sexy were half as impressed. What are you working on?"

"Covering a press conference with police and the county attorney." Elena logs on to her computer. "They're announcing arrests in a retail shoplifting ring." She pushes her chair back. "Speaking of shopping, check out my new kicks." She jiggles a foot.

"Whoa, I need shades."

Silver glitter coats her low-top sneakers, the soles gleaming with beaded pearls. Elena's the queen of comfy-cool footwear.

My talent is digging into a story, and I direct my boring flat shoes to Sexy's desk.

"Hey, got a minute?"

David looks up, but his fingers keep flying across the keyboard.

"I want to run something by you."

"Go."

"The city has been notified that a lawsuit could be coming. A small-business owner is alleging corruption."

David's fingers freeze. His hands plop on armrests and he swivels my way.

"Is this supposed to be news? Because most people assume city hall is corrupt."

"We're not in the business of assuming, are we? We should be investigating."

He gives me the cue to wrap it up: moving his hand in a circle with an index finger straight up.

"This guy claims the city was working with his competitor, giving him an unfair advantage to win contracts."

David makes a face. I don't know if it's because of my pitch or the morning show director passing by with a bag of burnt popcorn. David asks how much money is involved.

"A million dollars," I say.

"And how much is the city's annual budget?"

"Do you mean the general fund only? Or enterprise and revenue funds, too?"

David's head lolls back and forth on his chair. "News flash: this isn't NPR. We don't do ten-minute budget explainers." His head goes still as he stares at the ceiling. "Tell me the budget normal people think of, not convoluted government speak."

"That would probably be the general fund only. That's money from property and sales taxes that goes to police, fire, parks, libraries—"

"Yeah, yeah, how much?"

"I don't know the exact amount off the top of my head—"

"We're not going on the air with it. Give me your best estimate."

"About two billion dollars a year."

"And you're talking about a million-dollar contract? That's less than one percent of the budget. Much less if you combine the other stuff you rattled off. Most people wouldn't bat an eye."

"But it's our tax dollars. There are a million reasons why people should care. It's our job to make them care."

"Right now, I care about our newscasts having enough content. Would you like to help by attending the editorial meeting and pitching a story you can turn today? Or are you going to make progress on the cupcake investigation?"

"David, this is a story everyone can relate to: a regular guy taking on the government. It's worth looking into."

"Get me video of someone handing bags of cash to a politician—preferably clear bags so we can see the money—and I'll give you five minutes at the top of the show."

"You're on."

"But today, get those cupcakes."

I grab the undercover gear and text Pamela, the intern, a reminder to take extra batteries when she heads out. We split a list of twenty bakeries and my first stop is a strip mall as outdated as my kitchen. Before leaving my car, I double-check the equipment and place a recorder the size of a smartphone inside a black purse. Clipped to the outside is a camera disguised as a pen. My stomach is growling but my brain knows better than to eat anything from this place. The guy behind the counter alternates between pushing buttons on the register, brushing hair out of his eyes, and selecting cupcakes—all without wearing gloves.

I squat and prop the purse against my chest to get a close-up of a sign that promises GLUTEN-FREE and duck-walk to shoot video of a sign that reads, FRESH BAKED.

After ordering one gluten-free chocolate cupcake with chocolate frosting, I imagine Pamela filling a box with sprinkles of every hue: pink and purple, blue and green, red and yellow. Sprinkles shouldn't impact the tests but the lack of uniformity could influence audience perception. I text her to only order cupcakes with plain frosting, no toppings. She responds by asking what flavor cupcake.

Doesn't matter.
          What about frosting?
Doesn't matter.
          Can I mix them up?

These are not the hard-hitting questions I expected after landing a job in a top TV market.

You can do any cupcake & frosting flavors. No toppings.

She replies with a string of emojis I'm struggling to decipher when a text from Alex stumps me more.

963. Need you to go.

Why does Alex want me at a car accident? Maybe I got the code wrong.

Crash?
          Fatal.

Unfortunately, deadly car crashes are not uncommon. What's less common is sending me. As a hybrid reporter, I'm fortunate to usually work with a photographer, but my streak is about to end. Time to pull double duty. I call Alex to find out what's going on.

"Bad crash," he says. "We're short-staffed."

"I only have undercover gear."

"William is there. You can use his camera. He needs to take off."

Among some reporters, William Slater is known as Woman Hater, a nickname he earned after a bad breakup led him to offer unsolicited comments about half the population. Mercifully, I won't be stuck working with him. I park in a church lot and instantly notice what is not there: no vehicle, no skid marks, no obvious signs of a crash except for yellow tape circling crushed concrete blocks.

"Hey, I gotta run," Woman Hater says. "My dentist charges if you're ten minutes late and makes you reschedule. Trying to screw the working man. I gotta find a new dentist."

"How'd you end up here?"

"Stories have been falling through all day. Alex sent me because traffic was backed up. Don't know when they'll reopen the lane."

"What did you shoot?"

"Tow truck was leaving as I arrived. Probably got ten seconds of it pulling away. No damage visible, just the back of a white pickup."

"Thanks. Is the PIO around?"

"Nope. Not coming but an accident reconstructionist was here taking photos and measurements. It was a single vehicle. One occupant."

I lower the tripod and record tight, medium, and wide shots. Easy peasy. Until danger creeps into my viewfinder in the form of a gray-haired, glasses-wearing, notepad-carrying super reporter named Scott Yang. Why is one of the most respected journalists in Arizona covering a crash? He approaches a man holding a surfboard-shaped sign that reads: WE BUY GOLD. He's in his twenties with stringy hair parted down the middle and tucked behind both ears.

"Hey, Scott." My voice is ragged from jogging across the street to jump on the interview.

"Hi, Jolene. This is Tommy Crump. He saw the crash."

"Tommy, can you give me a second to get situated?"

"Sure, man, no worries."

"Scott, I'm surprised to see you." I open the tripod's legs and check the camera's focus. "Is everyone at the capital behaving themselves?"

"Never. But I was nearby and drew the short stick." He pulls a pen out of his shirt pocket and a notepad out of his pants pocket. "Ready?"

I nod and defer to Scott for the first question since he found the witness.

"Tommy, you told me you were working when the car went through the intersection and crashed. Can you describe what you were doing and what you saw?"

"Oh, man, it was crazy. I was just doing my thing, you know?" Tommy tosses the sign to his other hand, twirls it over his shoulders and through his legs before propping it under his arm. He pauses like he expects applause. When none comes, he continues. "So yeah, I'm just spinning like I always do and the car just blew across two lanes." He makes a swooshing sound and jumps back. "He almost hit me. I would've been toast, man."

"Excuse me," I say. "Tommy, can you do me a favor and put the sign down? I'll get video of you spinning after we talk."

"No problem." He sets the sign on the ground and studies his hands before letting them fall against his legs. "Feels kinda strange not holding something, ya know?"

"What did you think when you saw the car coming your way?"

"Like I was going to die, man. It was wild. The driver looked scared to death. I thought he was going to nail me but I jumped back like this." Tommy bounces out of frame and I jerk the camera to get him back. "And, then, he like, swerved and pow! Smashed right into the wall."

"What happened then?" Scott asks.

"I ran over to the car. So did another guy, but we couldn't open the driver's door. I called 911 and the other guy went to the passenger side. Got that door open but the guy was a mess, man. Air bag went off but it didn't do any good. His neck was like this—" Tommy flings his palm up and slaps it down. "It snapped."

I zoom in to keep Tommy's hands out of frame.

"Were you here when paramedics arrived?" I ask.

"Oh yeah. They worked fast and all but, like I said, he looked like a goner. Did he die?"

"Nothing's been confirmed," Scott says. "You can check azcentral for updates."

I chime in and say we'll have updates on our newscasts and online, which reminds me to post to social. But a text from Alex stops me. For the first time, Alex is not using police code.

WTF? Where R U?

He knows where I am—he sent me to cover the crash. Maybe Sexy is mad I'm not collecting cupcakes. But that's not my fault. Alex wants to know when I'll be back.

On my way. What's going on?
Woman claims u promised tour.

Shit. That's what my neighbor Norma was excited about. I forgot I agreed to show her and her friends around the station.

Sorry. Back in 20.

Part of me hopes Norma isn't getting on anyone's nerves but another part hopes Sexy is losing it. When I burst into the newsroom, I do a double take. Norma is center stage, basking in the admiration of her friends and—wait, is that Sexy laughing with them?

"Oh, David is such a dear," Norma gushes to me.

She's changed her hair color from watermelon to pineapple and added orange lipstick. Her friends sport a mix of ebony, brown, and red hair.

"He showed us all around the station and we got to sit in the same chairs as the anchors and take pictures! We even stood in front of the green screen to see what it's like to do the weather. It's been a lovely visit. Jolene, I can't thank you enough for arranging it."

She hugs me and I get a nose full of Aqua Net hair spray.

"You're welcome, Norma."

As she releases her grip, I brace for David's glare. But there's something indecipherable in his eyes. For anyone else I might peg it as interest or amusement. But Sexy? He's hiding something.

"Norma was just telling me about her job with the county," he says.

Her smile reveals a slash of lipstick on a front tooth. I've heard some of Norma's experiences as a former health inspector. She relishes talking about violations she witnessed and, from the looks of it, Sexy has been devouring stories about moldy meats and soap-less sinks.

"Norma mentioned our station used to do a weekly segment called 'Off the Menu,'" he says. "Before your time here. Mine, too."

"Such a shame it ended," Norma says. "The anchor did an outstanding job. He would use our reports from the county and highlight the five worst restaurants every week. Then, every month he announced the worst of the worst." She turns to her friends. "Ladies, do you remember what it was called?"

The brown- and red-haired women shake their heads and ebony says, "Culinary Cautions."

Norma snaps her fingers. "That's it! My late husband, Thomas, and I always watched. He used to joke that I should be the reporter because of all the inspections I conducted."

"How many restaurants did you inspect?" Sexy asks.

"Oh, easily thousands. Whenever we ate out, Thomas wanted me to give the restaurant a once-over before we ordered. We wouldn't even sit down before I checked out the restroom. That's the key. If management allows a public bathroom to be dirty, you can bet the kitchen is subpar."

"Maybe I should take you along next time I dine out," Sexy says.

Norma giggles. "You just name the time and place."

Am I trapped in a *Twilight Zone* episode? What happened to my rude manager?

"If the segments were so popular, why did they end?" I ask.

"The reporter left," Norma says. "I can't recall where he moved to—do you, ladies?" Headshakes all around. "Sadly, they never resumed. That was around the time Thomas and I started watching Channel 2 News."

"Well," I say. "We should probably let David get back to work."

"We sure enjoyed seeing the station and visiting with you, David. Didn't we, ladies?"

They murmur appreciation. Norma is the pack leader. She's earned respect for the behind-the-scenes tour.

"It's been a pleasure, ladies," David says. "I hope I've convinced you to become loyal Channel 4 viewers."

"I was always taught not to make promises you can't keep," Norma says. "My husband was a faithful fan of Channel 2 News. I'd feel like I was letting him down if I stopped watching."

My mind cannot comprehend Sexy's expression. Is that a teeny hint of compassion?

"My mom and dad watch the same newscast every night before going to sleep," he says. "How about this? Would you consider splitting the time? Watch us, say, twice a week? You can do that, right?"

"Oh, you sweet talker." Norma pats his arm "I'm sold. You know, Carol here always watches your station. And Kirti and Marcia, you alternate, don't you?"

"Yes," Kirti, the ebony-haired friend, says. "I like Channel 2's morning show."

"And their weatherman at night does a nice job," Marcia, the redhead, says. "But I like your anchors better so I mostly watch your station—except during monsoon season."

"See?" Norma says. "You're not doing too bad with my crowd."

David playfully wags a finger. "Then it's you we need to focus on."

Norma howls in delight and waves goodbye. As I lead them out of the newsroom, I wonder who has invaded the body of my micromanaging, social media–loving executive producer. False alarm. There's been no alien invasion. In the five minutes it takes to escort Norma and her friends to the door, Sexy's back to his demanding self. He's added stretching to his workplace routine since he started running.

"So." He swings a foot on his desk. "Where do things stand with the cupcake investigation?" His eyes stay on me as he leans over his leg.

I want to remind him it's only been a few hours since we talked and I visited one bakery before I was sent to the car accident, but what's the point?

"Making progress," I say. "Same with the contract dispute story."

Sexy straightens his torso, slides his foot off the desk. "Is the contract thing going to pan out?"

"Yes," I say, faking confidence.

He swings the other leg up. "If it's not sexy, we need to move on. We have plenty other stories to pursue, stories guaranteed to attract an audience."

He bends over to stretch, which saves me from saying something less than professional. I head to the assignment desk, an elevated platform that offers the only clear view of the entire newsroom.

"Alex, I'm sorry I forgot about my neighbor and her friends touring the station."

"All good. They arrived when the police scanners were blowing up and I was distracted. One of them—maybe it was your neighbor—kept calling from the lobby. That's why I texted you. How'd it go?"

"If I didn't know better, I'd say Sexy has a crush on her."

"He cranked up the charm again, huh?"

"Again? Are you telling me you've legitimately seen David display human emotion beyond annoyance?"

"Oh sure."

"He's never shown me."

"Ah, Jolene. Sometimes you are such a novice. Unlike your friend, you are a member of the media. That distinction automatically excludes you from any Nielsen Meters that measure our ratings. Ergo, you do not count."

But my stories count. David may not believe questionable contracts using tax dollars is sexy, but if I can add murder to the mix, he'll get behind it.

CHAPTER
5

I wake up before my alarm goes off, ready to tackle gluten-free cupcakes and the murder of a well-known lobbyist.

"Hello, Emmy." I tap her wings. The golden statuette from the Rocky Mountain Southwest Chapter of the National Academy of Television Arts and Sciences serves as the kitchen table's centerpiece and sentry, watching over the purse with the hidden camera. I pop fresh batteries in the recorder. The sooner I get cupcakes, the sooner I can focus on my biggest investigation since the talk show host's murder.

"Emmy, if things go as planned, you'll be getting a roommate."

Oscar gives me side-eye. Or maybe it's a weird reflection from his bowl.

"Don't be jealous, Oscar. You're one of kind."

While brushing my teeth, I scroll through news feeds. Video of two coyotes destroying a backyard garden. A garage fire extinguished before it spread to a house. A Phoenix eighth grader on his way to compete in the National Civics Bee. I click on Scott Yang's story about yesterday's car crash. He has the same information I have—with one exception.

A big one.

He has the victim's name: Carlos Rios. It's the same name as the guy I talked to at Home Sweet Home Mobile Home Park. The same name as the person who filed a bid-rigging complaint against the city. My heart ticks faster and I have to remind myself more than 40 percent of Phoenicians identify as Hispanic or Latino/a/x. There's definitely more than one Carlos Rios. I check emails for an update from the police PIO, but there's nothing new. The original email lists the unnamed victim's age as forty-eight. That matches my estimate. I call the Wright Legal Firm and ask Whitney if it's the same Carlos.

"Yes, it's awful," she says.

"Any idea what happened?"

"His wife thinks he might have had a medical emergency. Of course, we won't know for a couple days until an autopsy is performed."

I put her on speaker and open my closet. "What does this mean for your case?"

"We no longer have a complainant," Whitney says. "But, depending on how Carlos's business was set up and his family's wishes, we could still pursue."

I choose black pants, one of four black pairs I own, and ask if she's heard anything from the city.

"No. Typically, they wait until the thirty-day deadline to respond. Who knows by then whether we'll have a case?"

"What can you tell me about Kris Kruger, the guy who got the contract?"

"Contracts. Plural. That's the issue."

I reach for my favorite sweater, oversized and orange. "Have you talked to him?"

"No. We were just getting started. After the city responded to our complaint, we planned to investigate the entire process starting with the IFB—you know what that is?"

"No."

"Stands for invitation for bid. It's a public notice for businesses to submit proposals. We were going to track it all the way from when the IFB was issued to when the contract was awarded."

"And now?"

"We do nothing until Carlos's wife directs us."

In the background, someone calls her name.

"Whitney, can I ask one more thing before you go?" This is the worst part. "Can you share contact information for Carlos's wife? In case she wants to talk."

"In light of what she's going through I'm not comfortable doing that. But I will give your cell and email to the family and, should they feel up for it, they can contact you."

I hang up and hurry to the door, but my feet backpedal to the mirror where a giant Halloween bag stares at me. After trading the orange sweater for gray, I search Carlos's name on crowdfunding sites. A family friend has set up a campaign to raise money for funeral expenses. Carlos is described as loving and loyal, the loss unbearable to those who knew him. In his wedding photo, one of Carlos's hands is in a pocket, the other around his wife's waist. I recognize the bridge at Encanto Park where a younger Carlos poses with two girls and a boy nearly as tall as him. It reminds me of the photo I took of Carlos and Nana. It might be his last one. I pull it up on my phone. Carlos's smile isn't quite natural, it doesn't reach his eyes like Nana's smile. Her hands are wrapped around his, like she never wants to let go.

I check Scott Yang's Facebook account, his only social site. His last post was three months ago, which makes me relax but only for a second. If Scott knows about Carlos's complaint against the city, he would never tip anyone off before his investigative report is ready to go public.

The website for Mijo's Flooring lists a street address and

phone number I jot down before moving on to Carlos's competitor and former boss, Kris Kruger. His website is bare bones but a Facebook business page includes photos from residential and commercial projects, mostly carpeting and laminate, with a spattering of tile work. It lists a post office box for an address and a phone number that I dial.

"Hi, I'm trying to reach Kris."

"He's working from home today. Can I take a message?"

If I try to explain why I'm calling, it will never be relayed correctly. I keep it simple, give my name, number, and a request for Kris to call me about a story. But if Kris is getting city business through illegal or unethical methods, he's not going to voluntarily talk to me. I pivot to plan B.

On the assessor's website, there are no properties listed for Kris Kruger, but the corporation commission's site lists an address that comes up as a house. Gotta be his. I search for Carlos's company and track the address to an accountant that filed his paperwork.

In order to apply for city work, businesses must be licensed and bonded, so I check the Arizona Registrar of Contractors website. Carlos has zero cases or complaints against his company while Kris has one case marked as "Resolved/Settled," meaning both parties agreed to close the complaint. Most likely Kris addressed the customer's issues and fixed the work or refunded money. Since the case is closed, I don't expect any explosive information, but to be safe, I file a public records request for details. An automated reply says my request will be handled in the order it was received, generally taking twenty-one to twenty-eight business days.

"Oscar, looks like I have a busy day ahead." I shake flakes into his three-gallon home. "Wish me luck."

On the way to work, I shuffle between three radio stations to catch their newscasts. They all lead with different stories and none includes Carlos Rios. Maybe Scott Yang got lucky getting Carlos's name. Or maybe he's way ahead of me. Either way, I need to dig deeper and know just the person who can help.

I head straight to the assignment desk where the newsroom's digital guru is reading a hard copy of the *Arizona Republic*. The station canceled the physical subscription years ago, but Alex has an old-school streak and brings it from home. My grandma taught me to clip coupons from the Sunday paper, but I haven't touched one since she died.

"Hey, Alex, what's new?"

He flicks a page. "Jack Daniel's is on sale."

I drop into the seat next to him and a police scanner blurts out a string of numbers and letters. Alex throws the paper aside.

"Stand by." He cranks up the volume. "Possible 417-G at a school."

Oh, no. 417-G is subject with a gun. Images of school shootings hijack my mind. Sobbing students, terrified parents, and candlelight vigils, followed by national coverage of memorials before network crews are called back to their home bases, only to repeat the cycle again in a different city. For several minutes, we don't move until Alex lowers the volume.

"False alarm," he says. "You can breathe again."

I want to cover exciting, important stories but if I manage to go my entire career without covering a mass shooting, I will be forever grateful. Alex picks up the paper and folds the pages.

"Alright, Jolene, what do you need?"

"Do I have to need something? Can't I just say hi to my favorite person in the newsroom?"

He takes a slow slurp of coffee. "First, the flirty stuff doesn't work—not your style. Second, you are definitely not my type."

"Ouch. Remember that if Christopher kicks you to the curb. You won't get any sympathy from me. Unless, of course, you help me out."

"Let's hear it."

"Can you run background on a guy named Kris Kruger? I have a business name and home address."

Alex has access to databases the rest of us don't and knows how to use them like no one else.

"What's the deal with Kruger?"

"There are questions about how he always wins city contracts. There might be civil cases against him. Maybe you could run a criminal background check, too?" I curl my lips like it's the best idea he'll hear today.

"ASAP is not possible."

"Whenever you can. I appreciate it." I check the whiteboard where assignments and crews are listed. "Can I take Nate? Being friendly and efficient are necessary traits. We're going to Peoria."

"You know the story behind Peoria?"

Alex loves to play history teacher and I'm happy to indulge if I can work with my favorite photographer.

"As a Midwesterner, you should know this." He takes a swig. "After the Europeans pushed the Yavapai out, some families from Peoria, Illinois, made the trek here. The government gave them land and they named the area after their hometown."

"Did that come from a database?"

He taps a temple. "This one."

Let's see if I can keep the momentum going. I power walk to David's desk where he's bouncing on his toes. We're in prime race season. Between November and February, every weekend offers a buffet of K's: 5K, 8K, 10K, 15K, along with a selection of marathons.

"Hey, David, remember the bid-rigging complaint I told you about? Guy fighting the city over a contract?"

He bends a knee and reaches behind to grab a foot. "Yeah."

"He was the victim in yesterday's crash."

"So?"

"So maybe there's something we can do today. Beloved small-business owner dies unexpectedly. He was active in the community. We have crash-scene video and witness sound. And I can talk to his former employer. Maybe his family, too."

David releases his foot and stretches the other side, watching the seconds on a digital clock near the news set. Okay, I'm going to have to go there.

"What race are you doing?"

"Anthem Turkey Trot for a practice run. Still debating whether to do the half or full Phoenix Marathon."

"Wow. A marathon. That's impressive. I've only done a 5K and it was tough. I think Carlos, the business owner who died, might've been a runner. Or maybe he supported local races."

"You definitely get an A for effort." David's foot hits the floor. "I actually liked your pitch before you tried to stroke my ego."

"Thanks. You can tell everyone during the editorial meeting. I'll head out with Nate so we can stay ahead of the other stations."

"Good plan, Jolene. Keep me posted."

It will be interesting to hear what Kris Kruger has to say about the guy who quit working for him, started his own business, and then complained about Kris getting lucrative city contracts.

CHAPTER

6

While waiting for Nate to load his gear, I search the city's website. A single-page summary provided to the council recommended approval of a million-dollar contract to Paloma Flooring, Inc. Kris Kruger is listed as president and CEO.

I click on the page to request public records. In the description box I write: *All documents related to the procurement process, recommendation for award, and acceptance of award for a two-year contract worth $1 million.* I hope the city doesn't put Paloma Flooring on the same level as the Phoenix Suns and Phoenix Mercury. When the city was negotiating with the teams' owner to renovate the arena, neither side would provide details. As a private entity, the Suns and Mercury didn't have to, but the arena is city-owned and, for months, leaders refused to share numbers with reporters. If details got out, Phoenix argued, the city could lose bargaining leverage and that could potentially cost taxpayers more. After a public backlash, the city ultimately revealed the financial breakdown showing who would pay for what.

"You look like you could use some sunshine."

I shake my head to clear out the jargon and take in Elena's latest creation.

"Ta-da!" She presents a round cake covered in yellow frosting. Googly eyes and a black licorice mouth make up the sun's face.

"What are the rays made of?"

"Waffle cones. Frosted, then rolled in yellow sugar. The eyes are white frosting with brown M&M's."

"What was your inspiration this time?"

"Manny and I are spending a three-day weekend in San Diego where I plan to worship the sun."

"You know we're nicknamed Valley of the Sun for a reason, right? We average three hundred days of sunshine a year."

"Yeah, but we don't have the ocean. And the sun feels . . . I don't know, better when you're on the beach." She holds up a knife. "Want a piece?"

"Maybe later. I'm heading out in a sec."

"Your loss. Don't cry when it's all gone by the time you get back."

Free food in a newsroom goes faster than Sha'Carri Richardson in the 100 meters. "Save me a slice, please."

After sending an email to the city manager's office asking for comment on Carlos's bid-rigging complaint, I meet Nate in the garage.

"Hey," he says. "Today's high is supposed to be eighty degrees, so I figure we're safe taking Crazy Eight."

Managers refer to live trucks by numbers, but we came up with nicknames for a select few. Crazy Eight because we're convinced there's a ghost constantly messing with the air-conditioning. Sometimes it's like being trapped inside a frozen-food case. Other times, it's a hair dryer blowing on the hottest setting.

After filling Nate in on the plan to interview Kris Kruger, he says, "Are we talking to this guy about the crash or the contract dispute?"

"Both. The crash is the hook but I'm interested in his reaction to his competitor's allegations."

While Nate drives, I read an email from a city public information officer acknowledging my request for comment about the contract. Says he'll aim for a response before our four o'clock newscast. I check online for Scott's reporting. Nothing since he identified Carlos as the crash victim. Doesn't mean he's not working the story.

"Jolene, don't make me start."

"What?"

Nate wiggles a thumb in my face. "Would you like to talk to Sophie about how she stopped sucking her thumb?"

"No need to get your five-year-old daughter involved. Besides, I'm not sucking my thumb. I was chewing on the side."

"Okay, what's making you chew?"

I lift a shoulder, let it drop. I can't tell Nate why I care so much about a guy I spent ten minutes with. No one knows my story. But they should know Carlos's story. And if there's something unethical or illegal going on with city contracts using tax dollars, the public should know that, too.

The navigation system alerts us to take the Bell Road exit off Interstate 17. We pass a string of car dealers and shopping centers before taking a right onto Rudolph Lane.

"There it is," I say. "On the left. Second house with the citrus trees."

As Nate pulls to the curb, a man next door watches us. When a news crew shows up in your neighborhood it's a safe bet, we're not there for a feel-good story. I give him a "Hey, we're just here to talk to your neighbor. He didn't die or kill anyone" wave. The man scurries into his house.

Nate and I are halfway up the driveway when we spot two legs sticking out from underneath a truck. The legs are covered in blue jeans and what I hope is red paint.

"Hello," I call out. "Excuse me, we're looking for Kris Kruger."

A four-letter word erupts as feet barrel toward us. Scuffed cowboy boots serve as brakes for the cart. Hands pound the concrete, and a man rolls to his side, pushing himself up with a growl. As we introduce ourselves, he studies our faces like he might have to identify us in a lineup.

"Well, Jo, I'm Kris. What do you want?"

For you not to call me Jo.

"Have you heard about Carlos Rios?"

"What about him?"

"He died yesterday in a car accident."

From a shirt pocket, Kris snatches a rag covered with black and blue and purple splotches. "That so?"

"Yes, he hit a block wall. He may have suffered a heart attack, but there's no definitive cause yet. Since you worked in the same field, we thought you might be able to share a memory or information about Carlos."

Kris picks at gunk under his fingernails. "Whaddya want to know?"

"We'd like to talk with you on camera if that's okay. If you want to clean up a bit, we're happy to wait."

"Nothing wrong with getting dirty." He jams the rag in a back pocket. "Sign of an honest working man. This country'd be a lot better off if people relied less on machines and more on their hands."

Nate sets up the camera and I hand Kris a lavalier mic.

"You can clip it to your collar and let the cord run down your back. Then, plug the cord into this box. You can clip the box to your waistband or put it in your pocket."

"How about you put it in my pocket, Jo?"

I pretend not to hear him, but Nate responds. "Need help with the mic?"

"Nah." Kris winks at me. "I got it."

Once the microphone is in place, Kris describes Carlos the way most people talk about a neighbor or co-worker who dies unexpectedly: a nice guy who worked hard.

"What about your professional relationship with him?"

"What about it?"

"Did you ever have problems? You must have been surprised when Carlos left your company."

A pale pink tongue slides across chapped lips. "Listen, little lady, I had no beef with Carlos. We were competitors, yeah, but that's capitalism, the American way."

"Do you know why he felt you had an unfair advantage?"

"Nope."

He didn't ask what I meant about having an advantage. Carlos's attorney filed the complaint only forty-eight hours ago. That means Kris Kruger must know. He must have an inside connection.

"My business is doing just fine."

"What did you think when Carlos warned you about your former accountant playing with the numbers?"

He blows a sour breath. "My business is my business. Carlos was a good man and did solid work. But you can't win 'em all. I'm sorry about what happened to him and express my condolences to his family. That's all I got to say about it."

"Hey, everything okay over there?"

Kris looks over my shoulder. "All good, Peter."

The next-door neighbor who ignored my earlier wave gives one of his own before retreating back into his house.

"Peter's my chief elf."

"Excuse me?"

"He helps with Christmas decorations." Kris's cheeks crease and his tone gets lighter. "We go all out in this neighborhood. Starting the day after Thanksgiving, people come from all over to admire our display. C'mon, let me show you around."

I glance at Nate.

"Go ahead," he says. "We could use some B-roll to set up his interview. Keep the mic on and I'll follow you guys."

Kris leads us to the side of the house. It looks like a crime scene and all the victims are inflatable characters. Frosty the Snowman's mouth appears frozen in mid-scream, his body slumped on the ground. Next to Frosty is Santa, flat as a pancake, as if his insides have been ripped out. Reindeer faces are smashed into the ground, legs spread wide. It can't be the Grinch's fault—his limbs are as twisted as his soul when he stole Cindy Lou's Christmas tree.

"These are the first ones I pulled out," Kris says. "I have a storage unit full of lights and decorations and the neighbors store things, too. Peter, the guy next door, helps a lot."

"Most of your neighbors like to decorate, huh?"

"Not most—all. It's a requirement." His tone is no longer light.

"What do you mean?"

"Before anybody moves in, I have a little talk with them, explain how we do Christmas here on Rudolph Lane. Anybody who moves to this block knows to get along you play along. Know what I mean?"

"So, everyone decorates?"

His smile returns. "Yep. Been doing this so long, I got a real smooth system. First, we test all the lights, then we add the big inflatables like the ones on the ground here. Then, it's the medium ones like Charlie Brown and Snoopy." He's talking faster and louder. "We got candy canes, penguins—even a train. We highlight new stuff every year, and the neighbors add their own touches." He waves for us to follow, pointing out houses like a tour guide. "Peter and his family do a display with a Scrooge theme. Next to them, the Webers like to do a 'Reason for the Season' theme. And over there, the Shaffs sell cocoa and cookies to raise money for charity."

"What about Rudolph, your street's namesake?"

Kris beams. "That's the best part." He leads us to the curb. "It's kinda tough to visualize, but we have an entrance welcoming people to our winter wonderland. We string lights across the street and spell out Merry Christmas." He points to a two-story tan stucco house. "Santa's sleigh is parked on top of that house facing the next house. And the next house is where the reindeer start and it keeps going until the fourth house. That's Rudolph's spot."

"Sounds enormous."

"You gotta sec it to believe it."

Nate whispers, "I'm done."

"Kris, thank you for taking time to talk and show us around. We'll work up something for our newscasts today."

"What time will it be on?"

"I don't know, but if you miss it, you can find it on our website. Or I can text you when I find out what time." I open my phone's contacts. "What's your number?"

"That's alright," he says. "If I catch it, I catch it."

Nate offers to collect the mic and Kris hands it to him without comment.

Halfway down the driveway, I stop. "Hey, I was wondering if you've heard from any other reporters."

"Worried about competition, huh? Told you, it's the American way. Don't worry, Jo, you're the only one I've talked to, but come Thanksgiving, when our display goes live, don't expect an exclusive interview."

Nate loads his gear into the truck and asks where we're heading next.

"Let me call Carlos's business and see if anyone wants to talk."

I need someone who knew Carlos to discuss his character—someone with more compassion than Kris Kruger.

"If he's half the guy described on the crowdfunding site, it should be no problem finding an interview," Nate says.

I hop in the passenger seat and dial the number listed on Carlos's website. The man Kris called his chief elf is pretending to examine a fuchsia bougainvillea while watching us.

"Hello?"

I must have dialed the wrong number.

"Is this Mijo's Flooring?"

"Yes." The voice is hoarse, like someone who's been yelling or crying. After introducing myself, I feel like doing both. It's Carlos's wife. I purposely didn't call the number Carlos gave me because I wanted to be respectful and avoid directly contacting a family member.

"I'm sorry for intruding during such a difficult time. I want to let you know we're working on a story about your husband and wanted to see if you or another family member would like to share anything with us."

A sniffle fills my ears.

"We are devastated. Carlos had a heart attack last year and that scared him, you know? He started eating better and exercising. Everything was going so well."

She struggles to take a breath. I force my eyes wide to keep tears from pooling.

"I don't know why this happened. I can't . . . I can't talk about it."

"I'm so sorry. I understand and don't want to cause more pain."

"Carlos was a good husband and father. He was a very good man."

"If you have any photos you'd like to share, we can use them on air and online. We'll make sure people know you provided them."

It's so quiet I worry she's hung up.

"Mrs. Rios?"

She draws in a breath. "I do have some."

I give her my email address and apologize again before hanging up. Nate understands and we sit for a moment before he says, "At least we don't have to knock on her door."

I scan emails and click on a message from the city manager's office confirming they received a letter of intent from the Wright Legal Firm but offering no comment because their lawyers haven't yet reviewed it.

A rap on the passenger-side window startles me. The face smashed against the glass spooks me. I swing toward Nate. "Thanks for the warning. Glad he's not pointing a gun."

"Hey, I didn't see him. Must've come from behind."

I lean away from the window and crack it open.

"Sorry to bother you folks." He points past our truck. "I live three houses down and I'm curious about what's going on."

"We talked with your neighbor about a man who died in a car accident yesterday."

"That's too bad. Is he okay? I mean the neighbor you talked to. The other guy's clearly not okay."

"Yes, he's fine. They worked in the same industry."

"Oh, like you work with JJ Jackson?" His eyes glow with excitement.

Nate snorts.

"I guess you could say that."

"My husband and I love her. Really her whole station. They seem friendly and fun to be around. JJ's the best."

I guess when you play a reporter on TV instead of actually doing the legwork, you come across as fun.

"So, what's JJ like?"

Is he running for president of her fan club?

"She's JJ." I don't even try faking a smile. "If you'll excuse us, we have to go."

"Oh yeah, sure. No worries." He starts to step back and catches himself. "Hey, you guys have any station swag? Like stickers or water bottles?"

"No, sorry, they don't give us anything."

"Too bad. I got an autographed photo from JJ."

Of course you did. She probably carries a stack 24/7.

"It was from a camera guy. We saw him at Lake Pleasant Park. He was there for a hiker being rescued. A diamondback bit him. The hiker, not the camera guy. Anyway, I asked if JJ was around and he said no but gave me her photo. And we each got a pen with the station's logo on it. The ink ran out after three times, but I still have JJ's picture."

Nate starts the truck.

"Well, I know you guys are busy." He moves back. "If you see JJ tell her Walter says hello."

As Nate pulls away, I turn to wave to Kris Kruger, but he's already slid back under his truck.

CHAPTER

7

Nate heads east from Peoria to Phoenix, never veering off Bell Road. I don't ask where we're going because it's his turn to pick a lunch spot and I'm more focused on figuring out how to tell Carlos's story. I have diverse elements—an energetic sign spinner describing what he saw and how he reacted to the crash, and Carlos's former employer. But it lacks the emotional pull Carlos deserves. I need to convey how he made a difference in people's lives.

Nate makes a left turn and says, "You're welcome."

"For what?"

"My strategic cuisine selection. You may have noticed we're only a block from the accident scene. After we eat, we can stay here and work on the story. Be close for refills and a bathroom break before leaving for our live shot."

"And that's one reason all the reporters want to work with you."

"What are the others?"

"Uh-uh. Not telling. We have enough egos in this business."

"Must be my charming personality." He raises an eyebrow. "Or chiseled good looks."

"Chiseled? Where'd that come from?"

"Probably the vocabulary words plastered around the house for Sophie."

"Let's just say we reporters have a nice nickname for you."

"The bar must be pretty low considering the others."

I grab his elbow as he reaches for the door. "Wait, how do you know about the nicknames?"

"Even though reporters want people to tell them things off the record, some of you can't keep quiet."

"Don't you dare tell William we call him 'Woman Hater.'"

"What about Roger Hale? Or should I say Roger Snail?"

I give his shoulder a soft punch. "I don't know who told you but they shouldn't have."

"Unlike your comrades I can keep my mouth shut—if you give me something in return."

"Okay, I'll buy you lunch. And you can have my snicker-doodle."

"Nope."

"That's a generous offer."

"I want something that'll cost you more."

"That's not fair," I say.

"Who said life was fair?"

The lot is filling up. We need to get moving. "Okay, I'll buy two lunches."

Nate shakes his head.

"Three. And that's my final offer."

"I am literally and figuratively in the driver's seat here."

"What do you want?"

"My nickname."

I cross my arms. "No way."

He picks up his phone. "What will William Slater—oh excuse me, Woman Hater—have to say. Shall we find out?"

"Fine." I spit out his nickname.

"What? Didn't quite catch that."

"Nate. The. Great."

He rubs his chin. "Nate the Great, huh? I like it. I do strive for greatness with every story."

What I don't tell him is we sometimes use the nickname sarcastically when he acts a bit holier-than-thou. Occasionally, Nate gets carried away preaching about being the best husband and father he can be. His wife, Brandy, got pregnant at seventeen, they married when she was six months along, and, in Nate's words, he spent years messing up. Somewhere along the way Nate found God, asked Brandy for forgiveness, and got serious about putting his family first. Sometimes his comments can come off a little self-righteous. Considering I can be annoying, it's a small price to work with an excellent photographer and exceptional human.

"Maybe I'll come up with a new nickname for you," I say.

"Nah." He opens the door to Chino Bandido. "Nate the Great works."

Decades before fusion cuisine became commonplace, Chino Bandido was offering a mix of Chinese, Mexican, and Caribbean flavors with fourteen meat choices, five rice styles, and two kinds of beans.

"Jolene, don't pretend you're not getting the two-meat combo. The question is whether you do a burrito or quesadilla."

"That's where you're wrong. I'm definitely doing a quesadilla. I can't choose between machaca, jerk chicken, or jade red chicken."

"Jerk and jade," Nate says.

"Hey, those could be our nicknames."

"You must be Jerk," he says with a laugh.

I have time to debate my choices because the line reaches the Great Wall of Chino. Black frames pop against purple paint, showing off awards and reviews, signed photos from professional athletes, and a loyal customer posing in a custom-made shirt that says BODY BY CHINOS.

"Ready?" Nate says.

"Yep. I'm getting the jerk quesadilla and jade chicken."

"What about sides?"

"Fried rice and black beans. How about you?"

Before he can respond, my phone vibrates. I don't recognize the number.

"Can you order for me? I need to take this."

I step outside to answer. It's Carlos's son. I immediately apologize.

"When I called the business number, I had no idea your mother would answer."

"It's okay. We've been getting other calls. I told Mom to stop picking up, but she says Dad would want us to take care of his customers. Did you know my father well?"

The midday sun is fierce. Squinting doesn't help and my glasses are locked in the truck.

"I just met your father. I talked with him and his grandmother about the luxury apartments that are going to replace her mobile home park. It was obvious how much your father cared about her."

"Yes, Nana raised him and my aunts. We are grateful for Nana. Her love led to Dad raising me and my siblings."

"Were you in foster care?" I blurt without thinking. He answers without offense.

"Yeah, I was the oldest in the group, just like Dad. My sisters and I were separated, too." He pauses and takes a breath. "I was on my way to a group home until he saved me. I don't use that word lightly."

The sun's rays pierce my eyes, making them water. I take cover on the patio.

"Anyway, I called because I want to make sure you get what

you need. People should understand how amazing Dad"—his voice breaks—"how amazing Dad was."

I press knuckles against the corners of my eyes. Damn sun.

"I am sorry for your loss. And I apologize for what I'm about to ask, but it's my job. Are you up for doing an interview?"

"No, none of us are. I can email photos as you suggested to Mom and include a statement from the family, if that's helpful."

"Yes. Thank you."

"We appreciate you helping us tell Dad's story. This is a huge loss not only to our family, but the community."

Many people say that after a loved one dies. In Carlos's case, it's no exaggeration. He survived foster care, built a successful business, and rescued children from a system ill-equipped to provide what they need most: stable, loving forever families.

"I'll send an email in the next hour," he says.

An employee delivers our food and Nate looks for me, but his back is to the patio. I wipe my eyes and make another call.

"Thank you for contacting the Wright Legal Firm, Phoenix's only brother-and-sister law firm. How may I help you?"

The receptionist says Whitney is taking a deposition and she'll check with the team's other half. After a minute on hold with Whitney and Marcus gushing about how they're right for me, I get to find out for myself.

"Marcus, thanks for taking my call. Did Whitney tell you how we connected?"

"Yes, the stuck elevator at city hall. I told her she should've stayed around in case someone got hurt. Might've picked up a client, you know?" He produces a fake laugh. "But she bailed once she found out it was the mayor. No case to be had there. City won't sue itself."

Nate twists around and spots me. He jabs a fork at my bowl as if I can't see it. I raise a finger and mouth, "One minute."

"When I last talked to Whitney, her assistant was going to

send contact information for an accountant who used to work with Carlos Rios and Kris Kruger, but I haven't gotten it yet. Can you help? The accountant's name is Simona Park."

"Give me a minute."

Back on hold, Whitney describes how, even though she's the younger sibling, she taught Marcus right from wrong. She tells a story about him cracking their mother's crystal dish and hiding the chipped corner so it faced the back of the cabinet. He got away with it for seven months—until Thanksgiving. Just as Whitney is about to reveal Marcus's fate, he picks up the phone.

"Simona Park works for a company called Bentley Flooring."

He gives me a general email for the company and a Phoenix phone number. I ask Marcus to keep me posted if they move forward with Carlos's complaint.

"Sure," he says. "You know, Carlos's accident reminds me of a bad divorce case I handled."

Divorce? On the phone, Carlos's wife sounded crushed.

"Whitney never told me Carlos was getting a divorce," I say.

"He wasn't. It's his accident that reminded me of the case. The soon to be ex-husband cut the brake lines on the car belonging to his wife's future husband. He was lucky he wasn't going fast when he lost the brakes. He ended up in a ditch instead of a morgue."

My mind flashes to Carlos's former boss, Kris Kruger, looking comfortable and confident working on his truck.

"How did you prove it was the ex-husband?"

"We couldn't. Neither could the cops. But it was the only explanation."

Nate's burrito is gone and he's unwrapping his snickerdoodle.

"Before I go, can you tell me about the crystal dish?"

"Huh?"

"The dish you chipped when you were little. The recording cut off just as Whitney got to Thanksgiving."

This time, Marcus's laugh is real. "That's one of her favorite stories. My mom pulled out the dish for Thanksgiving dinner. It belonged to her grandmother and she only used it for holidays. Mom spotted the chip right away and asked us what happened. I could tell by the way Whitney looked at me she knew I did it. It wasn't the first time I'd broken something. But it was the first family heirloom."

"Did you confess?"

"No. I was adamant I didn't know anything. The more Mom looked at us, the more I dug my heels in. Then she started crying. And that's when Whitney apologized and said she accidentally dropped it. Mom thanked her for telling the truth and gave her a hug. Whitney gave me a look that, at the time, I couldn't describe, but now understand was complete disappointment. And it made me spill my guts."

"How did your mom react?"

"Good ol' Mom. Said she was glad I took responsibility, that it was the right thing to do, and we should always remember that."

"She must be proud of you both."

"Yes. We're lucky to have her. And our father for providing a surname that perfectly fits our business."

All I got from my father was a surname that makes many people assume I speak Spanish or come from a close-knit family. I call Bentley Flooring and get a recording to leave a message. If I don't hear from Simona, I'll try again in the morning.

Despite bordering on cold, the quesadilla satisfies the hunger in my stomach. But the nagging in my gut persists.

"What's eating you?" Nate asks. "Pun intended."

"I can't shake the feeling there's something more to Carlos's death." I slide my cookie to Nate. "The witness said he didn't even brake."

"Wouldn't that happen if he suffered a medical emergency?"

"It seems like a person could hit the brake. And what about that asshole, Kris Kruger, who always gets the contracts?"

"I agree with that description," Nate says.

"He knows his way around vehicles. Maybe he messed with Carlos's truck."

Nate takes a bite, brushes away the crumbs.

"How many people have a toolbox the size of a compact car?" I tick off points with my fingers. "No slowing, no stopping. No one's investigating Kruger, a master mechanic, who threatened Carlos, who happened to be Kruger's competitor. Something's going on."

"Maybe you just want something to be there," Nate says.

I look down and mix my rice and beans. "What's that supposed to mean?"

"Going back to covering things like road construction delays and credit card skimmers at gas stations must seem kinda boring after Larry Lemmon's murder."

He's not wrong. The attention and accolades from the talk show host's case had me riding high for days until the sparkle eventually faded. Still, when I call up the memories, validation dances through my body. I'm doing what I'm meant to do: exposing bad guys and breaking stories.

"My instinct says Carlos's death and the dispute over city contracts is worth pursuing. I don't know how David can't see it."

"I understand," Nate says. "But you have to accept local news is like a bad boyfriend. You can't change him. He may talk a good game and act interested in what you have to say, but at the end of the day, he's not willing to invest and do better. It takes too much time and energy. In the case of local news, it also takes money and the only money being spent now is on hiring people who offer ways to cut budgets even more."

"FYI—you just blew one of the reasons reporters like working with you."

"What?"

"You're known for having a positive attitude."

"How about this? I'm positive you'll have a great live shot."

"Thank you."

"Seriously, Jolene, we only have to be live for the four o'clock newscast. We'll be done by five. When was the last time your workday ended that early? Take the victory."

Maybe Nate is right. Maybe I'm trying too hard to find something suspicious about Carlos's crash. But he can't say that about Rich Gains. There's no disputing the lobbyist was shot and killed in his home. Who pulled the trigger and why are still unknown. On the drive back to the station, I search for recent coverage about Gains's case. There is none. Initial news reports don't include the address for the murder scene, only the nearest cross streets. It's in a less than desirable location for a wealthy widow. Yes, I'm stereotyping based on the photo of Rich and Stacey Gains in the business magazine. She had the air of an affluent zip code, not a neighborhood kindly described as on the upswing. I pull up the assessor's website, convinced I can pinpoint the address on my own. Except I can't. People with money know how to hide it. The Gains Family Trust shows nineteen results. And that's just what the family is willing to publicly reveal. It's going to take a super brain and supercomputer to narrow the possibilities.

CHAPTER

8

As I enter the newsroom, Alex bolts out of his chair, cups his hands around his mouth, and shouts, "Attention! Chopper's on scene. Repeat: chopper is on scene!"

David charges toward the news set. "Showtime! Let's go, anchors!"

Rachel and Rick dash out of the makeup room, cords from their earpieces slapping their backs. A producer hands off scripts as smoothly as an Olympic sprinter passing a baton.

"Any witnesses?" David's voice carries throughout the newsroom. "We need the anchors talking to someone."

"Standing by," Alex yells over the scanner traffic. "Llama rescue group should be calling any minute."

"What about police?"

"PIO's on the way." Alex faces a bank of monitors lining the wall behind the assignment desk. "Chopper's on scene. Anchors should be live."

David races to his desk, shoves his face inches from the monitor. "Is that guy trying to lasso a llama?" He zips past me on his way to master control. "What's the holdup? Why aren't we on the air?"

It's an ideal time to help Alex. And of course, once we wrap up llama drama, he can help me.

"What can I do?"

"Call the llama farm." He tosses a notepad with numbers scribbled on top.

"Is the area code five-two-oh?"

"Yeah. They're in Bisbee. We want 'em for Q&A with anchors ASAP."

After two rings, it goes to voice mail and, while I'm reciting the newsroom number, Alex pounds the desk.

"Damn! Channel 2 got the farm!"

I finish the message, even though it's a long shot. Once a station has a key interview during breaking news, they keep them on the line. That way they can always go to them for new developments. Plus, they keep competitors from getting the interview. Even without a llama farmer on the line, Rachel and Rick have compelling video to talk over. Two llamas—one black, one white—prance through a retirement community and gallop across a golf course. Two carts carrying confused players swerve to avoid hitting them, but the maneuver is unnecessary. The llamas zigzag over the greens, oblivious to balls flying through the air.

"I guess the llamas don't understand the word 'fore,'" Rick says with a chuckle.

I field calls from people who want to share the news. After explaining our chopper is over the scene and they can watch it live on Channel 4, I grill them like a detective.

"Where are you? What do you see?"

But no one provides a valuable vantage point, only fleeting glimpses of the wily, wooly animals. No one comes close to a llama farmer's perspective. And he's still on Channel 2.

Alex slams down a phone, cursing under his breath.

"What's wrong?"

"David assumes I care that llamas are trending."

"I wouldn't have thought they were sexy enough. It's not like they have a giraffe's long legs."

I drift closer to the TV and boost the volume to catch our anchors' play-by-play. It's not pretty. Despite the station promoting Rachel and Rick as besties, a competitive current occasionally bubbles to the surface. Like now, as they trample on each other's comments to sound the most informed about a domesticated pack animal of the camel family. I got that description courtesy of an online search. I also learned llamas are social animals and like to travel in herds. Two probably don't constitute a herd but they are sticking together, ignoring traffic rules and bystanders trying to corral them. While I'm no fan of car chases, there is something captivating about watching law enforcement officers, arms stretched wide, trying to reason with llamas. What will the cops do if the animals walk up to them? Cuff them?

"Now that they're off the golf course, it looks like there'll be a better chance of securing them," Rachel says.

"Let's hope so," Rick says. "If they keep heading in the same direction, they're going to run into a busy street and that could quickly turn dangerous."

Thirty minutes of commercial-free coverage later, it appears the llamas' freedom is coming to an end. A man riding in the back of a pickup truck manages to lasso one while the other llama bolts into a carport with no way out. Trapped by vehicles, the llama is lassoed by a man wearing overalls who comes out of nowhere. Our anchors seize the opportunity to create a narrative.

"You know, Rachel, this wouldn't be the first time someone saw Channel 4's chopper and tuned in to learn about a situation unfolding in their neighborhood."

"That's right, Rick. Perhaps this man caught our live coverage, grabbed a rope, and rushed to the scene to help."

No doubt every station will lasso him for an interview. As Rachel and Rick prepare to sign off, they stress no people or animals were hurt and answer the question everyone's asking: Where did the llamas come from?

"Apparently, a rancher had taken them to an assisted living facility as a form of therapy for residents," Rick says. "All went well until it was time to leave. When the rancher started loading the animals into the trailer, a nearby car backfired, spooking the llamas, and off they went."

"We're thankful everything ended well," Rachel says. "And we'll see you back here at the top of the hour for our regular newscast."

Now that the llama show is over, I trot over to Alex. "Can you help me?"

"Gonna cost you this time," he says.

"I'm way ahead of you." I present a bottle of Coke. "Your favorite."

"Is that all?"

"Stand by."

Sixty seconds later, I drop a handful of chocolate on his desk.

"Stealing from Elena's jar does not demonstrate a good-faith effort." He unwraps a Milky Way. "For the record, you'll need to do better next time."

"Duly noted." I pull a chair over and sit next to him. "Out of nineteen addresses I found, I'm trying to nail down where Rich Gains was killed and where his wife lives."

"Isn't he the lobbyist who surprised a burglar in his house?"

"That was the early theory," I say.

"Ah, sounds like Channel 4's Jolene Garcia believes there's more to the story." Alex leans back, his legs crossing at the ankles. "Let's hear it."

"There's nothing to tell. I'm just getting started."

He unwraps a mini Reese's and says, "Write down the

widow's name and your best guess for the murder house, listen to the scanners, and flag anything important." He pops the candy in his mouth and slips in earbuds. "I'm going in."

Peeking at Alex's computer is futile because he uses a privacy screen. I envision him hacking into websites and gaining access to classified areas teeming with personal details. Compared to llamas on the loose, the scanner traffic is dull. A call about someone who's fallen at home and can't get up, a dumpster fire, a medical emergency at the library.

"Here you go." Alex slaps a sticky note on the desk. Neatly printed in black ink are two addresses. "Top one is the murder house."

"How'd you narrow them down?"

"I don't reveal my secrets."

I take the note and scan the newsroom. David has corralled the producers to talk llama coverage. Manager averted. But turns out, it's not David I need to avoid. Pamela Worthy, the intern, appears to be on a sugar high. "Guess who I saw? Nina and Allysa!"

"Who?"

"Nina and Allysa. You know, the Lopez twins."

When Pamela registers my blank look, she says, "They went to my high school in Chandler. Not when I went there. The twins are, like, in their forties. Anyway, they used to be professional wrestlers and they've been on a ton of reality shows. Their podcast about *Love Island* is lit."

I'm not familiar with *Love Island,* but Pamela doesn't notice.

"I went into a bakery to get a cupcake for our story and they were there. Can you believe it? I heard Nina—or maybe it was Allysa—they're identical, if you didn't know. Anyway, they told the clerk they're back visiting for a week. I wanted to get a photo with them so bad but I told myself, 'Pamela, you're a working journalist and need to be professional.'"

David would be more impressed with video of the twins than anything I'm working on.

"Well done," I say. "Can you get more cupcakes tomorrow?"

"Yep."

"Thank you. Let's get together then and plan our next steps."

As Pamela saunters away, a grunt floats over from the next cubicle. "Why are you lying to that girl?" The grunter is Gina, our station's most popular reporter. She gets as many invitations to emcee events as our anchors.

"I'm not lying. I'll hit some bakeries in the morning."

Gina flashes a smile that helped secure her title as second runner-up in the Miss America pageant. "Keep telling yourself that."

"I'm serious. The sooner I get cupcakes out of the way, the sooner Sexy will let me focus on real news."

"What are you working on?"

"Promise not to tell anyone?"

"What are we promising?" Elena says as she sinks into a chair across from us.

"Not to talk about Jolene's story."

"You mean the grand gluten investigation?" Elena titters. "How will *60 Minutes* know to offer you a job if you keep it a secret?"

"Elena, be nice or next time I won't stop Jolene from emptying your candy jar." Gina nods at me. "Go ahead."

"I'm looking into the murder of that lobbyist who allegedly surprised a burglar at home."

"Allegedly, huh?" Elena opens her candy jar. "What do you think happened?"

Good question. At this point I only have Whitney Wright repeating a rumor about a staged scene and her opinion that the media aren't paying attention.

"I don't know, but his work upset plenty of people."

"If anyone can get to the bottom of it, it's you," Gina says.

"If anyone can take advantage of llama drama and leave before six o'clock, it's me." Elena pops a Hershey's Kiss in her mouth. "I'm sneaking out the back. See ya tomorrow."

Driving home I replay Gina's comment. I will get to the bottom of Rich Gains's murder. And I won't forget Carlos. Kris Kruger was mad Carlos left his company to start his own. On top of that, Rich Gains taught Carlos how to compete against Kris for city contracts. Kris had a sweet setup until Carlos tried to get in on the action, and his mechanic skills would make it easy to tamper with Carlos's truck. Based on Kris's abrasive personality, I don't think him going after Rich Gains is out of the question. I can't wait to hear what Kris's former accountant has to say.

CHAPTER

9

Bentley Flooring opens at eight o'clock. Three minutes later, I call and press zero to bypass the recorded options. On the second ring, someone answers and, after asking for Simona Park, I'm put on hold. Unlike the Wright Law Firm, there's no entertaining banter. Only the faint swish of water from my goldfish's bowl.

"Simona speaking. May I help you?"

I introduce myself, explain I'm working on a story about city contracts, and would like to get her thoughts.

"About what?"

I need to tread carefully. If she did embezzle from Kris Kruger she's not going to want to talk. As the accountant who worked with Kris and Carlos, she can provide insight no one else can.

"I'm looking at the city's bid process in general, and specifically at a flooring contract Kris Kruger and Carlos Rios bid on. I know you worked for Kris."

"Yes, but what does your story have to do with me?"

There's an edge in her voice. I keep my tone friendly and light while pacing from my refrigerator to the kitchen table.

"I'm just gathering information, trying to understand how the process works. Translating government speak isn't easy. You know the system and I'd love to get your input. Can you spare a few minutes?"

"Afraid not. I'm busy."

"I can come to your office any time or we could meet wherever is convenient for you."

"I don't have extra time."

And I don't have a backup plan. "I can call back later. It'll take five minutes max."

She exhales a heavy breath and shuffles papers.

"Alright. I can give you five minutes. Call me at ten."

"Thank you. Can I get your direct number?"

"The main number you called is fine."

Now I know where she'll be so I can show up in person. It's harder for people to say no to your face. Until then, it's back to the newsroom where I avoid a face-to-face with Sexy and come face-to-face with beauty.

"Hey, Jolene." Gina glides past my desk like a ballerina, wearing a dress the color of honey. She glows like the first morning light. "What's going on?"

"Just procrastinating," I say.

"You know that's Elena's specialty," she says.

"I can't dodge the bakery investigation much longer."

"Be sure to bring back doughnuts."

Elena drops her bag on her desk. "Who has doughnuts?"

"No one," I say.

Elena says, "Has the Food Network offered to make you their chief bakery correspondent?"

"Don't you guys have work to do?" I ask.

"As a matter of fact, they do." Alex has snuck up behind me. "Who wants to check out a 459-V?"

"We'll let you know when you tell us what it is," Gina says.

"Vending machine burglary."

Gina gives him a "You're joking" look.

"David finds it funny," he says. "That's why I'm sending a crew. It's five minutes away. The would-be burglar's hand is stuck in the machine. Fire was just dispatched."

"So?" Elena plops in her chair.

"Did I mention the vending machine dispenses condoms and it's located at Attractions?"

"There's no way they'll let us shoot video," Elena says. "Even if they did, we'd have to blur most of it. That's an adults-only store."

Alex's finger moves like a windshield wiper. "Technically, they call themselves a boutique specializing in lingerie."

"Well, I call BS," Elena says. "That's not a story."

"Okay, I'll send Nate by himself."

Gina and Elena respond at the same time. "I'll go."

"Elena, you've already worked with him this week," Gina says. "It's my turn."

"I'm not getting into the middle of this," Alex says. "Last time I picked one reporter over another to work with Nate someone poured salt in my coffee."

All eyes fix on me.

"C'mon, Alex. You know it was an accident. I'm not the one who put salt right next to the sugar in the breakroom. My brain was fried that day."

"Your brain may be baked, not fried today." He hits a pretend drum rim. "Here comes Sexy."

"Remember, I like apple fritters," Gina says. "I'll be sure to ask Nate what he wants. Ciao!"

Sexy struts to my desk. "Hey, Jolene, what's the status on cupcakes?"

"Going well."

Out of the corner of my eye, Elena's shoulders shake as she stifles a laugh.

"That's what I like to hear." Sexy's heels bob up and down. "When will you get lab results?"

"Pretty soon." I motion to the undercover gear on my desk as if it holds hours of fresh video. "When we have twenty samples, we'll drop them off at the lab and have results within two days."

He stops bouncing. "When will that be?"

"Way before your turkey trot," I say. "Have you decided whether you're doing a half or full marathon?"

Misdirection is a reporter's secret sauce with certain managers.

"Haven't decided yet. I'd like to do the full but don't know if I can get all the training in. I've been doing tempo and pace runs and know I'm ready for a half. I'd like to try a full, if I can squeeze in enough long runs. Maybe if I incorporate fartlek training."

"What's fartlek?" I say, throwing him off the scent of cupcakes.

"Sounds funny, huh?" Sexy pumps his arms. "It's alternating between slow and fast runs. I could add it to my training, but if I do a full marathon, I need to make sure I have enough time for tapering. Speaking of time, I better get ready for the editorial meeting. Keep me posted on the investigation."

"Will do."

When Sexy is out of earshot, Elena claps. "Bravo."

I take a bow. "Thank you."

"Are you still on for lunch this weekend?"

"Yes," I say. "What about Gina?"

"She'll be there. Unless her latest beau whisks her away to a private island."

Gina's personal life is the stuff of legends. She's dated professional athletes and famous musicians, wealthy CEOs and successful entrepreneurs. Once a Silicon Valley executive sent his personal jet to fly her to Maui for a weekend. Gina has it all: brains, beauty, family.

"I'm heading into the editorial meeting," Elena says. "Wish me luck."

I open my drawer and pull out a bag of Goldfish crackers. "Want some to pop in your mouth so you don't pop off at Sexy?"

"No, thanks." She pulls a Baby Ruth out of her candy jar. "Chocolate is more soothing. Remember that when you order my cupcake. Chocolate cake and chocolate frosting, please."

I shove my laptop in my bag and head to the escape room, officially called the greenroom. It was created when the station launched a daily lifestyle show that didn't last. Now it's mostly used by reporters who want to hide but have to stay close in case there's breaking news. A complaint over a city contract may not excite Sexy, but exposing the killer of a high-profile lobbyist would. And it would get me off the cupcake beat.

The scheduled demolition of the Home Sweet Home Mobile Home Park isn't the only recent controversy connected to Rich Gains, the murdered lobbyist. I find a story about another development by Jessica "JJ" Jackson, my least favorite reporter. She hired a marketing firm to run her personal YouTube channel where she posts hair and makeup tips and espouses advice on living your best life. Easy advice to give when you come from money. JJ manages to be on every platform 24/7 while I struggle to add text to an Instagram reel. It's hard being a millennial who suffers from social media incompetence. I click on JJ's story.

"Residents tell me an apartment complex—even a luxury project—would destroy the character of their neighborhood," she says as the camera shows a lawn big enough to house a Walmart.

Despite wearing stilettos, JJ moves elegantly on packed dirt. "This tree-lined path is a point of pride for neighbors. Years ago, it was a horse trail. Today, it's enjoyed by walkers and runners."

JJ introduces Rich Gains, who addresses the developer's plan to bulldoze two houses to build two hundred apartments.

"We are confident our high-quality project, which aligns with Phoenix's goal of increasing housing options for everyone, will be welcomed at city hall," Rich says.

A check of our newsroom archives reveals we chased JJ, essentially airing the same story a day after her broadcast.

"We support development, but it needs to be the right development," a resident told my station. "This area is not meant for a big box apartment complex. It's a safety issue. We already have signs alerting drivers to children at play. Adding hundreds of extra cars will lead to tragedy. Does the city really want blood on its hands?"

The five-month-old story is our station's only report. Whitney Wright was right about lack of follow-up, but in this case, it's understandable because an MMJ, or multimedia journalist, covered it. When one person has to research, drive to locations, conduct interviews, shoot video, write multiple versions for different newscasts, record audio, and edit the video, there's little chance to dive below the surface. Mostly, you hope you don't miss anything obvious or make a glaring error as you rush to meet deadlines.

I try another search using the project's address and get a hit. An arson from six weeks ago with a single script that aired during our morning news.

"Only Channel 4 Eyewitness News is bringing you video of this overnight fire. Our exclusive video shows just how fast the flames spread through the construction site. We're told an apartment complex was being built. Fortunately, no one was injured. No word yet on a cause though officials describe it as 'suspicious.'"

My initial thought is someone may have accidentally caused it while using drugs or setting a fire for warmth. But this is a neighborhood that's managed to insulate itself from shopping carts and panhandlers. Some residents could view the apartment complex as the beginning of the end of their paradise. Maybe someone felt threatened enough to set the fire.

I text the arson address to Tony, a firefighter I briefly dated and occasionally bug for information. If he's on a call, it could be hours before he gets back to me. After sending a public records request for the investigative reports into the arson, I search for neighborhood groups registered with the city. The arson falls within the boundaries of the Nirvana Association. The group's contact is Fred Nimby. I send an email asking him to call.

The Nirvana Neighborhood Association has a private Facebook page that requires an administrator's permission to join. I don't know anyone who lives in the neighborhood and call on Alex, the newsroom's version of Alexa. He picks up everything.

Rick lives there.

Not surprising our main anchor calls Nirvana home. I file that nugget in case I need access to the group's page. Moving on to the personal page for the group's leader is eye-opening. In his cover photo, Fred Nimby holds a sign that reads SOS! SAVE OUR SOCIETY!

The newest post is titled: "Protect property rights! Down with developers!" and the post before it reads, "Your neighborhood is next!" They're tame compared to his videos.

"This is what's coming to every Phoenix neighborhood unless we fight back!" Nimby roars.

The video cuts to shots of an overflowing dumpster, a car with four flat tires, and a frayed cord running from an apartment, across a sidewalk, to a battered RV.

"Dragging electrical cords along pedestrian paths is appalling and dangerous," he says. "Illegal camping, blight, and biohazards place us all at risk. Cramming more people into small spaces is not the answer. We must defend our neighborhoods and preserve the value of our single-family homes."

Fred's comments began a year ago when the neighborhood learned about plans for the apartment complex.

"The developer has hired a powerful lobbyist to ram this project through without taking into account the concerns of residents who've invested millions into their community. Anyone who works on these projects is complicit in destroying our lifestyle. It's time to take back our neighborhood!"

He posted a photo of Rich Gains with his phone number and encouraged people to call.

"Tell Mr. Rich Lobbyist that he better stop this project or he'll regret it because we will not be silenced. We will not stop fighting."

He has similar posts with phone numbers and emails for the mayor and council members. I wonder if police have been monitoring Fred Nimby. I don't want to call in a favor to my best police source this early into my investigation, so I text the mayor's chief of staff. Faith, the most effective media liaison ever, calls within five minutes. She never puts anything in an email or text that she wouldn't want broadcast on every TV, radio, and social media channel.

"Hi, Jolene, what can I do for you?"

"I'm looking into Rich Gains's murder and want to pick your brain."

"Have you talked to the police department's PIO?"

The public information officer is not going to give me anything and she knows it. The department will only release details after they make an arrest or if they've run down every lead, hit dead ends, and need the media's help to generate tips that could lead to a suspect or arrest.

"No PIO yet. I'm just getting started and want to talk to you."

"Off the record?"

"How about on background? That way I can use information you provide without attributing it to you."

"Let me think about it." Faith suggests we meet at Fair Trade Café in a couple hours, giving me time to visit Simona first. As I hang up, a text from Tony appears.

No info but had a call near the site yesterday. They're rebuilding.

Hmm. The fire didn't stop the project, so maybe someone decided to stop Rich Gains. According to information lobbyists are required to publicly file, Gains's firm represents dozens of companies. I recognize a handful of names from construction sites, billboards, and sponsorships of major events. Forty minutes later, after trying to decipher legal documents and reports designed to reveal the bare minimum, my shoulders are as hard as steel. Pinpricks in my temples are on their way to becoming jackhammers. I call Alex.

"If Sexy asks, I'm on the great gluten investigation, but I need a favor."

"Shoot."

"Can you run background on a guy named Fred Nimby?"

"You already asked me to check on another guy. Kris Kruger. He was clean."

"Yes, and I appreciate your help. Now I need info on a guy named Fred Nimby."

"You know I'm not your personal assistant, right?"

I don't answer because he drops the receiver on the desk to answer another call. I log off my laptop and grab a water out of the minifridge.

"What's your deadline?" Alex says.

"No rush. Email whenever you can. I'd like Nimby's phone, address, and any civil and criminal cases, please."

"Copy that."

"Thanks a lot, Alex. Remember, if anyone asks, I'm working on cupcakes."

Here I come, Simona.

CHAPTER
10

The smell of dirt and oil seep into my car's vent as I exit Interstate 17 at the Grand Central Industrial District. Parking spaces are as rare as good hair days during monsoon season. I pass a sand and gravel supplier and a company that rents traffic barricades before snagging a spot in front of a cannabis dispensary. Norteño music flows out of an auto upholstery shop. I check directions on my phone and cross the street. Next to a business that sells truck parts is a single-story building in need of a power wash. BENTLEY FLOORING appears in small letters above a tinted glass door.

Inside, a brown table with sharp edges pins a plastic chair against a wall. A calendar rests on a heavy oak desk, the kind used by teachers in old TV shows. No one's turned a page in four months. A note directs me to ring a silver bell for service. A minute later, a woman wearing a turquoise suit and a pearl necklace with matching earrings greets me. Her shoulder-length hair has multi-tonal highlights. I know this because Gina, the newsroom fashionista, has suggested I get them.

"May I help you?"

"Yes, I'm here to see Simona Park."

"And you are?"

"My name is Jolene Garcia. I spoke with her about a story I'm working on."

No need to explain that Simona expects me to call, not visit. My plan is to tap into her experience as Kris Kruger's former accountant to get a better sense of the man who consistently wins city contracts.

The woman glances at a bracelet watch before offering a hand. "I'm Simona."

She smells clean and refined and rich. The exact opposite of Kris Kruger.

"I was in the area and thought I'd pop in."

"It'll have to be quick. Follow me."

Simona walks with the confidence of a runway model. We pass an open door where a man is hunched over a desk studying a document.

"Have a seat."

Her furniture is sleek and modern. On a clear shelf, a gold award glistens. EXCELLENCE IN ETHICS, it says. Simona gathers papers, places them in a green folder, and sets it on the upper left corner of her desk, perfectly straight. She deposits a pen in a drawer, turns her phone over, and slides it to the upper right corner.

"What can I do for you?"

"Given your experience, I hope you can walk me through the process of submitting a bid to the city."

"It's public record. You can find all the steps online."

"Yes, but city speak and contract language aren't my thing. You have inside information that I don't."

Her back stiffens. "What do you mean by that?"

Take it easy, I remind myself. Simona doesn't know that you know she's a thief. Alleged thief.

"I just mean you know the drill. I don't."

A muffled voice carries from the next office. Something about regret.

"That's Chuck," Simona says, fiddling with her watch. "He's had a rough year, going through a divorce and trying to help his sister save her business."

"Is his sister in flooring, too?"

"No, she runs a janitorial services company. Maybe you've heard of them? Volenec's?"

"Sounds familiar," I say even though it's not.

"Textbook example of overextending." Simona moves her phone a fraction to the right. "She grew too fast and didn't plan for contingencies. I've offered to help go over her books but it's likely too late. Speaking of time, I need to get going."

"This'll only take a couple minutes. Can you please walk through the steps when you submitted bids for Kris Kruger?"

"Why are you asking about Kris? The process is the same for everyone."

Her eyes flash with distrust. Time to get off the Kris and Carlos train.

"There could be a connection to a story I'm working on. Do you know an attorney named Rich Gains?"

"No." She brushes her bangs to the side. "Should I?"

"He represented developers with zoning cases before the city."

"You're using the past tense. He's no longer an attorney?"

"He was killed when he surprised a burglar at home."

"That's terrible." She rubs a thumb over perfectly polished nails. "But I'm afraid I don't understand your point."

The voice next door is definitely threatening someone.

"I can't get into details because my information is preliminary and I don't want to say anything that could be wrong. I'm trying to find out if Kris Kruger ever worked with Gains or knew him."

"Rich Gains, you said." Simona opens her laptop. "Did he do something wrong?"

"I'm not saying he did or didn't. At this point, I'm simply looking into his professional relationships."

She taps the touchpad. "Hmm. Now that I see his photo, he strikes me as familiar. Yes, I recall seeing Kris with this man. But Kris was always very secretive about their meetings. He never added it to his calendar and never introduced me to him."

"Was that unusual?"

"Kris's other meetings were always on his calendar." She looks away and doesn't speak for a long moment. "One time I had a doctor's appointment and returned to the office earlier than expected. Kris didn't know I was there and I didn't know Rich was in Kris's office. They had a fight. About what, I couldn't tell you, but I'd never seen Kris so angry. I was afraid he might hurt—" She snaps her laptop closed. "I didn't mean . . . listen, getting upset was not unusual for Kris. I understood how he operated. He would shout to blow off steam and then he would move on."

Maybe he couldn't move on from his argument with Rich. The idea that Kris could have something to do with Rich's death seems less far-fetched.

"How long did you work for Kris?"

"About three years."

"May I ask why you left?"

"I'm warning you!" The voice next door startles us, but I won't let it end our conversation. I need Simona to keep talking. I ask if Kris did something to make her quit.

Her lips part to release a puff of air. She folds her hands and leans forward. "Let's just say Kris Kruger was not the most ethical businessman."

"What do you mean?"

"He played with numbers too much."

"Does that include bids for city work?"

She hesitates. "So that's what you're after?"

"Information is what I'm after. And someone who can provide context."

"I don't want to speak out of line. We run in the same business circles."

"From what I've learned, it sounds like he didn't follow standard operating procedures."

"I'm not comfortable talking about this." She stands and straightens her jacket. "I really should get back to work."

I don't get up. "Kris's bids were too low and he couldn't break even with the prices he quoted. As his accountant, you had to know that. Aren't you obligated by ethical standards or rules to say or do something?"

"Are you insinuating that I acted inappropriately?"

I stand, but she's still looking down at me. "No. I'm not trying to drag you into anything. I won't use your name. I'm looking for someone to confirm whether the bids were out of line."

Her eyes skip to a shelf full of photos. A girl grips a trophy in one hand, hockey stick in the other. A teenager holding a wrench poses next to a race car. Mom and Dad, dressed in power suits, stand behind mini versions of themselves. A quote from Michael J. Fox is etched at the top of the frame: FAMILY IS NOT AN IMPORTANT THING. IT'S EVERYTHING.

She looks at me and says, "All I can tell you is that I organized the documents and it never failed, an hour before the bids closed, Kris would have me lower the price."

"Occasionally or was it a regular habit?"

"The first time I thought maybe he was trying too hard to get the job. I told him the bid was too low, but he was dead set on it. He was the boss. What could I do? The next time it was the same thing. On the last day to submit bids he had me change the numbers. Not quite as low, but lower than I thought we should submit. That's when I realized he must have an inside track to keep beating everyone else."

"You mean he knew what other people were bidding and undercut them at the last minute?"

Her eyes drift above my head as if the correct answer is on the wall. "I don't know that for a fact, but it was problematic for me and I decided to leave."

Smart move before you got busted for embezzling, I think. But I skip the accusation since she's finally opening up. Besides, I'm more interested in who killed Rich and Carlos. "You're not the only one who couldn't keep working for Kris. Did you know Carlos Rios?"

"Only by name. He left Kris's company to start his own business."

"Carlos complained about the bid process. His attorney recently filed a letter of intent with the city, a precursor to a lawsuit."

"It was only a matter of time before someone else noticed. I bet that set Kris off—even more than when he blew up at Carlos for leaving him." Simona's innocent routine dazzles like the diamond on her finger.

"Carlos's complaint may not go anywhere because he died in a car crash yesterday."

"That's too bad." She reaches for the folder on her desk. "I don't mean to be rude but I need to get back to work."

"Of course. One last question: Do you know who's handling bids for Kris now?"

"Probably his daughter. Or maybe her husband. On second thought, not her husband. He's not the sharpest knife in the drawer and making a decision would require effort, another area he's lacking."

I hit the voice memo app on my phone and ask for their names.

"Peyton and Caleb. His last name is Davis. Peyton uses a hyphenated name. Kruger-Davis."

"They both work at Kris's office?"

"Showing up in person would be too much for Caleb, but Peyton goes into the office occasionally. They don't have to because they're so close to Kris if they need him. They live down the street, which Kris loves because they can help him with Christmas decorations."

"I've heard about his neighborhood display. Sounds like every house has its own holiday theme."

"Peyton and Caleb use their family ties to incorporate a nontraditional theme. They celebrate ASU with an inflatable Sparky."

"Simona, do you—"

The voice barges through the door a split second before the body appears. The man stops short and shoots Simona a questioning look.

"Chuck, this is Jolene Garcia. She's a reporter for Channel 4. Jolene, Chuck is our CEO and president."

"Nice to meet you, Chuck."

Chuck is broad shouldered, with muscles that have mellowed. He ignores my outstretched hand. "What's this about?"

"Simona was kind enough to help me with a story I'm working on."

He glares at Simona. "Why are you talking to the media?"

"It's not about your business," I say. "I'm working on a story about Carlos Rios, the owner of Mijo's Flooring. He died unexpectedly."

I pause for the obligatory condolences, but Chuck responds with a shrug, as if to say, "So what?"

"Carlos gave back to the community. His death is hitting people hard."

"Never met the guy."

Obviously, you've never met empathy, either.

"Carlos had an outstanding reputation. I guess since he's not around, your business will benefit. Less competition for city contracts, right?"

"What the hell are you implying?" His voice rumbles like thunder.

"Not implying anything." Other than you're a jerk. "Just stating facts."

"Simona, I want her out of here—now!"

She points to the door. "I can show you the way."

CHAPTER

11

It's the kind of day the Chamber of Commerce loves to promote: blue skies and seventy-five degrees with Thanksgiving and Christmas right around the corner. Phoenicians will delight in months of holiday cheer without shoveling snow. As people lounge outdoors sipping hot cocoa and iced coffee, variations of the same conversation echo across the Valley of the Sun: this is why we live here, this is why we endure summers. I'm glad the mayor's chief of staff suggested meeting at Fair Trade Café so we can soak in the sun.

But my plan is thwarted by a woman sitting on the curb near the entrance. She's wearing more layers of clothing than necessary, backpack hugging her shoulder. My insides twist as she sifts through a white plastic bag, the kind I use for kitchen trash, and pulls out a spiral notebook. Her attention shifts to me and I say hello. She doesn't respond. Clear eyes and clean clothes. She's new to the situation. If I guessed her age, I'd be within five years. Giving myself a mental shake, I open the door, and breathe in cinnamon, sugar, and vanilla. I order the Phoenix with extra agave and sit on a purple bench closest to the counter. Along the opposite wall, a wooden bench supports a row of customers fixated on their laptops. Pendant lighting twinkles, bouquets of fresh flowers dot the tables, and local artwork warms the walls.

I'm early for my meeting with Faith Williams and check emails. A reminder from Sexy about our mandatory social media meeting. Delete. A politician praising herself for doing her job. Delete. A fender bender creating a traffic jam on Loop 202. Delete. Laughter interrupts my flow. Three teenagers rumble in and place orders loud enough to disturb a customer wearing headphones.

Meeting with Simona has me convinced Kris Kruger caused Carlos's death. And possibly Rich's, since Kris kept their meetings secret and Simona caught them arguing. Learning that Kris's daughter and son-in-law work for his company sounds like progress, but I'm not sure how much having their names matters. I take a sip and return to emails. I'm probably getting rid of more than I should, but with an inbox topping twenty thousand, some days I have to delete, delete, delete. Until I spot the city's response to my public records request. I click on the solicitation document. It requested qualified vendors submit bids for a two-year deal not to exceed $1 million. The bid would cover all labor, materials, and equipment to remove and install flooring on an as-needed basis. Kris Kruger, Carlos Rios, and Chuck Baxter were listed as qualified bidders. I click on a document titled "Preliminary Bid Tabulation." The left side lists labor costs, like removal and disposal, installation, and emergency repair and replacement. The right side lists the companies and their prices. Kris's hourly rates are all lower. In a couple instances, half the amount. The attachment marked "Public Notification of Award Recommendation" said the offers had been evaluated and Kris's company was found to be the lowest responsible bidder.

The final attachment doesn't make sense at first. It's a change order request. Citing unforeseen increases in labor and material costs, Kris requested an additional $200,000. The bottom, marked "Paid," is dated months after Kris won the contract. The extra payment put him in line with Chuck's and Carlos's bids. Someone was either careless—or careful—to include the document in my request. It's all coming together. Thanks to an inside source, Kris managed to submit substantially lower bids than his competitors and then made up for it by sending a $200,000 bill later. I need to figure out who signed off on the extra payment and who has access to all the bids.

I pull up the city's website, determined not to get lost in legal language and five-syllable words. The process starts with someone posting a public notice that the city's looking for bids. Next, someone confirms receipt when a company submits a bid. Once bids have been determined to meet requirements, they're sent to a committee for review. Maybe I should look into who sits on the committees. No, their review comes too late in the process. It's got to be someone early on. My mind closes in on one person. Even though nearly everything can be submitted electronically, there's still a human touch, a person who confirms receipt, someone who sees the bids as they come in.

I email the PIO for the finance department and ask for the name of the employee who officially accepts and records bids. The response is an immediate phone call, which means, like the mayor's chief of staff, the PIO doesn't want a written record of our conversation.

"Paul Gullifor here. I got your email and was just wondering why you need an employee's name?"

"Is that person a public employee?"

"Yes."

"Then I'd like to get their name."

"Sure, sure, I hear ya." He sounds like a car salesman about to explain why the more expensive model is the better deal. "Is this for a particular story?"

After being kicked out by Simona's boss and constantly having to explain to Sexy why this story matters, I've reached my limit.

"Paul, as I understand it, I'm not required by law to explain why I'm seeking public information. Can you please get me the name?"

"As you know, the city is always happy to provide public information." His tone is now a salesman who lost the deal. "Let me check with my supervisor."

"Thank you. I hope to get it by the end of today."

"I'll do my best." Translation: don't hold your breath.

Maybe Alex the brainiac can come up with another avenue for me to explore. I'm about to check the menu board for a sweet bribe when Faith walks in and is greeted like a rock star. She waves me over.

"Jolene, do you know the owner, Stephanie Vasquez?"

"It's nice to meet you, Stephanie. I've read about your successful business ventures."

"And I've seen your reporting. Thanks for coming in."

"Stephanie was an early supporter of Mayor Ace's campaign," Faith says. "We sometimes held strategy sessions here."

"Best guy in the race," Stephanie says. "I still have the campaign button."

An employee asks Faith if she's having her regular.

"Yes, please. And can you add a veggie burrito and bottled water? Jolene, feel free to take a seat." Faith taps on her phone. "I'll be just a minute."

A light rail train stops at the Roosevelt/Central Avenue station and the woman outside rummages through her backpack. She pulls out a brush and ties her hair into a ponytail. Faith sets her coffee on the table, says she'll be right back, and walks out the door. She approaches the woman and says something that makes her shrug. Faith sits next to her on the curb. The woman closes the notebook, slides it into the plastic bag, and hooks the drawstring around her wrist. Faith hands her a business card and, after the woman nods, Faith shows her phone to the woman. She studies Faith for a moment and gets up. Faith pockets her phone and hands the water to the woman.

A red Ford Explorer pulls to the curb, an Uber sign on the windshield. Faith opens a back door and makes a "May I?" motion before placing the plastic bag inside. She smiles as the woman accepts the burrito and climbs in the back. After the Explorer leaves, Faith returns.

"What's her story?" I ask.

"Brittany lost her apartment a week ago. She's been staying with friends but it's not working out. I got her a ride to a place that'll help her."

"That was nice of you."

"A lost job, bad luck, or a poor choice and that could be any of us. Not everyone is fortunate to have a strong support system when they make mistakes." She glances around. "I thought this would be a good place away from city hall ears, but it's pretty busy." She removes the lid. "Suppose it doesn't matter much since I'm leaving."

I almost choke on my drink. Faith is connected with a capital "C." She could get elected mayor.

"It's time for a change. Mayor Ace is moving on and so am I." Faith blows on her coffee. "You said you wanted to discuss Rich Gains's murder. Are the police any closer to catching the burglar?"

"I'm not convinced it was a home burglary that went wrong."

I'm also not convinced it wasn't, but sometimes you have to act like you know something in order to get something.

"Why are you not convinced it was a burglary?"

"A reliable source thinks otherwise."

Not a lie. Whitney Wright is reliable—she took my call and gave me information.

Faith takes a tentative sip. "What are you hearing?"

"It's not only what I'm hearing but learning. Rich was the face for developers who wanted to build as fast and cheap as possible, with the least community involvement. Those tactics can backfire when residents find out."

Faith nods and says nothing. I'm not falling for that. I gave her something, now it's her turn. I take a sip. A slow sip.

"Jolene, I respect your reporting and I'm sure you can respect my position. I'd like to help but need assurances that my name will be kept out of your story. Can we talk off the record?"

Conversations off the record should be rare. Off the record means I can't use the information unless I get it from another source. There's only one person I regularly work with off the record and it's not Faith.

"How about on background? Anything you share that's pertinent to the story I can attribute to a city hall insider."

She swivels her cup while considering my offer. "I would prefer you only attribute it to a source. The rumor mill at city hall is worse than high school. It would take no time for someone to whisper my name and I'd be called to the mayor's office."

I don't like it, but I need her help.

"Even saying a source could be enough to land me in trouble," Faith says. "Maybe we should skip this."

Well played, chief of staff.

"You know, just because you tell me something doesn't mean I'm going to run with it. I would need to be one hundred percent confident it's accurate, and ideally, confirm it another way. I can't imagine anyone would identify you as the source. Unless you tell me the mayor killed the lobbyist."

Faith makes a noise under her breath and scans the shop. A corner table has opened and I suggest we move. The privacy pays off.

"Rich Gains was one of the first people I met when I started working at city hall," Faith says. "That was maybe a dozen years ago, when Ace was a councilman, and before we decided to run for mayor. Even back then, Rich knew how to schmooze. He donated to everyone's campaigns and supported their favorite nonprofits. Always bought Girl Scout cookies from Mayor's Ace's grandchildren." She lifts her cup to her mouth and pauses. "Until Ace cut off contact with him."

Mr. Unavoidable for Comment stopped talking to Mr. Rich Lobbyist?

"Why?"

"Mayor Ace wasn't comfortable with how Rich's influence had grown. Over the past few years, we've seen Rich box out competitors and lure their clients to his firm. He went from being moderately known to becoming the dominant lobbyist. His fingerprints were on all the major projects and the mayor didn't want a hint of impropriety."

"Sounds like he worked the system to his clients' advantage. Anything illegal or unethical?"

A flicker of doubt passes over her face.

"This is background," I remind her.

She looks at me like she's debating something that has nothing to do with my story.

"On background then," she says. "With no attribution to me. Deal?"

"Deal."

"Rich's firm got into trouble for not registering as lobbyists. I take that back—not really in trouble because at that time the city had no penalties for lobbyists who didn't register. Mayor Ace—then Councilman Ace—led the charge to put teeth in city ordinances to hold lobbyists accountable. He believed the public should have easy access to find out who's representing which companies and who's donating to which candidates. Of course, the donation information is kind of moot because all lobbyists donate the max."

"To every candidate?"

"It's the way the system works." She raises an index finger. "Except for Mayor Ace. He was so uncomfortable with Rich's ethics and morals, he refused to accept any more contributions from him."

Mayor Ace Logan likes to be liked. And he believes in second chances. Logan publicly forgave the man who drove impaired and killed his wife. For the mayor to distance himself from Rich Gains means Rich must have been an awful person.

"In my research, I found some of Rich's projects pit neighbors against neighbors. What about council members? Any animosity?"

Her look of hesitation is forced. She's giving off an energy, something she's dying to spill.

Faith leans in and says, "I'll let you in on a secret—if you agree this part is off the record."

I give her a "C'mon" look.

"Or not."

"Fine. But if I get the same information from someone else, I'm going to use it."

"As long as my name is never affiliated with it." Her phone chimes an incoming text. "Good. Brittany made it to the shelter." She places her phone face-down on the table. "I'm confident she'll get back on her feet. Now, where was I?"

"An off-the-record secret."

Faith takes in the space and gives a slight nod. "Certain council members like to publicly appear as if they're pushing back on developers, especially when neighborhood groups show up to meetings after they've spent months, sometimes years, battling a project. It can be a full-time job for residents trying to understand the process, all the city departments involved, what's required and not required of developers. When it comes time to vote, certain council members will say things that sound like they're siding with residents but act like their hands are tied. Really, their hands are behind their backs, ready for the next campaign donation. Almost always, council members know how the others are going to vote on controversial projects before the meeting even starts."

"So, all the public presentations before the council votes are just for show?"

"It is required by law, but basically, yes. That's why listening to Rich's presentations could be nauseating. It's heartbreaking to see residents who've invested so much time, effort, and sometimes financial expense by hiring their own attorneys, all for nothing. No trees saved. No historic buildings preserved. They would have more impact if they behaved less like grassroots organizations and more like lobbyists by donating to council campaigns."

Outrage surges through my body. I can only imagine how residents who are directly impacted feel. "Any cases raise concerns among the city council over their safety?"

"There have been verbal threats promising to vote them out of office. But again, elected officials know that very few residents have the resources to follow through, so the chances they won't be re-elected are next to nil. Besides, voters have short memories."

The urge to argue claws at me, but I stay on track. "What about the project in the Nirvana neighborhood?"

"Those neighbors are more organized than most. Their leader is a firecracker. Can't recall his name."

"Fred Nimby."

"That's it."

"What can you tell me about him?"

"Not much. Nimby fancies himself as a future council member, but doesn't realize his major obstacle is thinking he can get elected through neighbors backing him. It takes dollars to win votes."

"I hope to talk with him soon. His Facebook posts contain strong language."

"Understandable. It's a frustrating system. Mayor Ace wanted to revamp the process, require all developers to notify residents up front and keep them informed about the size and design and construction timetable. Right now, they only have to notify property owners within five hundred feet of a project and that's only if they request a change in zoning."

"Five hundred feet doesn't sound like much."

"About a tenth of a mile."

"When you're talking hundreds of apartments or a commercial project, someone could argue the impact reaches beyond five hundred feet."

"Exactly. But Mayor Ace couldn't get enough colleagues interested in changing the system because it would likely mean taking on state lawmakers. As you may know, it's not uncommon for the legislature to pass bills that preempt city laws. At the state capitol, developers and their lobbyists dominate. Requiring developers to include more residents early in the process would be a herculean task. It would involve extensive outreach and public participation. That's more work for developers, who, as you've noticed, have quite the influence."

"Did Rich Gains have special influence over anyone in particular?"

Her head shake says she's not going there. I let the silence settle between us. An employee wipes down a nearby table. Someone is chatting with the owner, scrolling on a tablet, giving off sales vibes.

"How about off the record?" I suggest.

Faith's fingers drum her cup as she stares at a framed message touting the economic impact of supporting a local business. It reads: You are doing so much more than just buying a cup of coffee.

"I will not report anything you're about to say unless I can independently verify it."

"Okay." She lowers her voice. "Quite a few people surmise Rich was especially cozy with Councilwoman Zoey Patterson."

"What do you mean by cozy?"

"You know she's a real estate agent?"

I did not. Phoenix council positions are officially considered part-time. Some members have other jobs, some do not.

"I can't give you hard evidence, but the impression among many people is that Councilwoman Patterson benefits from her relationships with developers, particularly Rich Gains. She buys and flips houses—that's her specialty—and she gets work done quickly, even at her own home. Whispers—again, that's city hall for you, so it may simply be rumors—but when most people, myself included, have to schedule renovations months in advance and she manages full kitchen remodels in three weeks, it raises eyebrows."

"Given her job, why is she voting on real estate developments? Isn't that a conflict of interest?"

"She deals solely with single-family houses. Developers are building subdivisions, multi-family housing, and commercial spaces. Technically, she doesn't need to recuse herself. But the optics are. . . ." She wiggles her hand like "so-so."

"Did the councilwoman and Rich Gains ever have disagreements?"

"I can only speak to what I witnessed. Once, while waiting to talk with her, I overheard raised voices from inside her office. I couldn't make out what was being said, but it was heated.

When the door opened, Rich stormed out. Who knows why? I didn't ask and Zoey never offered."

"Anything else about their relationship? Or Rich's relationship with anyone else at city hall?"

"The only time I saw—or I should say heard—any real anger was between him and Zoey." She takes a thoughtful sip. "You might say Rich is known for being passionate beyond his business."

"Are you saying he and Zoey had an affair?"

"I would never say that. But his reputation for affairs is as strong as his reputation for muscling projects through the city."

That's a new angle to consider. Let's see how much tea Faith is willing to spill.

"A source told me Rich would meet discreetly with a contractor who regularly wins city contracts. The source found it strange because the contractor never hid other work-related meetings."

"I'm not sure where you're going," she says.

"My source says the contractor—his name is Kris Kruger—may be winning city deals by not playing fair."

"Forgive my confusion," she says. "Are you investigating this Kruger person? Or Rich Gains's murder?"

"Both. The day the mayor was stuck in the elevator I learned a contractor is accusing Kruger of gaming the system."

She nods like maybe it's a common complaint. "I get it now. The contractor's attorney is Whitney Wright who happened to chat with you at city hall."

Shit. I shouldn't have mentioned the day.

"Do you know anything about Kruger's contracts? Or his relationship with Rich Gains?"

"I do not." Her phone quivers and she reads a text. "You'll have to excuse me."

I thank her, promise to protect her name, and consider my

next move. I had expected our conversation to provide a clear path forward for me to investigate Fred Nimby as a potential suspect in Rich Gains's murder. But Councilwoman Zoey Patterson is piquing my interest. A public official who cut deals with a lobbyist to get personal construction work done. A lobbyist she argued with and may have been romantically involved with. Time to call my super source.

CHAPTER

12

Jim Miranda is my most valuable source, but not the most willing. Our relationship is complicated. On this day, my optimism is unusually high because it's only been twelve minutes between my text and his call.

"How's life in the SIU?" I ask.

Jim's in charge of the Special Investigations Unit or, as he calls it, "Someone is Unhappy." Cases that land on his desk are labeled high-profile because they're monitored by the police chief and city leaders. They're cases that have either generated publicity or cases they hope to keep out of the public eye.

"I was doing okay until your text. Don't tell me another talk show host has died."

"No, I'm looking into Rich Gains's murder."

Jim lets out an exaggerated sigh and says, "I thought we were even after Larry Lemmon's murder."

Jim helped with my investigation into the talk show host because he owed me for sitting on another story at his request. Agreeing to back off the story ended up biting me. JJ Jackson got the scoop and reported what should've been my exclusive.

At the time, I was pissed, but helping cops catch the talk show host's killer and winning an Emmy made up for it.

"Jim, let's not keep score. Besides, you know you can trust me."

Whenever we talk, everything he says is off the record. When Jim's done sharing whatever crumbs he's willing to drop, we negotiate what I can report. It's a system we created when he was a PIO and we bonded over our low tolerance for bullshit. Because of our jobs, we'd never describe ourselves as friends, but we can be friendly on the rare occasions we get together for lunch. Not only does Jim know where to find the best kimchee, he's a kickass interviewer. After sharing that he grew up with an absent father and overworked mother, he got me to open up about my childhood. He's the only person who knows the real story.

"It's been a couple weeks since Gains was shot. Isn't there someone you're looking at?"

"Can't tell you anything more than what you guys reported," he says. "It appears he surprised a burglar."

"How about this?" I offer. "Tell me what you have and I'll tell you what I have. Bet you'll be impressed."

"Really? Let me call my lead investigator so we can tap into your expertise. Unless you've already identified the killer. Then, by all means, do share."

"I sense you're not in the most giving mood so I'll get to it. I had a conversation with a source who pointed out a special relationship between Rich Gains and Councilwoman Zoey Patterson. Can you ask your guy about it?"

"The lead investigator is a woman."

"Thank you for the clarification. Can you ask her about the relationship between the councilwoman and the murdered lobbyist?"

"What about it?"

"Okay, I give up. I'll just talk to council members myself. I know they get regular updates on high-profile cases."

There's a beat of silence before Jim speaks.

"Not much to share. Whoever shot Rich left no evidence."

His words come out too fast.

"What about security video?"

"Negative. Perpetrator jammed the system and blocked signals."

"Video from neighbors?"

"One camera caught a handful of cars coming and going around the time of his death. Detectives ran their plates. No connections, nothing out of the ordinary."

"Any other houses hit in the area?"

"Negative."

Now he's trying hard to sound nonchalant. Jim's holding back. As I dig through my bag for a notepad, I tell him I just started working the story and found people who aren't shedding tears over Rich's death.

"Jolene, he was a lobbyist. Of course, not everyone liked him."

"You must have a list of persons of interest." I flip to a fresh page, pen locked and loaded. "Care to share?"

"No.

"What about fingerprints?"

"Found a lot in his home. Not unusual considering he liked to entertain. Got hits on two sets through the federal system for white-collar crimes. People more likely to arm themselves with charm and wipe out your bank accounts than pull a gun and steal your wallet."

"Just because they ripped people off without physical violence doesn't mean they wouldn't go that route."

"We checked them out, Sherlock. Both had solid alibis."

I hate when he calls me Sherlock. It's never meant as a compliment. "Any other prints of interest?"

This pause lasts two beats.

"Jim?"

"We are still off the record."

"Absolutely." I close my eyes and tune out the hum of the coffee shop.

"Two people from city hall."

My eyelids snap open. "Who?" I hear him breathing. I keep my mouth shut.

"Councilwoman Zoey Patterson and Mayor Ace Logan."

"What?" I clamp a hand over my mouth, but no one noticed my shock. Thank you, headphones and earbuds. "Their prints showed up when you ran them for priors?" Mindful of our agreement, I jot down their initials only.

"Don't get worked up. Their prints are on file with the state because their volunteer work required background checks. Logan's been part of a children's literacy program for years and Patterson used to visit nursing homes."

Patterson's prints make sense if she accepted kickbacks—and possibly kisses—from Rich, but not the mayor. If, as Faith claimed, the mayor disliked Rich so much he wouldn't accept campaign donations, there's no reason his prints would be at the lobbyist's house.

"I heard Mayor Logan wasn't a fan of Rich Gains."

"Are you implying the mayor killed him?"

"No." But the new information warrants a closer look. "Patterson argued with Rich and she has a reputation for cashing in."

"Is that a question?"

"Yes. What do you think about her relationship with the dead lobbyist?"

"I don't have a public opinion."

A woman carrying a panini and wearing no headphones slides into a nearby seat. I toss the notepad in my bag and head out the door. "My source thinks Zoey Patterson engaged in un-ethical, possibly illegal behavior."

That may be a stretch but I need more from Jim.

"Good luck with your story. I have to get back to work."

"Can I call you after I talk with council members?"

"Why would you do that?"

"They're familiar with the victim. He appeared before them countless times seeking support for his clients' projects."

"I need you to not go there."

Something in Jim's voice shifts.

I plop down on a bench. "Why?"

"You know, some days I really regret giving you my per-sonal cell number."

Pressing a finger against my ear, I try to block out the traffic.

"Jim, if there's not a good reason for me to back off, I can't."

He curses under his breath and reminds me we're off the re-cord. "We suspect Patterson has been promising contracts if the price is right."

That supports the rumors about remodeling work done at Patterson's properties, but it can't be easy.

"There's a public bid process for city contracts," I say. "She can't award contracts on her own."

"Not every deal goes through a formal process. If a contract is worth less than twenty-five thousand dollars, the department can handle it internally. If it's between twenty-five and fifty, it needs city manager approval."

I scribble notes using my shorthand version of mostly drop-ping vowels.

"That means the councilwoman could subtly—or not so subtly—let her opinion be known on contracts up to fifty thou-sand," I say. "Does that sound right?"

"I'm not describing anything as right or wrong in this off-the-record conversation."

"What about deals worth more than fifty grand?"

"Goes through the formal process," Jim says. "But there can be exceptions if time is of the essence or if there are only one or two businesses that offer a specific service or item the city needs. In those cases, departments can send contract proposals directly to the council for approval. Almost always, they're approved with no discussion."

"What kind of evidence do you have against Councilwoman Patterson?"

"I've already told you too much and I'm not going to jeopardize the case. Besides, we're still gathering evidence."

"Okay, tell me if this is reasonable: you have someone who will testify to bribes. Or you have undercover video. Or both?"

"I'm not revealing specifics."

"Do any of those examples sound reasonable?"

Jim says nothing.

"So, they are not reasonable?"

Silence.

"You can at least tell me why Phoenix is investigating one of its own. Isn't the Arizona attorney general supposed to investigate public officials?"

He huffs a response. "Yes. Unless there's a connection to murder."

The notepad falls from my hand. "You think Councilwoman Patterson is involved in the lobbyist's murder?"

"That is not what I'm saying."

"Then what are you saying?"

"Our priority is investigating Gains's murder. As part of our investigation, we uncovered information about possible bribes and alerted the AG's office. They've taken the lead on the corruption investigation and we're providing support as needed."

"Sounds like the AG's investigation goes beyond the councilwoman and the lobbyist."

"You would have to ask the AG's office."

"And you know I won't get a response. Based on what you've said, it's clear Patterson isn't the only elected official being looked at. Who else?"

"All you're getting from me—off the record—is that the investigation is ongoing and widespread."

"Okay," I say. "For now, I'll avoid any reporting on bribe allegations and pitch a follow-up story about the investigation into Gains's murder. My manager will go for it and that would be my way in to talk to council members."

"Jolene, I need you to stay away from the council."

"I'm not going to accuse anyone of breaking the law. Just ask if they have ideas about who killed Gains. You can't still believe it was a burglar."

"I believe my investigators need to do their jobs without you interfering. Councilwoman Zoey Patterson is a person of interest, but she may not be the only one. We can't have you getting in the way."

"I appreciate you sharing so much, but please appreciate my position. What am I supposed to do?"

"I'm not telling you what to do. Only that you can't use anything I've given you. And since that included the council connection, you need to stand by our agreement. That means avoiding the council."

But Jim didn't ask me to stay away from the scene of the crime.

CHAPTER
13

The house where the lobbyist was shot is off Grand Avenue, a diagonal outlier in a city built on a grid system. For decades, hotels and restaurants along Grand Avenue served travelers heading to Los Angeles, but after Interstate 10 was built, traffic slowed, along with business. After Phoenix invested heavily in its downtown, developers began sniffing around Grand. Some property owners welcome what they see as progress, while others remain protective of the area's quirkiness. Art galleries, yoga studios, and vegan restaurants mix with used car dealers, repair shops, and drive-through liquor stores. Die-hard preservationists take comfort in zoning ordinances that don't allow for high-rises. A reporter might suggest they pay attention to city council meetings because zoning gets changed. A lot.

That outlook is presumably what led Rich Gains to buy the property I passed twice. The first time I didn't trust my phone's directions, the second time I didn't trust myself. A single-story redbrick house stands between two empty lots: one consisting of a cracked concrete slab, the other surrounded by a chain-link fence. The thrum of cars and exhaust fumes from the interstate add to the ambiance.

A FOR SALE sign supports my theory that Rich's widow isn't here. But someone is. I park behind an older-model pickup with a ladder mounted on top and follow the sounds of a leaf blower past a security sign and hedge of yellow bells. I peer through a partially open gate, debating how far to push it. Arizona consistently ranks near the top of gun-friendly states, and walking into someone's backyard without an invitation isn't the safest move. Still, the house is for sale so a stranger showing up shouldn't be a total surprise. One thing is certain: if I do nothing, my story goes nowhere. Not an option. Opening the gate is like sneaking into a five-star resort. Luscious grass leads to a fountain that rivals the Bellagio in Las Vegas. A covered patio protects a kitchen with granite countertops, tile backsplash, and a flat-screen TV. Cushions as thick as my mattress are tucked into chairs around a fireplace built into a marble wall.

"Hello!" I shout to the landscaper. "Excuse me!"

From behind me, a voice booms, "Can I help you?"

Hopefully the guy who followed me belongs here.

"Hi, I'm looking for Stacey Gains."

"She's not here."

"Do you know when she'll be back?"

He removes sunglasses, revealing tan lines around his eyes.

"Do you know Mrs. Gains?" he asks.

On my shoulder, the angel of ethics flutters her wings. Technically, I don't know Mrs. Gains, but I know of her. And Mr. Gains. That counts for something.

"I haven't been by since her husband died and wanted to offer my condolences."

"Mrs. Gains doesn't live here."

"Of course, she's at the other house." Now's my chance to test my assignment editor's accuracy. Alex nailed the murder house. Let's check the widow's residence. "Do you have her address?"

The guy squints and his tan lines crinkle like fries.

I raise my hands. "Don't have my phone on me." No need to mention it's in my pocket.

He pulls out his phone and my hands relax. Until he speaks.

"We don't give out personal information, but you can call her."

The angel of ethics shakes her head. Or is she laughing?

"That's okay. My phone's in my car. Thanks for your help." Strike one.

He follows me out the gate. At the end of the street, I pull over and check the rearview mirror. Two minutes tick by. I'm confident he's not coming after me. But someone is coming out of a house across the street. I push my door open and break into a jog.

"Excuse me, do you have a minute?"

"I'm not interested."

"Oh, I'm not selling anything. I'm a reporter for Channel 4 Eyewitness News."

The woman's pace picks up. "We had enough media when that poor man was killed. Go away."

Strike two.

I understand where she's coming from, but my job is to gather information and that only happens by asking questions.

I spot a house that's sure to pay off. A camera on the side points in the direction of Rich's home with two more in the front. I follow a walkway and pass a sign that warns would-be burglars about a twenty-four-hour security system. And then I discover how powerful that system is. As I prepare to knock on the screen door, a ferocious growl erupts, so deep it strangles my throat. The monster lunges and I flounder backward. My phone goes airborne and my elbows slam against pavers. It jumps on hind legs, massive body towering over me, claws ready to slice through the screen. Saliva drips from a jaw snapping open and closed. The barks are no longer detectable over my pounding heart. I scramble for my phone and sprint to my car.

Strike three. I'm out.

By the time I reach Luana's, my palms are no longer sweaty, but my muscles are twitchy and my mind cannot let go of the fangs. I read somewhere it can take a half hour to recover from a fight-or-flight response. It didn't say how long it takes if a dog attacked you as a child.

I order the beautiful chaos drink for me and the number thirteen for Alex. It's my secret weapon. A few sips into my peanut butter and salted caramel mocha, the twitching has stopped and Alex's order is ready. He's going to love me. I sneak to my desk and hide the bribe before hitting him up.

"Alex, all I need is the name of an employee in the city's finance department. It's the person who works in procurement and confirms whether a bid has been submitted."

"Going to cost you this time." He picks up a stress ball that reads, OH, YOU'RE STILL TALKING?

"You know liquor is not allowed in the building," I say.

"But cupcakes are." He tosses the ball and catches it. "How's the investigation going? Ready to bust bakers? Be careful chasing them into the kitchen. Don't want you sliding on sugar and wiping out."

"You seem fixated on cupcakes. Does that mean you're not interested in what I have to offer?"

I catch the half-second pause before he continues tossing the ball. "Depends what it is."

"Stand by."

Halfway to my desk, Sexy corners me about cupcakes. I tell him we're close to taking them to the lab for gluten testing. I know I need to work on that story, but first, I've got to wow Alex. His eyes flit between two computers and he doesn't notice me until I ask, "What's your favorite number?"

"Don't have one."

"Bzzzz. Wrong answer. Let's try again. If you had to pick a favorite number, what would it be?"

Alex stares at me.

"Maybe a number between twelve and fourteen?"

"Okay," he says. "Thirteen."

"Ding, ding, ding. Alex, I may not remember every history lesson you give, but your love of Mu Shu Grill stuck with me." I have his attention. Mu Shu closed years before I moved to Phoenix and Alex still grumbles about how no one can match their version of General Tso's chicken. When Luana's replaced Mu Shu, Alex swore he'd never step foot inside.

"You know, carrying a grudge isn't healthy," I say. "You should give Luana's a try. There's a velvet orange chair where you'd feel right at home. It belonged to the owner's grandfather and he used to sit in it and watch CNN. The chair has a prominent place in the center of the action. Just like your seat here in the newsroom."

"Unless they're serving my favorite, I'm not interested."

"Lucky for you, Alex, I happen to be willing to share an inside scoop."

I explain Luana's got the recipe for General Tso's chicken from Mu Shu's owner and added it to their menu, using the same number as Mu Shu: thirteen.

"Any guess what I brought you?"

He rubs his hands together. "Where is it?"

When Alex opens the container, his head bows and his chest expands as he breathes in the sweet and spicy aroma. "Got a fork?"

"Not so fast," I say. "How about helping me get the name of the city employee who handles bids?"

"No sweat. Listen to the scanners and write down anything that sounds important. I'll be right back."

Why's he leaving? I expected him to log on to a secret site.

Two minutes later, Alex slaps a sticky note on the desk.

"There you go."

"This is my city worker?"

"Yep." He drops into his chair and rips open a plastic fork.

"How'd you get his name so fast?"

"I don't reveal all my methods."

"I won't tell anyone."

He jabs a forkful of chicken into his mouth.

"I brought your favorite. Isn't that worth a little extra info?"

His eyes slide my way as he swirls the rice. "Let's just say sometimes old-school is most effective."

"C'mon, what'd you do?"

"Used the phone for its original purpose."

"Wait, you called and they just told you?"

He finishes chewing and says, "Why wouldn't they tell a business owner calling to confirm receipt of his bid the name of the person he should talk to?"

"But we're supposed to identify ourselves as journalists. I don't know if that's ethical."

"Aren't we supposed to be uncovering injustice and holding the powerful accountable? If you want to take the high road, be my guest. There's plenty of room since the llamas were lassoed."

I pluck the note off the desk, ready to investigate the city employee, but my plan is derailed.

CHAPTER

14

"Hello, Jolene, how are you?"

"Hi, Hussein. I'm doing okay."

Hussein Aden manages mail and deliveries and serves as a security guard. More than once, he's calmly handled someone barging in demanding to talk to a reporter.

"How are Mumina and your children?" I ask.

Hussein's family moved to Phoenix as part of the federal government's refugee resettlement program. His wife, Mumina, developed a strong fan base in the newsroom after sharing her homemade sambusas.

"My family is good," he says. "Me, not so good."

"What's wrong?"

"I got in trouble at my other job."

Hussein also cleans cars at the rental center next to Sky Harbor Airport. He works so much that last year his manager made him take time off.

"My new manager thinks I steal. He says I take money from cars, but I follow the rules."

"What are the rules?"

He checks the clock on the wall. It's time for his rounds and

I offer to walk with him. As we enter the parking garage, Hussein explains when items are left in rental cars, he takes them to the manager.

"Then the manager writes it down and I sign the book. After one month, if nobody calls to say, 'That is mine,' then I get to keep it." Hussein's face shines with eagerness. "I have many lawn chairs and sunglasses. Would you like some?"

"That's nice of you to offer, but I don't need any. What happens if you find money?"

"The coins fall under seats or they get stuck. I pick them up and turn them in. Sometimes I find dollars. One time I found a wallet in the back seat. There was a driver's license, credit cards, and forty-eight dollars."

"And you turned it in?"

"Yes, yes."

Out of the garage now, we head toward the station's entrance. Hussein pulls on a thick metal gate to make sure it's locked.

"My manager—a different manager—found the owner of the wallet and sent it to him. I didn't get to keep anything then." He grins. "But another time I found a fifty-dollar bill and I got to keep it."

"Do you find money often?"

His face scrunches. "Maybe two times a month."

"How much have you kept—if you don't mind me asking."

"You mean since I started working there?"

"If you know."

"Yes, I keep track. Almost nine hundred seventy-five dollars. The most I found at one time was sixty-three dollars. No one reported it and I got to keep it." He frowns. "But that was my other manager. She was a good manager. This manager is no good."

"Why do you say that?"

"He fired my friend. He said my friend steals. We do not

steal. If my friend needs money, I will help him. If I need money, he helps me. That is what the Koran teaches."

"If your manager accused you of stealing, what can you do?"

He shrugs. "I don't know. He told me I cannot work until the investigation is done. It will be ten days. Maybe longer. Mumina is worried because she is going to take time off of work after the baby is born. We need the money."

We walk in silence for a moment. I ask Hussein who he thinks is taking the money.

He looks down. "It would not be right to say because I do not know for sure."

"Where does the money go after you turn it in?"

"There is a box in the manager's office. He puts it in there and locks it."

I say what Hussein will not. "The manager could be stealing."

"I do not know who else has a key to the box."

"What about the book you sign when you turn in money and other things?"

"That was with my last manager. Only sometimes with this manager. He's been my manager for three months and I signed the book only one time."

"Let me get this straight: He fired your friend last month and now he's accusing you?"

"Yes." He opens the front door and we greet the receptionist who buzzes us in.

"Hussein, do you know anyone in human resources?"

He nods. "Will they help me?"

I recall what a producer told me not long after I started in TV news: HR's job is to protect the company, not employees, so if a manager is slimy, unethical, or incompetent, you either find a way to deal with it or leave. At the time I thought the producer was disgruntled—and he was—but he was also right. The rental car business might be less brutal than TV news, but

I don't want Hussein to risk it. And maybe he won't have to. A solution comes from a monitor behind us. A commercial urging me to contact the Wright Legal Firm.

"Hussein, how about this? I'll call an attorney and get her advice. Maybe she knows a group that can help without charging you. If I find someone, I can have them call or text you. Is that okay?"

"Yes, thank you."

I add Hussein's number to my phone and excuse myself to call.

"Whitney Wright speaking."

"Hi, Whitney, it's Jolene Garcia."

"Add it to the list."

"Excuse me?"

"We can talk about it tomorrow. Bye."

"Hello?"

"Sorry about that, Jolene. Just wrapping up another call. What can I do for you?"

I explain Hussein's predicament. "I would bet my reputation he's not stealing."

"No offense, but reporters don't have the best reputations. What makes you so sure he's not stealing?"

"My gut, I guess. Hussein works hard and seems devoted to his religion. He's told me that Islam stresses avoiding debt and supporting people in need."

"Glad you're not his lawyer. You could be making a case for why he would steal."

"I think he would ask other Muslims for help if he needed money."

"You say there was another guy fired? Was he Muslim, too?"

"I don't know. I can ask. Or I can have Hussein call your office and set up an appointment. Since this is a personal request, not related to my job, I'd like to cover his consultation. After meeting with him, if you decide to take him on, you two can talk fees and decide how to proceed."

"I'm due for pro bono work. I'll meet with him at no charge. Doesn't mean I'll take his case though. Have him call my office to schedule an appointment."

I share what I've learned about Kris Kruger, the guy who always wins the city contracts. I explain how Kruger worked the system by bidding lower than her client, Carlos, and made up the difference by later submitting invoices for "unanticipated" labor and material costs.

"I've got to hand it to you, Jolene, I was skeptical. You're renewing my faith in local journalism."

"Whitney, I know you haven't personally met Kris Kruger, but do you have any impressions based on what you know and what you've heard?"

"What are you getting at?"

"When I interviewed him, I got a weird vibe."

"Meaning?"

"Let's just say I wouldn't be comfortable alone in a room with him. He's definitely not pleasant and he got defensive when I asked about Carlos's complaint." I take a breath. "Plus, he's a mechanic. Do you think he could've had anything to do with Carlos's crash?"

"You suspect Kris did something to Carlos's car?"

"When you consider the timing of the crash—right after you put the city on notice—and no skid marks at the scene, it's suspicious," I say. "And your brother mentioned a divorce case where someone cut a car's brake lines."

Whitney is silent for a long moment. "You raise an interesting point," she finally says. "Perhaps Carlos's family was too quick to blame a medical issue. Just like reporters were too quick to accept the police department's version of a lobbyist interrupting a home burglar. Have you found a connection between Rich Gains and Kris Kruger?"

I recount my conversation with Kris's former accountant, Simona Park, about Kris's secret meetings with Rich, and their angry outburst Simona witnessed.

"After Carlos left Kris to start his own company, he began doing work for Rich's clients," I say. "Carlos told me Rich taught him how to bid on city contracts."

"Kris could have resented Rich for helping his competition. He had it made until Carlos showed up," she says. "I wonder if he could have been angry enough to go after both of them."

"Exactly what I was thinking."

"Once again, you've impressed me, Jolene. Sounds like you're onto a major story. Kris Kruger could've potentially lost millions in business if Carlos's complaint had been successful. And he might never have been in the situation if Rich hadn't walked Carlos through the bid process. Is there anything I can do to help?"

"Do you have any other documents or information?"

"You have everything from us. I haven't closed the file and won't unless Carlos's family directs me, and that conversation won't happen for a couple weeks."

"Okay," I say. "Thanks for all your help."

"You know, when we met, I didn't expect you would do anything. And now you're on the verge of exposing illegal behavior at city hall that likely led to the murders of a well-known lobbyist and a beloved small-business owner."

I'm glad someone understands and appreciates my work. Now if I can just convince my managers. Until then, I have to keep mixing cupcakes with city hall. I pack the undercover gear and swing by the assignment desk on my way out.

"Now who owes who?" I tell Alex.

"It's who owes whom," he says. "But I'll let your grammar go, because you remembered my favorite." He pats his stomach. "General Tso's chicken was delicious."

Alex's enthusiasm leads me back to Luana's where I order my own number thirteen to go. My grandma would be proud I made it all the way to my kitchen table instead of eating over the sink. She'd be less impressed with my dinnertime scrolling. I push my phone out of reach and focus on savory chicken chunks. They disappear faster than raindrops under a Phoenix sun. My phone buzzes.

Back off, Jolene. Stop investigating.

The text comes up anonymous. I type,

Who is this?

They don't respond. Not that I expected them to. Anonymous texts and emails aren't unusual. If I backed off every time someone wanted me to, I'd have nothing to report. Not going to happen. I'm on the cusp of breaking big news.

CHAPTER
15

The next day begins on a positive note—no anonymous text warning me to stop investigating. But I can no longer stave off Sexy's desire for cupcakes, so I devise a plan to hit a few bakeries before feeding my hunger for real news. With the help of Pamela, the intern, we should collect enough cupcakes today.

My first stop is Fairy Tale Cupcakes in Old Town Scottsdale. A banner declares it's home to the best local cupcakes. It's definitely home to the most shades of pink. Bubblegum-pink booths, magenta napkin dispensers, fuchsia molding on the walls. I cradle my purse like a baby, swaying back and forth so the hidden camera captures the shop's claim to fame. The audio track plays in my head: "They may be the best, but are they really gluten-free?"

Behind the counter, a woman pokes her head out of a swinging door and says, "Marty, can you handle things alone? I need to check on a catering order."

"Sure thing, Mel."

As Marty helps a customer, I stroll along the display case, angling the camera to record what I hope will be smooth video.

On the second pass, my phone interrupts the flow. The caller ID comes up as spam and I shut it off.

"Let me know if you have any questions," Marty says.

I place the purse on the counter to record the transaction.

"I'd like one chocolate cupcake, gluten-free, please."

"Any sprinkles or candy bar toppings?"

"No, thanks."

"Any nuts or fruit slices?"

"No."

"What kind of frosting?"

"Uh . . . regular?"

"Buttercream and whipped cream are our most popular."

"That's fine."

"Which one?"

"Whatever you recommend."

"Can't beat our whipped cream."

But I could beat my head against your counter. I remind myself Marty didn't assign this story.

"Whipped cream, please."

Marty's head bobs. "Magnificent choice. Anything else? As you can tell, our products are extremely popular. That's why we offer such variety. Just this morning, Mel—that's the owner—baked peach cobbler cupcakes and someone bought them all."

"Just one chocolate, please."

When Marty opens the display case, I hold a five-dollar bill in front of the camera, moving it in and out of frame.

"Here you go." He hands me a cupcake topped with a swirl shaped like soft-serve vanilla ice cream.

My stomach rumbles. "Can you make it two?"

Inside the car, I rewind the video. The money shots are excellent. So is the cupcake. Wiping crumbs off my phone, I notice two voice mails. The first is a robocall claiming my car warranty has expired. I delete it before "Susie" finishes her pitch and play the next message.

"Jolene, you are persistent." The voice is deep, a mediocre clone of Darth Vader. "Typically, an admirable trait in a reporter, but not in this case. Stop investigating or you will regret it. Do yourself a favor and stick to cupcakes."

My head spins like a Tilt-A-Whirl. Someone is watching me. Is it the person in the Jeep pretending to be on their phone? Was it the older man who held the bakery door as I walked out? Maybe it wasn't even an older man—but someone in disguise. Fear pricks my spine. The smart thing to do is get more cupcakes, as planned. Darth Vader will think I got the message loud and clear.

I stick to the posted speed limit. In a city of speeders, it's my best chance at spotting a tail. And I do. The only vehicle that doesn't pass me is a forest-green SUV. When I slow, it slows. When I flip on my turn signal, the driver does the same. Anger churns from my head to toes.

"This is how you want to play?"

I park between a bakery and a sandwich shop, tracking the SUV in my mirrors. If I don't recognize the driver, I'll get the license plate number and ask Jim Miranda to run it through law enforcement databases. The SUV pulls up to a business two doors down. Other cars block the view.

No more hiding. I'm going to get a real face to go with the fake Darth Vader voice. I grab the purse, hit the recorder, and smack my door open. My marching feet keep time with my thumping heart. I hear the SUV's door close. Then another. It's two against one. That's okay, there are plenty of witnesses.

"Hey," I call out to the driver.

He shoots me a look and moves toward me. As my mouth opens to yell again, a child carrying an Elmo backpack skips to the front of the SUV. He takes the driver's hand and they walk into a daycare center. Darth Vader must have been in a different car. The voice mail and anonymous text were meant to stop me from investigating, but what exactly? Carlos's deadly crash? Rich's murder? Both? The uncertainty has me craving control. Cupcakes I can handle.

At the next bakery, the blast of sweetness makes me woozy. When I crouch to shoot close-ups, I lose my balance and hit the floor.

"Are you okay?" An employee wearing a black apron with LISA embroidered in white cursive leans over the counter.

"Yep." I push myself up and adjust the purse. "I'd like one gluten-free chocolate cupcake with chocolate frosting, no toppings."

She clicks her tongue. "Sorry, we're out of chocolate."

"How about vanilla?"

"Ooh, we're out of those, too."

"I'll just take whatever you have that's gluten-free."

"Hmm." Her eyes track the display case. "Looks like we have lemon and strawberry. No, I take that back. No strawberry. But we have apple."

Ordering lemon is the best way to avoid temptation. They're meant for lemonade, not cupcakes. At the final stop, I order a flavor meant for salads: carrot. Mission accomplished. I decide the anonymous text and voice mail were aimed at my investigation into Carlos's death. Police have been all over Rich Gains's murder, so it's safe for me to look into it. Goodbye cupcakes, hello real reporting.

The Biltmore neighborhood is on Phoenix's east side, with beautiful views of Camelback Mountain. Multimillion-dollar homes that could easily house multiple families surround the Arizona Biltmore, a resort that's welcomed every sitting president from Herbert Hoover to George W. Bush. The Biltmore is long-rumored—but not definitively proven—to have been where

Irving Berlin penned the classic song "White Christmas." Residents who venture past towering oleanders and stately fences are treated to a jeweler's showcase, gorgeous emeralds courtesy of two eighteen-hole golf courses and brilliant sapphires thanks to man-made lakes.

Reaching the home of Rich Gains's widow is harder than a middle-class gated community, where you simply wait for someone to punch in the code and slide in behind them. When properties hit the million-dollar mark, gates come with guards.

I consider how to get past the guard while circling Biltmore Fashion Park. I slow for a woman strolling across the parking lot swinging Pottery Barn and Ralph Lauren bags. Maybe I can say I'm filling in for the regular housekeeper? Nah, my clothes aren't expensive, but they aren't meant for cleaning, either. I brake for a bronze Ferrari backing out of a space. Maybe I'm the nanny? Too risky since I don't know if they have kids—or a nanny. As I pass Macy's, a more realistic plan pops into my head. Floral delivery. Nothing suspicious about that. I'll offer condolences and introduce myself. In what I take as a sign from the universe, a prime parking spot beckons. I pull up the shopping center's app and scroll: J.Crew, MAC, Saks. No florist. Then it hits me. I already have the perfect prop. Five minutes later, I tuck my press ID under my shirt and smile at a man stepping out of the guardhouse.

"Hi, how are you?"

"Doing fine, ma'am. And you?"

"Could be better." I pick up the cupcakes from the passenger seat. "I meant to drop by Stacey Gains's house earlier, but the day got away from me. Bet you know how that goes."

"Oh, yes." He makes a note on a clipboard. "You know where the Gains's residence is?"

Thanks to an app, I do. "Take the first right, then the first left?"

"You got it. After that, it's the fourth or fifth house on your right."

"Thanks so much."

As I wait for the gate to open, he moves to the back of my car. Oh, no. He's writing down my license plate number. I should've known it wouldn't be this easy. Can I be charged with trespassing? No, the guard let me through. Impersonating a delivery driver? Not if I actually deliver something. When it comes to legal consequences, I'm in the clear. I ignore the ethical ramifications.

The mailboxes have no names or numbers and each house is larger than the last. The fourth house is hidden behind ficus trees. The fifth house is visible, along with a water fountain and circular driveway that promises a quick escape. I creep along gray cobblestone, praying my presence doesn't trigger alarms or a pack of dogs. My heart jumps when I spot the Mercedes's personalized plate: LOBWIFE. I close my door as if not to disturb a prayer service. I don't know if it's nerves or being around money that triggers the gentle closing of my car door and tender steps to the stone archway. Double doors constructed of steel and glass separate me from Rich Gains's widow. I want to know if she thinks her husband surprised a burglar or if his business relationships could've played a role. Holding the cupcakes, I take a deep breath, paste a half-smile on my face, and press the bell. It sounds like a musical entrance fit for the Queen of England. Or the Queen of Biltmore. A woman dressed in all black with dark hair pulled in a tight bun opens the door.

"May I help you?" She makes it sound like, "You have no business here."

"Hello, I'm looking for Stacey Gains. My name is Jolene Garcia."

The corners of her lips pull down. "Is Mrs. Gains expecting you?"

"No, but I hope she can see me. It's important."

"I don't believe that she is available." She eyes the box, thin brows drawing together. "May I tell her what this is regarding?"

"Her husband."

"Mrs. Gains is in mourning."

"I understand and I don't want to cause any more pain. But I think she'd like to know I'm here." I pull out my ID. "I'm a reporter looking into her husband's death."

"This is not the appropriate time."

Knocking on the door of a victim's family usually results in someone either appreciating the chance to share stories about their loved one or being disgusted with my appearance. Both responses cling to my skin for days.

"I understand this is a difficult time and you're doing your job. So am I. Can you just ask her? Please."

If the woman had chugged vinegar, her expression would be more pleasant than it is now. "One moment."

I'm rehearsing how to apologize and introduce myself when the door flies open. Heat spews off a woman who towers over me.

"How dare you come to my home?"

"Mrs. Gains, I'm very sorry to disturb you."

"You should be." Even in mourning, Stacey Gains could be a model for effortless chic. Caramel skirt with matching cardigan. Gold hoop earrings. Wavy bob.

"I'm following up on your husband's death and have a few questions. I apologize for showing up out of the blue. Truly, I am sorry. I wouldn't be here if it wasn't important."

"I have nothing to say to you or any other reporter. This has been a horrible time for my family."

"I'm sorry for your loss and I don't want to cause any more pain—"

"Too late."

But she doesn't close the door. There's curiosity in her eyes.

"Have the police given any indication they're close to making an arrest or identifying a suspect?" I ask.

"There's no shortage of suspects in that neighborhood. Too much riffraff and too many bleeding hearts letting them roam the streets, harassing people, and stealing from them." She shakes her head. "Rich thought it would look good to have a place to entertain clients so close to city hall. He even talked about buying the property next door and building a second office. He said it would pay off in the long run." Her shoulders sag. "Rich promised he'd only stay overnight if he had a late night and early meeting the next morning. Even after someone broke in when we were on vacation, Rich wanted to keep the place. And look what it got him." She squeezes her eyes shut. "I wish I'd convinced him to let it go. I should have tried harder."

I probably should've thought this through more. The cupcakes are bricks in my hands. "When you talked to the police, did they ask about anyone your husband dealt with professionally?"

She pulls a tissue out of the sweater pocket, dabs an eye, and asks what I mean.

"Did your husband have any problems with a colleague, a client, or anyone else involved in his work?"

"Do you mean Simona Park?"

I almost drop the cupcakes. How does Rich's wife know about Simona when Simona claims she didn't know him? I'm not sure what to say and go with, "Do you know Simona?"

Her shoulders go rigid and her mouth tightens. "I don't make it a point to learn a lot about my husband's mistresses. Simona was an exception. I had to understand whether her behavior was going to blow over or become a serious issue."

"Her behavior?"

"I didn't like Rich's affairs but as long as he didn't flaunt them in front of me or our friends, I could live with it."

I keep my expression neutral but she spots something.

"You're too young to understand. Rich and I loved each other and had a mutually beneficial arrangement. Simona didn't accept the rules. She would call and text at all hours and that was simply unacceptable."

"How did you handle it?"

"I tried to be civil. When we both attended a business event, I pulled her aside and politely asked that she stop sleeping with my husband. She balked, and called and texted even more. It was humiliating for me to be forced to have a conversation with Rich about breaking up with his mistress. Simona didn't take it well. She had the nerve to follow Rich home one night—here, to my house—and profess her love for my husband. When I threatened to call the police, she threatened us. I was bluffing, but I feared she was not."

My head is spinning. Simona said she didn't know Rich. Maybe acting, not accounting, is her true calling.

"How did Simona threaten you?"

"I am not going to relive that awful experience." Stacey Gains has aged ten years in five minutes. "I would like you to leave now."

"Mrs. Gains, I apologize for showing up out of the blue. Your information about Simona could be important to the case. Did you tell police?"

"Why would I? There's no reason to publicly bring up a painful affair. Rich is gone. The police need to find his killer."

"Yes, and—"

"Please go. Now."

I want to explain that Simona could be involved. When I went to Simona's office, she presented herself as a successful, ethical accountant, but she's an embezzler and a liar. Maybe she's a killer, too. But I can't form the words before the door closes.

I catch the housekeeper or maid, or whatever rich people call them, peeking through a curtain, shooing me away.

I stop at the guardhouse. "Mrs. Gains didn't want the cupcakes. Would you like them?"

"Are you sure, ma'am?"

"Absolutely."

"My sweet tooth thanks you."

At least one person doesn't hate me.

CHAPTER

16

With no cupcakes left and no interview with Rich Gains's widow, I react the way any reasonable reporter would—by heading to Filiberto's. Not to be confused with Julioberto's, Roberto's, Eriberto's, or any other "-berto's" that dot the Phoenix landscape.

"I'd like carne asada fries. Can you please make the fries extra crispy?"

"Yes. What kind of salsa?"

"Red and green, please."

The portion is generous enough for two people—or one reporter hungry for success. As I begin shoveling thousands of calories into my mouth, I watch a guy enjoy his burrito with similar gusto. At another table, a woman's eyes are fixed on a TV, her fingers fumbling for a taco. The telenovela's volume is off but the acting makes it easy to guess who's going to end up in bed together. The soccer match on the other TV is less exciting to watch but more exciting to hear. Making a scoreless match sound like the World Series, bottom of the ninth, bases loaded, full count is artistry in action.

As I dip a forkful of fries into guacamole, my phone chimes.

I savor the mix of grilled steak, cheddar cheese, and potatoes before checking the text. The message causes a coughing fit. An employee asks if I'm okay. I nod and gulp half my drink. Never in the history of local news has a reporter received a text from a news director marked "ASAP" that resulted in good news. I call Alex, counting on his newsroom radar to help me prepare.

"Stand by, Jolene. Code 100 at the convention center."

The receiver whomps the desk and the scanner crackles about a mattress on the freeway. I gobble another bite before he's back.

"False alarm," he says. What's up?"

"Any idea why Bob wants to see me?"

"Negative. What's going on with the cupcakes?"

"It's not about cupcakes."

"Sorry, can't help you. He's been in his office for the past hour. No one's gone in. Want me to transfer you?"

"No way. How are you doing for stories? Need me to pick up anything?"

"Nice try. If the boss wants to see you, better get back here."

Dread brings out my law-abiding side. I maintain the posted speed limit, stop at every yellow light, and watch snowbirds pass me. What should have taken fifteen minutes takes twenty-five. Another diversion comes in the form of an intern walking out of the station as I'm heading in.

"Hi, Pamela, how'd it go?"

"Great. I was able to get samples from five places."

Thank goodness one of us is making progress.

"Where are they?"

"In the break room," she says. "I got a cake box and put them in the fridge."

"Oh, no!" I run inside and catch a hand about to grab the pink box. "Step away and no one gets hurt."

The hand goes still.

"That box is for a story."

The body straightens and the face flashes with annoyance.

"There's no name on it," Sexy says.

Apparently, his race training fuels the urge for sugar.

"Just because it's in the fridge doesn't mean it's community property." I wave him aside, pull out the box, and peer inside. Whew. All accounted for. Like a mama bird protecting her eggs, I carry the precious cargo to my desk.

"Ooh, what did you bring?" Gina asks.

"Nothing." I grab a notepad and black marker.

She leans over the partition separating our desks. "Doesn't look like nothing."

"It's for a story." I snatch a roll of tape off my desk.

"Wow." Gina arches a brow. "I did not see that coming. You really were serious about working on the cupcake investigation."

"Pretend you never saw this."

"Saw what?" Elena crowds in. "What's in the box?"

"Nothing." I turn to Pamela. "Follow me."

We manage to make it out of the newsroom and into the greenroom without being accosted. I write DO NOT EAT on three sheets of paper and tape them to the sides of the box. I remove four water bottles from the minifridge.

"Is it going to fit?" Pamela asks.

Pushing the box all the way back leaves barely an inch of space.

"Piece of cake," I say, and write: WARNING: NOT EDIBLE and tape the paper on top of the box. "What do you think?"

"I guess it's pretty safe."

"Only pretty safe? Let's try layered security." I tape a note to the fridge's door.

"How about now?"

Pamela wrinkles her nose. "I don't know."

"What?"

"An out-of-order sign might make someone want to open the fridge and see if it's really broken. Or, like, maybe check to see if someone forgot to take off the sign."

I consider the thick capital letters. "You're right. It might draw attention." I toss it into the recycle bin.

"Okay, here's the deal: we need to get twenty cupcakes to the lab. We can't risk leaving food around news people. Understand?"

She nods.

"Bring your samples directly here. No stopping in the newsroom. And don't tell anyone where we're keeping them, okay?"

"Got it," she says. "Aren't you going to put your cupcakes in here?"

I would if I had some.

"An unexpected issue came up. I'll get some tomorrow. Thanks again for all your help. Let me know when you're able to get more, okay?"

I round the corner and roll my shoulders back the way Gina demonstrated to improve my posture. She also says standing like Wonder Woman for five minutes not only makes you feel powerful, but claims research has shown others perceive you as more successful. No time to channel Wonder Woman. I've run the clock and the buzzer is screaming.

As I approach Bob's office, he answers his desk phone. I imagine the person on the other end is a prison employee and Bob, the warden, is giving the order to start the execution. My mind fails to convince my stomach it's not that serious. Should've tried Wonder Woman.

"She sent the research this morning," Bob's telling whoever's on the phone. "I'll read it tonight."

I look at photos I've seen several times but couldn't have described. In the largest frame, Bob, his wife, and four kids stand side by side, parents in the middle and kids arranged by height.

Swap the tan khakis and sky-blue shirts for bold colors and they could be contestants on *Family Feud*.

"No need to focus-group the franchise," he says.

I scan emails on my phone, automatically deleting any with exclamation marks in the subject line.

Bob drums a pencil on his desk. "Earth to Jolene."

His standard friendly expression has been replaced with a look bordering on cold.

"Sorry, got lost in emails."

"And what is your excuse for intruding on a widow?"

Uh-oh.

"Stacey Gains is a close friend of Lou's wife. That would be Lou, our general manager. Who do you think Lou's wife called after listening to her distraught friend?"

He doesn't wait for a response.

"Lou also has a direct connection. He sits on the Chamber of Commerce board. So did Rich Gains." His fingers twist around the pencil. "What the hell were you thinking?"

"I can't tell you."

The pencil snaps and its point whizzes past my ear.

"Can't or won't?"

"I promised a source confidentiality and I needed to talk to Stacey Gains. The scenario we were given about her husband's death—that he surprised a burglar—doesn't ring true."

"Maybe I should have required you take time off after Larry Lemmon's murder."

A pain scrapes my insides, as if Bob's stabby pencil is piercing my stomach.

"Jolene, I'm worried about you. There's a line, sometimes a very fine line, between story passion and obsession."

"I'm not obsessed."

"No need to get upset."

My jaw clenches. I'm not the one breaking pencils.

"I'd like you to contact the employee assistance program." He raises a hand before I can open my mouth. "It's confidential and free. I think it will be helpful for you to talk to a professional. You were nearly killed, Jolene. That's got to affect you."

"What will kill me is talking about my job to someone who knows nothing about news. I need to be working. That's the best therapy."

"This isn't a compromise. I take partial responsibility for your erratic behavior."

"It's not erratic. It's being a good reporter!"

His hands go up like he's surrendering. Except he's not.

"I should have suggested it more strongly after the Lemmon case. Now I am requiring it." He pushes a document at me. "You don't have to contact them right this minute, but I would like you to reach out soon. Say, within the next forty-eight hours. For now, why don't you take the rest of the day off? Think it over."

I snatch the paper, fold it with a crease sharp enough to cut, and stomp to my desk.

"Are you okay?" Elena asks.

I cram the employee assistance information in my bag. "I'm fine." Except for the knife twisted in my back.

"What happened?"

"Nothing."

"Okay, I get it. You don't feel like talking."

I grab my laptop.

"Jolene?"

"What?"

"Look at me."

Elena produces a bite-size Twix and a full-mouth smile. I accept it and walk away, my eyes shimmering with tears.

It's going to take more than a piece of chocolate to shake off Bob's ridiculous request. On the drive home I replay our conversation and wonder what happened to my news director. He used to care about breaking stories and chasing real news. He used to trust and support me. Now, he thinks I'm unstable.

Oscar greets me with his usual grumpiness.

"I'm not even late," I say.

Maybe he knows my leftovers are better than shrimp flakes. My fries! After spending hours in my car, it's too late to save the sour cream and guacamole. Flinging the condiments into the trash, Bob's words taunt me. Counseling? Please. I've gone my entire life without therapy. I stick the fries in the microwave, slam the door, and watch the plate spin. Actually, when I was around ten years old, I was sent to counseling. But it was only because someone had to check a box in my case file. My foster parents took me twice before the therapist left for another job, and I never went again. Just like foster care, Bob wants to check a box. Didn't need it then and don't need it now.

The fries are mushy but it's okay because Jim Thornton is happy to see me. When *Wheel*'s theme song begins, so does my therapy session.

"From Sony Pictures Studio, it's America's Game!"

Unlike my news director, Pat Sajak is always supportive. Even when a contestant blows it, like tonight. Corey from Kansas doesn't guess the phrase in the bonus round. But I do.

Stay the Course.

CHAPTER
17

I don't need therapy to understand that going to bed mad and waking up madder is not healthy. Neither is jolting awake every two hours replaying my news director's callous words. The only way Bob will back off the idea I need counseling is if I break a big story. I know I'm on to something, but my thoughts are rattling around like puzzle pieces in a box. When my mind is muddled, it can help to shake things up.

"What do you think, Oscar?" I drop breakfast flakes into his bowl. "Should I try a hike?"

Even Oscar knows it's not going to happen. Maybe someday my fear of falling and having my rescue broadcast on TV and social media will be weaker than my need to push my body.

"Steele Indian School Park, it is. See you later."

The outer loop is just under a mile and I figure three laps should do the job. I have a love-hate relationship with running. I've never experienced a runner's high, but sometimes it's exactly what I need. Conditions are perfect: clear skies and sixty degrees when I pull into the Central Avenue entrance. I take a long drink and walk toward the Phoenix Indian School Visitor Center. When the historic Memorial Hall comes into view, I start running. The redbrick building, built in 1922, is dedicated to Native American students who served in World War I. Passing the parking lot, my gait feels awkward, my breath bumpy.

Carlos Rios's car crash was no accident. I'm sure of it. When Carlos quit working for Kris Kruger to start his own company, Kris got upset. Carlos's attorney said Kris threatened Carlos's life. I should have pressed Carlos more instead of letting him brush off Kris's threat. When I interviewed Kris at his house, he was clearly comfortable around vehicles. He could've tampered with Carlos's truck. With Carlos gone, Kris might avoid an official investigation into how he wins city contracts.

The more I learn about Rich Gains, the less likely I think a burglar killed him. Rich's reputation as a lobbyist who rammed his clients' projects through with little regard for residents made him a man some people loved to hate. Toss in Rich's affairs and there's no shortage of suspects.

A chaotic cocktail of barks quickens my pace. Thankfully, a high fence blocks their fangs, but the bluster coming from the dog park amplifies my pulse. Ahead of me, a guy walking a giant poodle and talking on his phone is oblivious to my panting and heavy footfalls. I detour in the grass, mindful of dog poop, and slide back to the pavement after establishing a safe distance.

Simona Park seems like a strong suspect for Rich Gains's murder—if the story Rich's wife told is true about Simona coming to their home and threatening them. Even if Stacey Gains exaggerated Simona's reaction to Rich calling off their affair, police always look at the ex-lover. Investigating all of Rich's ex-lovers could explain why detectives haven't yet made an arrest. If Simona would kill Rich, it's feasible she'd want to stop Carlos from blabbing about her stealing money from Kris Kruger when she worked as his accountant. Simona wouldn't want to jeopardize her fancy clothes and jewelry or her kids' auto racing and hockey tournaments.

As I approach the playground area, my plan to run up a hill goes out the window when I see a man, a young girl, and a dog racing uphill. Across the path, a woman calls out to a boy on a swing.

"Dalton, be careful!"

The boy looks on the verge of swinging backward over the bars. The woman yells for Dalton to stop and he flings his body through the air, landing with a thud on the rubber surface. A squirt of surprise hits his face, quickly replaced by jubilation, and his fists pump the air.

I keep running and consider Mayor Ace Logan. Cutting off campaign donations from Rich Gains might appear noble if the mayor's prints hadn't shown up at the site of Rich's murder. For years, Logan's image has been carefully cultivated. Since his wife died, he regularly makes most-eligible-bachelor lists, but he's never been public about a serious relationship. Doesn't mean he's not in a relationship. Or maybe he was and someone dropped him for Rich. And what about Councilwoman Zoey Patterson? She had a questionable financial relationship with Rich—and possibly romantic. Their relationship could've turned ugly. As the saying goes, there's a fine line between love and hate. Maybe Rich planned to turn on Zoey and help the attorney general's investigation into corruption. The AG could've offered Rich a deal to testify against Zoey.

The path takes me close to the bird-shaped lake where an old man is tossing bread to ducks and a woman is teaching a child to cast a fishing line. I startle as a runner passes me with the silent steps and soft breathing of someone familiar with a runner's high. After my second lap, I'm ready to call it quits, but tell myself I can leave after I charge up a hill.

With every step, my quads burn hotter. My breathing gets heavier, but my thoughts get lighter. I still don't agree with Bob trying to force me into counseling, but the anger that ripped through my body while sitting in his office has evaporated with my sweat. Trying to steady my breath, I gulp in the view of Camelback Mountain. Its shape resembles the head and hump of a kneeling camel. After almost three years in Phoenix, I'm still a visitor. The desert landscape is so different from Nebraska. It's why I love this park—because I can soak in the green grass. Outside the gate, rock gardens, gravel paths, and cacti are everywhere. I miss autumns in Omaha, but I have no reason to go back. My grandma was the only person there for me.

My moment of Zen is interrupted. Peals of laughter arrive seconds before two people join me. We exchange quick hellos and they start shooting social media reels.

"Hi, y'all, I'm king of the hill at Indian School Park in Phoenix."

Trekking down, I contemplate the next steps in my investigation into Carlos's and Rich's deaths. Rich helped Carlos compete for city contracts. That's their connection. That's where I should focus. I haven't looked into the city employee who accepts bids, and that's going to change.

Before leaving, I visit the memorial honoring four Phoenix journalists who died in 2007. Pilots Scott Bowerbank and Craig Smith and photographers Jim Cox and Rick Krolak were killed when their helicopters collided in midair while covering a police chase. Both helicopters came down in an empty part of the park. Someone has left a fresh bouquet of roses. Every year, local stations solemnly observe July 27 by airing file video of the scene. In my newsroom, only Alex worked with the men. The anniversary hits harder for him. Every year, Alex lists Scott's, Craig's, Jim's, and Rick's names on the assignment board and handles the newscast scripts. Alex won't let anyone else write their stories.

Walking back to my car, I check my phone. Elena wants to meet thirty minutes earlier for lunch than we planned.

No problem. See you soon.

I still have plenty of time to dig into Ved Patel, the city employee who accepted bids from Carlos and Kris. The only Ved Patel that shows up owning a home is in Sun City, the first master-planned active retirement community in the United States. Can't be the city employee I'm looking for. My Ved Patel is in his twenties. Sun City residents must be fifty-five or older. The house could belong to Ved's father. Maybe he lives with him. But that's a long commute to downtown Phoenix. Doesn't feel right. It also doesn't feel right that I can't get back the hour I've spent on his social media accounts. How many food photos can one person post? Handmade mozzarella at Pizzeria Bianco. Carnitas at Tacos Chiwas. Sunshine roll at Yama Sushi House. I'm about to give up when it hits me: most of the restaurants are within five miles of each other. Ved must live nearby. A slew of older photos and videos show Ved cooking in the same kitchen. I run three photos through a reverse imaging tool and get the same address. It's an apartment complex and I need his unit number. I'll have to chew on that because I have a lunch date with my colleagues.

From the Loop 202, I take the McClintock exit and brace for congestion from Tempe Marketplace, an open-air center with shops and restaurants. Still, it's more efficient than taking Rural Road, which runs through athletic facilities and housing for Arizona State University's main campus. I pass new apartments and pricey coffee shops before pulling into a strip mall decades past its prime.

"Hello, Haji-Baba, I've missed you."

Despite gentrification around ASU, Haji-Baba hasn't changed. It's a no-frills restaurant sharing space with a market that sells condiments and cookies and drinks and desserts from around the world.

"Jolene, over here!" Elena jumps up even though she doesn't need to. She's at our regular table, next to a mural of the ruins of Palmyra, an ancient city in Syria. A thirty-two-ounce cup stamped with a retro Pepsi-Cola logo awaits me.

"Thanks for ordering."

"I didn't have to," Elena says. "Omar's working. He knows what we get."

"One day I might try something different."

"Yeah, right. Gina will be here in a minute."

As I dip warm pita bread into hummus, I'm grateful my initial experience here was never repeated. It was my second day at the station and another reporter invited me to lunch.

"The plates here are large," she said. "How about we split an entrée?"

If this is a Phoenix thing, I remember thinking, I picked the wrong city. Since being the new person required positivity, I agreed. Giving up half a chicken kabob plate was a low point that first week. Fortunately, it turned out not to be a Phoenix thing, but a Southern California thing. Ms. "Let's split an entrée" moved back to San Diego where she's surfing, meditating, and sharing salads.

The people at the next table are staring. So is their server and everyone else. They're not checking me out. Or Elena's sparkly sneakers. They're trying to figure out who Gina is. The breezy way she enters the room and the positive energy she gives off make people assume she's famous. Gina's so used to it, she doesn't even notice.

"Your hair is beautiful," Elena tells her. "Love the curls."

"Thanks," Gina says. "I'm keeping it natural for a while. It feels right for tonight's concert."

"About Stevie Nicks's show," Elena says. "How's it feel to have front-row tickets?"

"Not front row. Third row."

"I stand corrected." Elena looks at me. "Gina's date is the chief operating officer for a cybersecurity firm. They're getting the VIP experience."

"It's not like we're going to meet Stevie."

"You're going backstage, aren't you?"

"I don't know."

"Gina, please."

"What?" she says. "Nothing is guaranteed."

"I'm guaranteed to have a blast with my mom," Elena says. "Our lawn seats will be perfect for twirling in our matching shawls when Stevie sings 'Edge of Seventeen.' I can't believe my mom's never seen her in concert. All I heard growing up was Stevie Nicks and Fleetwood Mac."

My grandma played country music from the seventies. I guess that's why my mom named me after Dolly Parton's song. Maybe I can ask her someday.

"So, Jolene," Elena says. "Got any fun weekend plans?"

"I was hoping to meet someone but it probably won't happen."

"Ooh, do tell." Elena moves her iced tea to the side and leans in. "Who is this mysterious someone? Tall, dark, and handsome?"

"I don't know about tall, but he has dark hair and he's pretty good-looking."

"Did you meet online?" Gina says. "Is he funny? Smart? Details, please."

"We haven't met. It's someone I want to talk to for a story."

Elena's face morphs into the face of my restaurant manager

during college. At the end of my senior year, my name wasn't on the schedule. When I asked why, the manager said it was graduation weekend. As if I didn't know.

"Don't you want to spend it with your family?" she said.

I had no family and needed the money. When I told her I wanted to work, the pity in her eyes shamed me. Thinking about it now makes my stomach cramp.

"You need to do something fun," Gina says. "You work too hard."

Working too hard is juggling multiple jobs to cover the basics. Or landscaping during Phoenix summers. Or standing on your feet all day to provide for the granddaughter you never expected to raise.

"You know," Elena says with a smile. "Manny's best friend recently broke up with his girlfriend."

"Wait a minute," Gina says. "We know your heart is in the right place, but your matchmaking skills aren't so hot. Remember your neighbor?"

They reminisce about Elena inviting her neighbor to the station to introduce her to Alex, our assignment editor. She thought they'd make a cute couple. Elena learned a lesson that day: never assume.

The scent of garlic, cumin, and paprika reaches our table before Omar does. He delivers chicken shawarma and steaming rice for Elena and shish kabob plates for Gina and me.

"How's Boo Boo?" I ask.

"Kitty is getting more spoiled every day," Omar says. "I don't know when she became the owner of me." He pulls a phone from his back pocket. "Look at this. She watches bird videos in bed."

"That's adorable," Elena says. "I know exactly what you mean. It's like catering to a baby all the time."

"Maybe you should try a fish." I squirt sriracha on rice. "They're less work."

"But a fish doesn't purr when you come home," he says.

"And you can't kiss a fish or snuggle with it," Elena says.

"Valid points."

After a moment chewing in delight, Elena asks Gina what she's heard about the weekend anchor position.

"My agent is still negotiating."

"Our weekend anchor is leaving?" I say.

They exchange a look and Elena says, "It's amazing how you can get scoops and exclusive interviews and not know what's happening in your own newsroom."

My mouth is full and I wave her on.

"Our weekend anchor has an offer from Pittsburgh and wants to move to be closer to her family."

"When will you take over and start anchoring weekends?" I ask Gina.

She presses a napkin against her mouth. Somehow her lipstick still looks fresh. "I don't know that I will. My agent says Bob's playing hardball. He wants to lock me into a three-year deal. My agent says I could probably get to a top-five market in the next year. Maybe even network. So far, Bob's not willing to include an out."

Having an "out" is what it sounds like: getting out of a contract under specific circumstances. Bob's no dummy. Gina embodies the perfect anchor. She's professional, charismatic, approachable. Everyone wants to be her friend. Or more.

"Maybe you compromise by accepting less money," Elena says.

Gina looks at Elena like she suggested we dine and dash.

"How much does your agent figure you can get for the weekend job?" Elena asks.

Gina's response makes me choke on my kabob.

"What?" she says. "It's only seven thousand more than I make now."

"You make four thousand more than me," Elena says.

They both earn more than me.

"Your agent needs to do better," Gina tells Elena.

"We parted ways last year," she says. "No need to give him ten percent of my paycheck when I'm happy here and not going anywhere."

I've never had an agent and wonder if Bob took advantage of that. My grandma taught me to work hard and not count on others, but we never discussed how to ask for more money. It's not her fault. Or Bob's. I was so excited to move from Omaha to a major market, I jumped at the first offer.

Omar removes my empty plate and leaves two foam containers. As Elena scoops leftover rice, Gina places a half-full skewer in her container and brings up SMH's visit. "What do you think she'll want us to do, Jolene?"

"Oh no, don't get Jolene worked up," Elena says. "I was worried she was going to get kicked out of the last meeting when SMH brought up the social media center."

"I will refrain from any outbursts at the next meeting."

Their expressions reveal they don't believe me.

"Honestly, I will do my best to keep my mouth shut. But sometimes Sexy tries to instigate things."

"Speaking of David," Gina says. "I couldn't believe how gabby he was with your friend."

"Norma's my neighbor. I forgot I promised to show her around."

"She captured David's attention. Maybe you should invite her to the social media meeting."

"Hard no. She's already too interested in my business."

Elena's phone chirps. "Mom's at my house. Better get going. I'd say see you later, Gina, but they keep us commoners far, far away from royalty."

"Oh, stop," Gina says with a wave. It's her trademark response whenever someone mentions her charmed life.

"I should go, too," I say.

They have musical legend Stevie Nicks and I have city employee Ved Patel.

Although I've driven by Ved's apartment complex dozens of times, I've never been inside. A steel fence serves as a fortress with chubby shrubs providing backup. The lone vehicle entrance is locked, accessible only to emergency responders. I park on the street and walk half a block past various shades of green before a narrow opening reveals a gate. I push and pull, but the dead bolt does its job. I'm about to give up when someone approaches. I whip out my phone.

"I'm right outside the gate," I say.

I smile as the person opens the gate and I slide in behind. One door down, another to go. A cluster of mailboxes in the middle of the complex offers no clues. Only unit numbers, no names. My frustration is short-lived as terror takes over. A woman tugs on a leash attached to what a veterinarian would describe as a large canine but what I call a beast.

"Brutus, stop!"

I yelp as a panting, drooling Brutus barrels toward me.

"He won't hurt you," she shouts over his barks. "Brutus, be a good boy."

I don't trust Brutus or the woman and bolt toward thick foliage. My breathing doesn't return to normal until the barking stops and Brutus is out of sight. I emerge slowly, checking both ways before stepping on the sidewalk. If not for Brutus, a sense of calm would be flooding my body. Mature trees and water fountains drown out traffic and drop the temperature by ten degrees. It's a hidden gem in the heart of the city. Beneath a southern oak, a gray-haired man rests in an Adirondack chair, reading a book. I peg him as a visitor due to his T-shirt, shorts, and flip-flops.

"Hello," I call out. "How are you?"

"Splendid," he says. "It's a glorious day, isn't it?"

"Yes."

"This will be my first winter here," he says. "I can't believe I didn't move sooner."

"From where?"

"Michigan. Outside Detroit."

"Lots of Midwesterners here," I say.

"You don't have to tell me. Neighbors on my left are from Indiana. My neighbor on the right is from Iowa."

Okay, Mr. Chatty, let's see how much you know.

"Any chance your neighbor is Ved Patel? I forgot his apartment number." I wiggle my phone. "He's not responding to my text."

"I'm guilty of that myself. Set it down and walk away, or forget I put it on silent mode." He pulls his phone out of a pocket and taps on it. "I don't know anyone here named Ved but I know who might." He presses the phone to an ear. "Hey, there. Quick question: Do you happen to know anyone in the complex named Ved? No, it's Ved, with a 'V.'" He nods at me and holds up a finger. "Do you know his unit number?"

Mr. Chatty is Mr. Come Through.

"Thanks. His girlfriend is looking for him."

I don't correct him.

"Ved's in unit 115."

I don't have to ask for directions because I passed it while running from Brutus the beast. I practice what I'll say when Ved opens the door. Apologize for disturbing him, introduce myself, and ask if he can provide background on the city's bid process. I'm about to knock and my mind flashes to the lobbyist's widow. Considering I haven't followed up on Bob's "suggestion" to attend counseling, it would be wise not to risk another complaint. Safer, too, since I don't know if Ved's a bad guy with a big dog. Rather than surprise him here with no one around, I'll visit him at work with plenty of witnesses. I head home to dive deeper into his social media platforms. But before I'm out of my car, my next-door neighbor is at my door talking turkey.

"I'm finalizing the Thanksgiving dinner list," Norma says. "I'm handling the turkey, Mr. Lee and Miss Kathy are bringing side dishes. Marcia, you met her when we toured your station, is baking apple and cherry pies. Everything is covered so you don't have to bring or buy anything. Maybe vanilla ice cream if it's not too much trouble. I do enjoy pie à la mode, don't you?"

"I have to work."

"Oh, darn. That's too bad." She picks up Tuffy, who's taking an unusual interest in the conversation. "I'll be sure to save you a plate."

"You don't have to. The station will have something delivered."

"Dear, that's not the same. You need a home-cooked meal."

Tuffy's look is unsettling. Like he can read my thoughts. Maybe Brutus sent Tuffy a message. Or maybe Tuffy can smell the fear that oozed out of my pores. I tell Norma I need to feed my fish and excuse myself.

As my door closes, I catch her parting words. "I'll mark you down as maybe."

It's not actually mealtime for Oscar, but I give him a treat before treating myself to a king-size Butterfinger and delving into Ved's digital footprint. Before becoming a foodie, he documented outdoor adventures: posing at Dobbins Lookout in South Mountain Park, taking in the sunset from Piestewa Peak, and hanging in the Hole in the Rock in Papago Park. Most of his followers are around his age. My scrolling picks up speed, images blurring until something clicks. I go back and slow down. Back some more.

There it is. I double-check the name tagged in a photo: Peyton Kruger. The same name as Kris Kruger's daughter. A tingle runs up my spine. Can't be that many Peyton Krugers in Phoenix. I click on her profile. Peyton loves felines as much as Ved loves food. She travels more than him. Videos on a cruise, beach, and boardwalk. Photos from an elaborate wedding in Italy confirm Peyton is Kris's daughter. The tingle turns electric. The wedding party includes none other than the city employee who records the bids that lead to Peyton's father getting lucrative contracts. Ved Patel is in several photos looking chummy with Peyton's husband, which is what you'd expect from the best man. Ved is going to have some explaining to do when I talk to him at work. It's finally starting to look like Sexy will have to eat his words and give me five minutes at the top of the newscast.

"Oscar, we are celebrating tonight. Bloodworms for you and pizza for me."

While waiting for delivery, I scroll news sites. Thanksgiving is more than a week away, but holiday stories are in full swing. St. Mary's Food Bank is seeking donations, and the Salvation Army and St. Vincent de Paul are prepping to serve thousands of turkey dinners. Fortunately, I won't have to cover "Thanksgiving Grandma" and her mistaken text sent years ago that led to an annual dinner because I am onto a blockbuster story. Never have I ever counted the hours until the end of my weekend. I'm close to exposing Kris Kruger as a cheater and a killer.

CHAPTER
18

On Monday morning, I text Alex that I'll be in late because I'm meeting a source. Not totally true but not totally false. I'm counting on Ved Patel to talk about his role in the city's contract process. After I get him to explain his job, I'll hit him with questions about the deals awarded to Kris Kruger. I practice on my goldfish.

"How do you think it looks for a key city employee to socialize with the winning bidder's children?"

Too clunky.

"Can you explain your relationship with the winning bidder's family?"

Better.

"Considering your close personal relationship with the winner's children, someone might question your role in the process. What would you say to them?"

That will work.

Driving along Seventh Street, I pass three construction projects, all box-shaped wood frame apartment buildings capped at four stories, so they "pencil out," as developers like to say when talking about costs and profits. Holding my breath, I creep up the ramp of the city-owned parking garage. Every floor is a crap-shoot. Oversized trucks and SUVs poke out of spaces built for se-dans, narrowing an already precarious path. My car crawls along, to the disgust of a Tahoe driver riding my bumper. Flipping him off is not an option because I don't dare let go of the wheel. As we near a corner to the next level, I move as far over to the right as I can.

"Go on, jerk. Pass me."

He can't because a car jets around the corner, almost hitting us. The Tahoe's horn blares as the car speeds down the ramp. I ignore an open spot between two SUVs and continue to the fifth level where I can back into a space for a quick exit. It's a tip I picked up during a week of reports the station called, "Get Out Alive." The series featured rare but terrifying scenarios to scare viewers into watching under the guise of protecting them-selves.

The ding of the elevator door is followed by jingling coins. A man shakes a dirty McDonald's cup at me. "Help me out?"

"No, sorry." I avoid eye contact and pick up my pace.

I've read reports about how homeless people are more likely to become victims of violent crimes than to commit them, but I also know the story of Donna Brady. During her morning walks, she befriended an unhoused man, often bringing him food. One day, he attacked Donna and stabbed her to death. Intense media coverage focused on Donna, a retired elemen-tary school teacher, grandmother, mother, and wife. Police de-scribed the suspect as violent and unstable and victims' rights groups argued Donna would still be alive if the suspect had served his full prison sentence for aggravated assault and not been released early. Left unreported by the media but recorded in court documents was a summary of the man's life before the attack. Shuffled through the foster care system starting at the age of three. A frequent runaway from group homes as a teenager. A high school dropout before graduating to convicted criminal. Society failed him long before he failed society.

Inside city hall, a woman follows me into the elevator.

"What floor?" I say.

"Nine, please."

She's wearing a city ID and I ask how the elevators have been working since the mayor's incident.

"No problems that I know of," she says before getting off.

I remind myself to think positively as I follow signs to the finance department.

"Can I help you?"

"Yes, thank you. I'm here to see Ved Patel."

"Is he expecting you?"

"No, but I just need a couple minutes."

"He's in a meeting. You can leave a message if you'd like."

"I'll wait. It's no trouble. I have emails to check." I zip over to a beige couch, eyes locked on my phone.

"Excuse me," the receptionist says. "Can I get your name?"

I offer my best "Just a regular person" smile and give her my name.

"And what is this in reference to?"

My cheeks stretch as if I'm thrilled she asked. "A story I'm working on."

She frowns and slides a hand under the desk. Is she signaling security?

"Have you talked to the PIO?"

"I have." My cheeks are getting tired and so is my act. I wiggle my phone. "Please excuse me a second." I perform several head nods and repeat, "Mm-hmm." It's a good trick if you remember to turn the ringer off. Once I got a real call during a fake call.

When the receptionist steps away from her desk, I trail her to a hallway, close my eyes, and tune out the drone from fluorescent lights. Did someone say my name? I might have heard "reporter." Definitely heard "Not here." When the voices stop, I sprint back to the couch.

"Excuse me, Ms. Garcia?"

Another pleasant smile. "Yes."

"Mr. Patel is not available today."

"Are you sure? I only need five minutes."

She cocks her head and smacks her lips. "Afraid not."

"How about tomorrow?"

"If you need information or want to arrange an interview, you're welcome to contact the PIO for this department."

Or I could just wait outside the elevator for him to take a break. Two hours until the first wave of clock punchers will pour out for sustenance, so I head to the lobby and settle into a chair. I pull up social pages for Ved Patel and imagine his face attached to a torso wearing a button-down shirt.

After ninety minutes of scrolling, reading emails, and the Associated Press app, I impersonate Sexy by stretching my legs. I contemplate climbing the grand staircase. Why not? I'm wearing my regular flat footwear, plus there's a handrail. Somewhere around the forty-fifth step, I lose track. Going down, I count seventy steps and two burning quads. My pulse is nearly back to normal when it ticks up again. Ved Patel likes his lunch early.

Ved strolls toward the exit with another tall guy. Their strides make me regret taking on city hall's StairMaster.

"Excuse me, Ved. Can you slow down, please?"

He either doesn't hear or he's ignoring me, but his friend stops, and I thank him as Ved turns around. His expression is open and questioning. I hold out a business card.

"I stopped by your office earlier. Can we talk for a minute?"

Ved looks at the card, but doesn't take it. "I don't have time."

"It won't take long at all. I just need clarification on a contract."

"I said no."

"Maybe you can explain your relationship with Caleb and Peyton Kruger. I know you were Caleb's best man. Did Caleb's father-in-law need help submitting bids?"

Ved's feet snap as he whips around. His friend casts a confused look before following. I could go after Ved, but he's not going to have a change of heart if I follow him into a restaurant or pounce when he returns to the office. I slouch against a wall and close my eyes. Now I have to deal with Sexy and cupcakes. My foot pushes off the wall and I bump into someone.

"Whoops, sorry."

"Quite alright." Mayor Ace Logan flashes a grin worthy of a toothpaste commercial. "Nice to see you again, Jolene."

"Hi, Mayor, how are the elevators working?"

Logan chuckles. "Is that what brings you here? Testing them?"

"No, but now that you mention it, who fixes the elevators?"

"I can't recall the company's name but if you check with the Communications Office, they can get it for you."

"Here's something you can probably help with: Why do city contracts have change orders? And what's the process for paying a company more than the original deal?"

He studies my face and says, "I have a few moments free. Why don't you come up to my office and we can talk?"

In the elevator car, Logan's eyes stay on his phone while his escape partner, Detective Martos, remains silent. I'm fine avoiding small talk. I have to figure out what questions will get the information I need without revealing too much about my investigation. When the door opens, a woman barges in.

"Oh!" She catches her phone before it hits the ground. "I'm so sorry, Mayor Ace."

"No worries, Julie. Just be sure to keep that off while you're driving, okay? Wouldn't want you to have an accident."

Logan's shoes click-clack on the tile. He waves at a reception-ist on a phone and, when we approach the seating area outside his office, a security guard springs up and practically salutes. "How you doing today, Mayor Ace?"

"Just fine, Nelson. How's your son? Is he over that ear in-fection yet?"

"Yes, sir. He's doing much better. Thank you for asking."

"Terrific news."

Logan tells his security detail he can take a break. Inside his office, he shrugs off a black suit jacket, loosens a maroon tie, and motions to a minifridge.

"I have regular water, sparkling water, and iced tea. What'll you have?"

"Nothing, thank you."

"How about coffee? I have a Keurig. Your pick of flavors."

"I'm fine."

"For your information, the coffee is a personal purchase."

He removes a bottle from the fridge, walks behind a mahog-any desk, and settles into a high-backed leather chair with curved armrests.

"Please, have a seat."

He waves to a mesh chair, the kind everyone claims provides wonderful back support but I can never properly adjust. I'm forced to look up at the mayor.

Logan twists off the cap, takes a long sip, and sets it next to a photo frame that reads OUR FAMILY. The number of kids and grandkids rivals the number of steps on the grand staircase.

"Tell me, what contract are you investigating?"

His directness catches me off guard. "I didn't say I was."

"You don't have to. Listen Jolene, I know people see me as the grandfatherly type—and I am. I love my family and I love this city."

He gestures to a wall covered with photos. There's Logan high-fiving a high school basketball player, buying Girl Scout cookies, and reading to a kindergarten class. Logan with the late U.S. Senator John McCain, another with former Arizona Cardinals player Larry Fitzgerald, and Logan posing as Wonder Woman alongside Lynda Carter, the original Wonder Woman. The star of the exhibition is the mayor with Hollywood director Steven Spielberg. The other photos circle them, like planets around the sun. Spielberg premiered his first film in Phoenix at the age of seventeen. Logan might've seen it. Now, he's probably hoping to get Spielberg as a guest on his talk show.

"I've been in politics probably longer than you've been alive," he says. "I know when someone's snooping, so why don't you tell me?"

"You know, I would like a water, please. Regular." When I smile, the corners of my mouth wobble. How can I not have a plan? What kind of reporter am I?

"I may be the last person who still gives these out." Logan hands me a bottle. "Bad for the environment and all. I avoid plastic straws but am simply not comfortable accepting a glass of water from someone who may not thoroughly wash the glass—or their hands." Back on his throne, Logan crosses his legs. "Are you going to tell me what you're working on?"

"I'm gathering information about how city contracts work and hope you can help."

He kicks his feet up on his desk. I know nothing about men's shoes, but the metal tip on his sole stamped GUCCI can't be standard footwear on a public servant's salary.

"As you know, I'm not running for office again. I have nothing to lose."

"Who does?"

I manage to hold his gaze but break the silence by twisting the bottle cap.

"You're different from the other TV reporters, aren't you?"

"In what way?"

"The others are more flash, less substance." He points a manicured finger at me. "You have more depth. You remind me of an old-school newspaper reporter back when everyone read them."

My grandma would burst with pride. For years, she consumed a daily diet of Walter Cronkite anchoring the *CBS Evening News*. In her eyes, he was the perfect man: informed, trustworthy, and reliable—he showed up for dinner every night.

"I do my best."

"Don't be so modest," Logan says. "It is abundantly clear that your best is superior to everyone else."

I sip water and contemplate how to get the conversation back on track. Logan's designer shoes slide off the desk. He sits forward and folds his hands.

"There's something else I've noticed about you."

"What's that?"

"You never call me Mayor Ace."

He waits for a response. I give a silent nod.

"Over the years my campaigns have invested a great deal of time and money in my name. In fact, we used the same slogan the last three elections: Vote for Ace."

"Wasn't it 'Vote for Ace, the best man in the race'?"

His finger and thumb make a gun. "See? That's what I'm talking about. You are sharp."

I take another sip.

"Oh, I think I understand where you're coming from. Were you concerned the slogan was sexist? Because it wasn't. I was the only man in the race, which, of course made me the best man in the race. If that's why you don't call me Mayor Ace, please put your mind at ease."

"I was taught to refer to elected officials by their title or use their last name. It's nothing personal. I don't use Barack, Joe, or Donald either."

"I can respect that."

There's a double knock at the door and his chief of staff pokes her head in.

"Mayor Ace, excuse me for interrupting but I need your signature." Faith approaches his desk. "Hello, Jolene, good to see you again."

"You, too."

"Jolene is interested in how city contracts are awarded," the mayor says.

Faith sets a folder on the mayor's desk. "What would you like to know?"

Her enthusiasm matches a fast-food worker asking if I want fries. The mayor would never guess she shared off-the-record information with me about how much he disliked the lobbyist Rich Gains. Or the rumors about Rich paying Councilwoman Zoey Patterson to support his clients' controversial projects.

"I'm interested in how someone bidding on a contract can get details about other bids before the contract is awarded."

"That's not possible," Faith says. "The process is confidential. Bid information is never released until it's been evaluated and determined to meet the criteria. Bids that qualify are then sent to a committee, which comes up with a recommendation based on a scoring system that applies to everyone."

Logan says, "Fairness and ethics are very important to us at city hall." He flips to a fresh page.

"What about optics?" I say.

His pen pauses. "What do you mean?"

"Let me give a hypothetical. Suppose a city employee has a close relationship with someone doing business with the city.

And suppose that employee has access to information that would help the business owner submit better bids than his competitors and ultimately win contracts."

The mayor's mouth opens in disbelief. Probably practicing reactions for his upcoming talk show.

"Jolene, we are in the business of public service," he says. "Our employees adhere to strict principles."

Faith gathers the signed documents, returning them to the folder. "Do you have proof of this hypothetical?"

If I had evidence, I wouldn't tip you off.

"Of course she doesn't." The mayor clicks his pen closed. "I stand behind every one of our fourteen thousand employees."

Now, he's in full politician mode. Every organization has questionable employees. The city pays out millions annually to settle claims involving employees' mistakes and bad behavior.

"In fact, my first television show will feature a thank-you to public servants. I've asked my producer to include video of city workers. It may be my show, but I could have never done it without the support of employees and the fine folks of Phoenix."

Especially Faith, who was savvy enough to get him in front of national media when they helicoptered in to cover the radio talk show host's murder.

"Mayor, since you have back-to-back meetings, I'm happy to talk more with Jolene."

"I do need to prepare," he says. "But, Jolene, I don't want to give the impression that I don't respect your work. Freedom of the press is fundamental to a healthy democracy." He presents a pen with the flourish of a symphony conductor. "Please accept this as a token of appreciation for your work."

An American flag is imprinted next to text that reads VOTE FOR MAYOR ACE. A vision of his fingerprints compels me to take the pen by the tip. I have no idea if I'll need to check his prints or if it's even possible, but I open my tote bag and drop it in a pocket lined with tissue.

"I enjoyed our discussion," Logan says. "Faith will help with whatever you need."

Outside his office, Faith speaks in a low voice. "You'll have to excuse the mayor. He's a little nervous."

"About what?"

She glances around before whispering. "Being a suspect in Rich Gains's murder."

When we met for coffee, Faith said the mayor disapproved of the lobbyist's tactics and distanced himself from Rich, but gave no hint Logan was worried about being connected to his murder. She must know Logan's prints were found at the murder scene. Maybe she's trying to tell me something without telling me.

"You didn't mention that when we talked."

"Jolene, I'm his chief of staff. Why would I volunteer such information?" She guides me away from the reception area. "Besides, Councilwoman Patterson is a much more viable suspect."

She takes a step back and bumps into a chair, sending the folder to the floor. Faith gathers loose papers and I pick up a notecard. It's addressed to Ved Patel. Typed words: *I appreciate your exemplary service to the people of Phoenix. Keep up the good work!* Personally signed by Mayor Ace.

"I'll take that." Faith snatches the card and shoves it back in the folder. "I don't mean to cut your visit short, but I also have a meeting. You have my cell. Feel free to call with any questions."

Boy, do I have questions. Like why is the mayor writing a love letter to the employee who handles city bids? The way she pried the card out of my hand reinforces Faith's priority is protecting her boss. She probably lied about Logan distancing himself from Rich Gains so I wouldn't entertain the idea of the mayor being rotten. Knowing he's nervous about being a suspect in Rich's murder changes everything.

CHAPTER

19

My mind's buzzing as I ride eleven floors from the mayor's office to the lobby. Finally, a crack in his public façade. Mayor Ace Logan is nervous about being a suspect in the lobbyist's murder. And he personally praised Ved Patel, the city employee who handles bids for million-dollar contracts that repeatedly benefit Ved's friend. Councilwoman Zoey Patterson may be the favorite subject of corruption rumors, but it looks like she's got company.

I hurry past three people waiting to get on the elevator, round the corner, and slam into one of the last people I ever want to see.

"Hey, watch it!" Jessica "JJ" Jackson snaps her makeup compact closed. "You heading to a fire or something?"

"Sorry about that." I ignore her question and ask my own. "What's going on?"

"Waiting for my photog."

My heart whops against my chest. The mayor ended our discussion to prepare for a meeting. Is it with JJ? If she knows the attorney general is investigating the council for possible corruption, I'm toast. JJ's charm has choked me on countless stories.

"What's wrong with you?" she says.

"Nothing."

"You're scratching your neck like you have fleas."

I pull my hand down. "Slept on it funny. You covering something interesting?"

"Not unless you call a shred-a-thon and canned food drive interesting." She peers behind me. "Where's your photog?" Now it's her turn to be suspicious. "Aren't you here for the press conference?"

A text from my news director saves me. "Gotta go." Bob wants to talk about the cupcake story. I respond that I'm on my way.

Waiting for a light at the intersection, I pull up Zoey Patterson's bio. It doesn't mention her job as a real estate agent but includes a bunch of awards from various development groups. She describes herself as a third-generation Phoenician and a lifelong public servant. The lifelong claim is questionable considering she's been on the council for three years and, before that, spent a year on the library advisory board. Maybe she counts public service in dog years.

As people push past me, I tap on the mayor's page. Halfway through the crosswalk, I stumble, limbs splaying on the way down. A car zooms by, so close the engine's heat might have singed my eyebrows. Gravel smacks my face, dust stings my eyes, and smoky tar attacks my nostrils. A blur of metal careens around the corner and disappears. My clumsiness may have saved me from becoming roadkill.

A woman sprints to my side. "Are you okay?"

"Yeah." I prop myself up, wincing at the pain in my hand. The palm is red and raw but not bleeding. I stretch my arm to reach my phone, but fall short. The woman hands it to me. A crack zigzags the screen, but I'm lucky it still works. Also, because I'm still breathing.

The woman scoops up my notepad and the mayor's pen, and jams them into my bag. So much for getting his prints. She takes my arm. "C'mon, we need to move. The light's going to change."

Wearing pants not only saved me from flashing my underwear downtown but protected me from road rash. Ten cautious steps and I'm on safer ground. The woman asks if she should call an ambulance.

"No, I'm okay. Thanks."

"I wish I'd gotten the license plate number to call police. It was like the driver was aiming right at you."

Probably because he was. It must be the same person behind the Darth Vader voice mail and anonymous text.

"What did he look like?"

She shuffles awkwardly. "I didn't really see the driver. Sorry. The window tint was dark."

"What about the car?"

She gives a strong nod. "It was a silver sedan. Medium size. Newer model. Maybe a Camry or something like it."

I contemplate calling Jim Miranda, my police source, but there's nothing concrete I can share. Camrys are among the most popular models in the United States and silver is a top color in Phoenix. Even if I tell him about the text and voice mail threats, he'd remind me his unit has actual crimes to solve.

My subconscious knows what I need and, before I realize it, I'm pulling into a strip mall with a pet supply store, bead shop, and bakery. I open a glass door and breathe in bliss.

"Welcome to Sweet Republic." An employee scoops almond buttercrunch into a cup for another customer and says, "Let me know if you'd like to sample any flavors."

Two toddlers burst in. A woman tries to hush them, but their clamors grow. I let them order first and the woman smiles in appreciation. I order two scoops of blue moon. My grandma would tease me that it tasted like Froot Loops. Sitting at an outdoor table, I remind myself not to wolf it down, to let the handcrafted flavor rest on my taste buds and soothe my nerves.

Four people leave a Chinese restaurant, joking and talking, and heading my way. One of them says, "You've got to try it." I'm starting my second scoop when my throat tightens. A silver Camry is circling the parking lot. When it slows at the bakery next door, I stop breathing. The passenger side is nearest me, but I can't make out anyone through the tinted windows. The driver hits the gas and something hits my lap. Ice cream. My fingers, blue and sticky, are squeezing the cup. I pick the scoop off my pants and toss it in the trash. I grab a wad of napkins and my phone goes off. Bob wants to know where I am.

Getting hit by a car might have been less painful than facing my news director. It's like two caterpillars are fighting above his eyes. I want to laugh at his seriousness over a silly story, but the vein pulsing at his temple warns me off.

"Where are the cupcakes?"

"Safely stashed in the greenroom."

"Why?"

"I don't want anyone to see them. You know how the news-room is—people will eat anything."

"That's not what I meant. Why are they here? They should be at the lab." He paws at a paper clip. "Actually, they should have been analyzed by now."

"They'll be at the lab end of today—tomorrow at the latest."

I have no idea if that's true. We haven't yet collected twenty samples, which was the plan before real news derailed me.

Bob jabs the paper clip at me. "No more stalling."

Okay, enough about cupcakes. A story that could bring down leaders in the nation's fifth largest city is way more important. I lean forward, pressing my hand on his desk. Ouch. Wrong hand.

"Bob, I understand you want the cupcake story, but you should also know that I'm working on something with major potential."

He folds his arms and says, "Let's hear it."

Not long ago, I would've felt comfortable talking openly with my news director. He started in the business as a reporter and should understand where I'm coming from, but more often than not, he sides with Sexy when it comes to story selection. Still, I know there's a reporter inside Bob—it just needs encouragement to come out.

"I can't go into detail. Not yet. But trust me, you'll be glad I stayed on it." As long as someone doesn't kill me first. On the drive to the station, I considered telling Bob about the car that almost hit me, but that's ammunition for him to harass me into counseling—or worse, pull me off the story.

"What are you working on that's so important?"

I chomp on a thumbnail.

"C'mon, out with it."

A sliver of skin comes loose.

"Jolene, I have other meetings today."

"I'm working sources on two different investigations but I really can't tell you any more than that right now."

"I am your news director and I've been a journalist longer than you've been alive."

I want to tell him about the threats to stop me investigating. I'd like to get his support, but the reporter in Bob is buried too deep. He's in full manager mode and I can't give him another reason to beat the counseling drum.

"You can trust me to keep information confidential."

I'm not sure. I've been in newsrooms when someone shares something and then, as sort of an afterthought, says, "But that's off the record." I've even heard someone hang up from a call and announce, "Off the record, so and so says . . ." That's not protecting a source. It's why I would never advise a friend to share delicate information with a reporter without thoroughly vetting the journalist. You've got to know who you're talking to before you can trust them.

"You have to promise me you won't repeat it," I say. "Not to David or anyone else."

Bob exhales a long breath. "I was a reporter before I was a manager. I understand confidentiality."

"All I can tell you is both investigations involve elected officials and no one else knows about them. That's why I need to keep digging. I don't want to get beat."

Left unsaid but hanging in the air is, "I don't want a repeat of the talk show host's murder where I had the early lead, lost it, and then nearly got myself killed."

"Are you talking about criminal investigations?"

I nod. If I don't say the words out loud it feels less like violating a source.

"You refuse to tell me more?"

I meet his eyes and shake my head. Bob drops the paper clip and leans forward.

"I'm proud of you, Jolene. While the manager in me is curious—and, frankly, irritated—the journalist in me respects you for sticking to your guns and protecting your sources."

My shoulders soften and the knot in my stomach begins to unwind. My news director still cares about news.

"I'll give you some time to pursue your story under three conditions."

Why so many?

"First, keep me posted. I want to know if this is moving forward or if you get stuck. If it's really as big as you say it is, we don't want to get beat."

"Thank you, I won't let you down." I stand at an angle so he doesn't see the rip in my pants and head toward the door.

"Jolene?"

I stop.

"The other condition is to get those cupcakes to the lab. Now."

"Got it."

"One more thing: make your counseling appointment."

At least he ranked the stories first.

CHAPTER
20

We get no pizza, no sandwiches, not even chips. Apparently, SMH's airline ticket swallowed the food budget.

"Since our last meeting about social media, I've noticed significant improvement," Bob says. "Referring to the audience as our friends or followers instead of viewers has been a game changer in getting everyone to think digital first. As you know, people aren't watching traditional newscasts as much, but they are getting content from our website, social media platforms, and breaking news text alerts. Our consultant, Shelley Munro Hammett, has been analyzing the data and I've asked her to share highlights so you can see where we're making progress and where we can improve."

SMH prances to the jewel of our newsroom: the social media center. After pressing a remote control, the magic—in her mind—begins. Using a seventy-five-inch screen, she dazzles Bob with a bunch of numbers showing various likes, clicks, and comments.

"Now, are you all ready to see my favorite?"

Can I click no?

"As everyone is aware, there's no proven formula to video

going viral. With one exception in this market being Jaime Cerreta reporting live in the middle of a ghastly dust storm. While Channel 4 Eyewitness News doesn't have that, I'm pleased to share the station's video of llamas on the loose got picked up by our network, the cable networks, and numerous online outlets like Buzz-Feed. While the llamas were trending on social, Channel 4's story attracted the attention of Instagram. Of course, many Instagram users liked it, but I'm talking about the platform itself. Instagram reposted the station's video on its account. Anyone want to guess how many followers the official Instagram account has?"

"Hundreds of millions," Sexy says.

"Close to seven hundred million."

"Take that, L.A.!" He punches the air like a boxer.

Shelley chuckles. "You'll really enjoy this. As of this afternoon, that single post has more than half a million likes."

SMH doesn't explain how it translates into money for the station, but the managers react as if every like generated a dollar into their personal bank accounts. As she drones on about engagement, my mind wanders to city hall. I need to dig more into the relationships between Mayor Ace Logan, Councilwoman Zoey Patterson, and the lobbyist Rich Gains. Logan disliked Rich enough to reject campaign donations and, according to his chief of staff, Logan is a suspect in Rich's murder. Zoey is rumored to have been taking kickbacks and having an affair with Rich. But I can't let Rich's murder distract me from Carlos's deadly car crash. Just because police aren't calling it suspicious doesn't mean it's not. Between the anonymous threats I've received and a car nearly running me over, it's obvious someone doesn't want the truth to come out. The sound of my name brings me back to the meeting.

"Jolene gets credit for this next idea," Sexy says. "If her friend hadn't been so captivating, we may have never revived our 'Off the Menu' franchise."

"What?"

I didn't realize I'd said it out loud until he snickers.

"For those of you who didn't have the pleasure of meeting Jolene's friend, Norma, let me tell you she is a treasure trove of information." Sexy is pleased he caught me off guard. "Our anchors will front the pieces and they'll air Sunday nights starting in two weeks."

"Wouldn't it make more sense to air them Friday as people head into the weekend?" Elena asks.

"Friday nights attract fewer viewers," David says. "Typically, we're strongest Sundays at ten."

I blurt out, "Thought we were digital first."

Bob jumps in. "Jolene, don't be a smart-ass."

Dozens of eyes bear down on me. No shuffling feet or shifting in seats. Even the scanner traffic goes silent. Bob rarely swears, which is unusual in a newsroom. Alex told me the last assistant news director used so many variations of the F-word that people only freaked out when she didn't use it.

"That's how you knew she was really pissed off," Alex said.

She applied for Bob's job and, when she didn't get it, accepted a news director job in New Orleans. Bob never filled her position, a money-saving move that secured his position for a couple years.

Bob scans the newsroom as if daring anyone to come to my defense. No one does.

Sexy continues the dining pitch. "Shorter segments and promos will post to social on Fridays. They'll continue through the weekend to boost engagement and, of course, we'll encourage people to watch for the full report on Sunday. Any questions?"

Even though I have no intention of speaking, Elena kicks my chair as a warning.

"We believe the 'Off the Menu' franchise will be extremely

popular," Bob says. "You all know how much people love learning about restaurant openings and closings."

"They're always the most re-posted content on social and get the most hits on our website," Sexy says. "Our research has also revealed another area for us to explore. People want restaurant news, call it the dessert of the news buffet, if you will, but they also want a main course, so they get a balanced meal."

"David is right," Bob says. "People care about quality journalism and I couldn't be more pleased to announce a new initiative. Channel 4 Eyewitness News will showcase watchdog journalism, exposing questionable behavior and actions by those in power. Research shows our audience wants the powerful to be held accountable."

That's exactly how I pitched Carlos's contract. Sexy yawned then but now he's a bobblehead.

"Jolene is working on a watchdog investigation that she's not yet ready to share, but she has my full support to pursue, while handling other duties as well."

Am I dreaming?

"If you have ideas for watchdog stories, let David or me know. We don't have unlimited resources, but we are committed to quality journalism."

Covering real news makes the cupcake investigation easier to swallow, for sure.

"We'll double down on what sets us apart, from 'Off the Menu' to whatever Jolene and others uncover, while keeping our viewers—excuse me, our friends—involved and engaged through our social platforms."

Bob pauses like he's co-anchoring with SMH and it's her turn to read. She nods at him, pivots to the audience, and delivers a smooth performance.

"The most successful newsrooms are nimble newsrooms,

willing to adapt and change as needed. We're going to modify a segment the station began after my last visit. Instead of having viewers vote for a story to cover every day, we'll have them vote on a story of the week. This will help Bob and David better manage resources, especially with greater emphasis on watchdog journalism."

"Thank you, Shelley." Bob looks like he's going to announce Phoenix will never break another heat record. "And thanks to our sterling sales team we have a new sponsor for the segment. The sponsor for our story of the week is Your Best Self."

"What is it?" Gina asks.

"It's a first here in the valley, a one-stop shop for cosmetic dermatology, surgery, and dentistry. They're excited about our new segment offering people choices and letting them pick what they want. It aligns with their business model."

Sometimes it feels like newscasts only exist to fill time between commercials. Archie's Arctic Air sponsors our weather segment, Arizona Accident Attorneys sponsors traffic, and Gyms for Real People sponsors sports. At this rate, we might change our name from Eyewitness News to the Wright News.

"Before we wrap up, I encourage you all to stay active on your social media platforms," SMH says. "Keep thinking about your audience as your friends."

"Remember, everyone should have a Facebook page affiliated with the station to share your work. Even better if you operate on another platform," Bob says. "You're welcome to get personal. Share dog photos if you want. Or cat videos if that's more your style. Vacation photos, your kids' pictures, what you're making for dinner. Our friends want to get to know you better. But let me remind you that personal does not mean political. Nor does it mean you should share opinions about social, economic, or other issues that would cause someone to question your objectivity as journalists."

"Excuse me, Bob, if I may?" SMH aims the remote at the monitor. "I'd like to show an example everyone here can relate to."

Elena's Instagram page fills the screen. She's no longer slouching. This was not pre-discussed.

"Reporter Elena Ramirez recently attended Stevie Nicks's concert. Here's a reel that shows her entering Talking Stick Resort Amphitheatre, the concession area, walking to the lawn section, and setting up chairs and a blanket. Very relatable for our friends."

"Teacher's pet," I whisper to Elena.

"She also posted selfies and photos of the show. Super fun. And, here's an exceptional post—I admit this is my favorite Stevie Nicks song, so I may be biased."

SMH plays a reel of Elena's mom twirling to "Edge of Seventeen." The shot widens out to include more twirlers. I glance at Elena, expecting her to squirm, but she's beaming.

"Elena nailed it here by showing her personality and including her mom."

Gina asks how often we should be posting.

"There's no magic number," Shelley says. "But through my work with other stations, I've found seven times a day is sort of a sweet spot."

Seven times? I want to ask how we're supposed to post seven times and manage to research, conduct interviews, write, edit, produce, and report news, but I don't need to be scolded by my news director seven times in a day.

Bob says, "Keep in mind, there's no pressure to get as elaborate as Elena's posts. Keep it simple. Slices of daily life. Ways to show people you're just like them. The more they can relate to you, the more the station benefits."

After the meeting breaks up, Elena announces she might create an Instagram account to show off her cakes. Gina sees the social media push as a chance to get her parents involved.

"Maybe I can do a weekly feature on Mama Robinson's nuggets of wisdom," she said. "What do you think, Jolene?"

I aim for a bland expression, but Gina mistakes it for sadness.

"Oh, I'm sorry. I was thoughtless."

No, I am conniving. My friends believe the story I told them, a lie I've been living since first telling it in college: my parents died in a car accident and that's how I came to live with my grandma. No one knows the truth. And I want to keep it that way.

"It's all good." I force a smile. "I'm excited we're going after serious news."

And I am. It proves how trusting your gut and not backing down can pay off.

CHAPTER
21

The next morning my excitement is as high as local news rat-ings in the eighties. Management's support of watchdog jour-nalism has me feeling like a kid who got their birthday pony. I float into the kitchen an hour before my alarm was scheduled and surprise Oscar.

"It's a big day." I shake flakes into his bowl. "Wish me luck." When he fails to respond, I tap Emmy's wings. "You might be getting a roommate soon."

I plan to be at city hall when it opens, but a fender bender puts a dent in the plan. Thankfully, not my fender. Traffic inches along Seventh Avenue until just past the accident, where anyone not speeding risks the wrath of tailgaters. Pulling into the city garage is like visiting a theater for a Monday matinee. Dimly lit and empty. But stepping outside the garage is like the opening sequence for a *Mission: Impossible* movie. The sun's rays pound my eyes. Horns hammer my eardrums. The air is like plastic wrap squeezing my throat. I feel the gravel and taste the dirt from my last time at this intersection.

What if the person who tried to run me over followed me? I watch as three people enter the crosswalk. My feet won't move.

I wait through two light cycles before I muster the courage to wedge myself in a cluster of pedestrians. Safety in numbers. On the other side, I release a breath I didn't know I was holding and shake it off.

When Zoey Patterson ran for council, her catchphrase was "Smart Growth." She promoted her knowledge of real estate, including the "tricks" developers play as a way to attract voters. Patterson beat the incumbent—another lifelong public servant if you believed his campaign signs—by fewer than four hundred votes. The next election is a year away but Patterson is already campaigning and exercising caution when dealing with the media. Like all politicians, she seeks attention when she's mastered the talking points. In this case she doesn't know what to expect, which is why I'm stuck waiting outside her office reading a brochure produced by the economic development department detailing why "Phoenix Is Hot."

An hour later, Patterson emerges with the same toothy smile from her bio page. Her attire is what my fashion-forward colleague Gina calls "on trend," styles you might find at a well-stocked Ross. But the councilwoman's clothes have no loose seams, straggling threads, or cheap fabric. Her clothes whisper Nordstrom. Patterson excels at fashion and dental care, but her eyes need work. Beneath arched brows, blended shadows, and black liner, suspicion lurks.

"You told my assistant you had something to discuss?"

Not waiting for an invitation, I move toward the door. "Yes, thanks for seeing me."

She blocks the entrance. "I'm busy. What's this about?"

I lower my voice. "It's confidential. Can we talk in your office?"

Now it's Patterson's turn to play 007. She peers down the hall and, finding it clear, steps aside to allow me in before quickly closing the door. No family photos on display but plenty with fellow politicians and what the media like to label "community and business leaders." Several faces I recognize but don't know their names. Like the woman standing next to Patterson in front of a display of State Forty Eight T-shirts.

"Wasn't she on *Saturday Night Live?*"

"Yes, that's Aidy Bryant. I shop at the boutique her mother opened and got a photo when she stopped by. That was taken when Aidy was still on SNL and before her mom sold the business. Both of them are extremely sweet."

I point to a photo of Patterson in a car showroom. "Who's that?"

"You don't recognize him?"

"No."

Disapproval crosses her face. "Rex Sanders is a local legend. I bought my first car from his dealership. Great guy. He supports dozens of nonprofits."

"Did you know Rich Gains?"

I hadn't planned to ask right away but the question seems appropriate since she's sharing experiences with movers and shakers.

Her smile falters. "I don't believe so." She moves to a sleek desk and swivels in a chair the color of sand.

"He was a regular at city hall representing developers. And his murder was widely reported."

"Oh, of course." A well-moisturized hand wiggles the mouse next to her laptop. "My brain must have short-circuited for a second."

She clicks twice, scans her screen, and leans back. I take it as an invitation to sit.

"What happened was unfortunate," Zoey says. "Like my colleagues, I knew Rich from his appearances before the council."

"Is that all?"

"Excuse me?"

"Didn't he donate to your campaign?"

I already know the answer from searching the campaign finance database. Gains had contributed the maximum. Plus, I found online photos where he attended fundraisers for her campaign.

"Off the top of my head, I couldn't tell you." She crosses her legs and smooths her velvet skirt. "It wouldn't be unusual. Many people who do business with the city donate to various campaigns. There's nothing illegal about that."

Who said anything about illegal?

"So, you only associated with Rich through city work?"

"Yes."

"Never socially?"

"Depends on what you mean by social." She straightens her legs and scoots her chair closer. "A business breakfast, an awards banquet, those types of things are professional but you can also develop friendly relationships." Zoey's elbows rest on her desk, her hands form a steeple at her chin, not a single tiny chip in her red nail polish. "Exactly what are you getting at?"

I'd like to know if you or the mayor had anything to do with Gains's murder, but I can't say that directly. Before I can come up with a response, Zoey's desk phone rings. Her eyes cut to the display and back to me.

"Please, take that," I say, hoping to buy time.

She answers, scans her computer, and shakes the mouse. "When?" After three clicks she tells the caller she'll be right out.

"Excuse me a moment."

It's just me and her laptop. An open laptop. Sliding it around for a peek wouldn't take more than ten seconds. The door appears fully closed. I would hear it open. But would it be enough warning to turn the laptop back? I scutter around the desk. Her email account is up. It's illegal to open someone's physical mail without their permission but this situation is murky. I opt for look but don't touch. Most of the inbox contains messages from the city's domain. The others have professional-sounding subject lines. What I see at the bottom of the page catches my breath. The sender is "PeytonAndCaleb" and the subject line is "Hello and meeting." The font isn't bold like the newer messages so she must have opened and read it. If I click on it, she'll never know. My fingers flutter above the mouse as the door flies open.

"What are you doing?"

"Um, I, I—" My voice croaks. "Dropped my pen."

I squat and pray for a pen. All I get are two pointy shoes coming at me like pitchforks.

"I don't see anything," she says.

"It must have rolled under the desk."

"You need to leave. Now."

My head bangs against the desk as the pitchforks close in.

"I'm late for an appointment," she says.

"Sorry." I uncurl my body and move kicking distance away from the pitchforks. "Just one more question: How well do you know Kris Kruger?"

Patterson squares her shoulders. "I don't know that name. What is this about?"

"Maybe you know his daughter Peyton?"

"I don't know what kind of games you're playing but I don't have time." She points to the door. "Go."

I may not have picked up much, but what I did learn was critical: Zoey Patterson is a liar.

She can throw me out of her office but not city hall. In the lobby, I join the line at the coffee kiosk. Nothing on the menu is going to soothe the bump on my head, but I'm counting on hot chocolate to ease my mind. I sink into a chair and wrap my fingers around the cup. At a minimum, Councilwoman Zoey Patterson and Mayor Ace Logan deserve more scrutiny. Both pretend they have no relationship with Rich Gains but their fingerprints turned up at his house where he was killed. Logan sends a personal note to the employee handling bids for city contracts and Patterson is friendly with the winner's family. That's no coincidence. I need to find out if they're working together.

I text Jim Miranda, my favorite former PIO, to call me, and pass the time by guessing the destinations of visitors passing through security. If they take an immediate right, they're headed to licensing services, which can make for entertaining people watching. The department issues licenses for a handful of activities—from auctioneers and street vendors to escorts and strippers. I take a last sip and toss the cup in a recycle bin. As I watch a guy begin climbing the grand staircase, my phone vibrates.

"What's up?" Jim says.

"That's what I was going to ask you."

"Your turn to go first."

"I didn't realize we were keeping score."

"We are," he says.

My calves involuntarily tighten as the guy on the stairs picks up speed.

"Would you consider it a big deal if a council member is friendly with the daughter of a contractor accused of gaming the system to win city contracts?"

A whack jars my ear, like a fist hitting a table.

"Jolene, we agreed you would stay away from the council."

Oof. Guess my excitement over the station's new support of watchdog journalism got the best of me.

"I didn't *say* I talked to anyone." The stair climber slows to catch his breath. "I was asking a hypothetical to get your take."

"What's going on? What are you working on?"

"There's a guy named Carlos Rios who was complaining about city contracts going to the same guy. Then, he dies in a car crash. Unusual crash—no braking, no skid marks. Can you check on it?"

"Have you forgotten my unit's workload? We're providing support to the AG's office on its investigation into potential corruption at city hall while also trying to solve the murder of a high-profile lobbyist. I don't need a Sherlock wannabe messing things up."

"But there's a connection between the lobbyist and Carlos Rios. Rich Gains helped Carlos bid on city contracts. Carlos was competing against his former boss, who happens to be the person who always wins the contracts. He had motive to silence Carlos. And—get this—he's a master mechanic. Can you check with the vehicular crimes unit?"

"No, Jolene. Every extra ounce of energy is spent in meetings acting like a team player and not going off on people's political posturing."

"Sounds like our newsroom meetings about social media."

"Please do not equate criminal investigations with Instagram reels."

Damn, Jim.

"I need to keep my unit focused on what we are assigned to investigate and that is Rich Gains's murder."

"Where do things stand with the murder investigation?"

"Making progress. Nothing solid yet."

My gut urges me to come clean about visiting Zoey Patterson, but when I open my mouth, nothing comes out.

"Remember to stay away from the council and don't screw this up for us."

Glad I kept my mouth shut. I'll keep investigating on my own.

When I return to the newsroom, Alex greets me. "No cupcake for me?"

"Don't remind me."

"Apparently someone has to."

"I'm working a story—no, I'm working two stories—that will make Sexy forget all about baked goods with gluten."

"Does this have to do with the city contracts?"

"Yep. It's big."

"I hope it's not Don Bolles big."

"Who?"

"Jolene, you disappoint me."

"Join the club." I pull up a chair next to a collection of Kung Fu Pandas.

"It's a crime we don't include his story in employee orientation. Every journalist should know about Don Bolles."

I pick up Alex's Slinky. "Tell me then. Did he work here?"

Alex takes the Slinky away, like a teacher demanding my full attention. "Don Bolles was a kick-ass reporter for the *Arizona Republic*. Covered organized crime and corruption in the seventies. Bolles went to meet a source at the Clarendon Hotel. The source never showed, Bolles got in his car and it blew up. He was hospitalized for several days before the injuries killed him."

"That's horrible. Did they catch who did it?"

"Three people were convicted. Bolles's murder was national news. You know about IRE, right?"

I nod at the reference to the Investigative Reporters and Editors organization.

"In response to Bolles's murder, dozens of journalists from all over came together to finish his work. IRE produced a series called the 'Arizona Project.' It ran in newspapers across the country."

"I feel stupid for not knowing about him."

"I didn't know as much until I visited the Newseum in Washington, D.C., before it closed. Bolles's car was on display. Powerful stuff. The Society of Professional Journalists named the Clarendon Hotel a historic site and there's a bust of Bolles in the lobby."

Alex answers a phone and I search mine for the Clarendon. On the corners of Fourth Avenue and Clarendon and Osborn Avenues are ceremonial blue street signs for Don Bolles Way.

"I'll let her know." Alex hangs up and gives me a "What'd you do now?" look.

"What?"

"Bob wants to talk to you."

"Probably wants to yell at me for not finishing the gluten investigation."

I walk into his office, ready to apologize and promise to absolutely, positively, no excuses, have the cupcakes to the lab within twenty-four hours.

"Sit down," Bob says.

It's twenty degrees hotter at his desk.

"What the hell has gotten into you?"

If Bob were a cartoon character, he'd have steam coming out of his ears.

"That's not a rhetorical question, Jolene."

"I don't know what you mean."

"Were you sneaking around Councilwoman Patterson's office and accessing her laptop?"

Oh, shit.

"She invited me in."

"Did she invite you to read her emails?"

There's nothing I can say that's going to help me here so I keep my mouth shut.

"Accessing and reading someone else's email is illegal."

"I didn't touch any keys. Her email was on the screen. And I didn't click on any of them."

Bob shakes his head. "I don't know what you were thinking. That behavior is reprehensible. As bad as harassing a widow."

I didn't harass Rich Gains's widow. Sometimes people want to talk. When she declined, I apologized and left. But I have enough sense not to argue.

"Have you made an appointment with employee assistance yet?"

I don't trust my voice and shake my head.

"It is not voluntary. You will go. Or you will be suspended without pay."

WTF?

A knock interrupts Bob's berating. I've never been so happy to see Alex.

"Excuse me, we have breaking news," he says. "Can Jolene head out when you're done talking?" he asks.

"What is it?" Bob says.

Doesn't matter. I'll take anything to get out of here.

"Fatal 2-49."

"English, Alex."

"Electrocution."

"At a business?"

"A house. It's strange. That's why I'd like to check it out."

"Go." With a flick of his hand, Bob dismisses me. "But remember what I said."

I resist the urge to hug Alex as I bolt out the door.

CHAPTER

22

I'm so grateful to be out of my news director's office I don't mind being assigned to work with Roger "Snail" Hale. Until I recognize the address for the electrocution death. It's the home of Kris Kruger, the guy who uses an inside source to win city contracts. My mind is moving faster than our truck. If Kris is dead, he may have gotten away with Carlos's murder. Possibly Rich Gains's murder, too. Unless someone killed Kris. Like his former accountant. Simona Park had reasons to silence all three men. Slow down, I remind myself. No one is calling Kris's death a murder. It could be an accident. Then again, that's what they said about Carlos's crash.

By the time we get to Kruger's house the sun has set, but we have no trouble finding the action. Three news trucks are positioned along the curb. My fists clench at the sight of a crew sporting the confidence that comes with being first on the scene and getting exclusive video.

"Look who finally showed up." JJ flips blond hair extensions off her shoulders. "Your assignment desk must have seen my live shot and sent you running, huh?"

Mother Teresa would struggle to stay curse-free around JJ.

"We're the only ones with the ambulance leaving." She bats eyelashes as thick as my bangs. "This is going to be a huge story."

Does she know about the contract dispute between Kris and Carlos? Maybe the Wright Legal Firm gave her the documents, too. I should ask. JJ won't stay quiet if she has an opportunity to gloat.

"My producer says the network wants to run my story."

Nope. Not asking. That would appear weak, like I need her help. The only thing JJ can help me with is hair and makeup and that's not the priority—information is.

"You know the network will post to social." Her eyes are as bright as the Hollywood sign at night. "Everyone will see it."

I push my pride down and cram a lid on it. "Is anyone talking?"

JJ cocks her hip to the side, slender fingers draping over it. "Yeah. To me." As she saunters away, I wish for her high heels to step on a pebble and send her to the ground. No such luck and I return to our truck.

"Ready, Roger?"

"Roger that." His chuckle is as slow as his driving.

To prod him along, I grab the mic and tripod. A handful of neighbors are gathered on the sidewalk.

I overhear JJ tell her photographer, "This is exactly what I need for my résumé reel."

She's always working on a résumé reel, a compilation of your best work that can lead to your dream job if the right person sees it at the right time.

"Jolene?"

Somehow, Roger has passed me and joined the neighbors. I hurry over, plop the tripod down, and introduce myself.

"Can anyone here tell us what happened?"

They come across as retired Midwesterners. Practical shoes, simple hairstyles, no Botox. Same as my grandma—except for the retired part. She worked in a beauty salon until the cancer sapped her strength.

A tall guy with a protruding belly finishes a swig from a Budweiser can and says, "Bad accident. Sounds like he was electrocuted."

A woman points to JJ. "That reporter said he fell and died."

"Was anyone around when it happened?" I ask.

"Not us," the shorter man says. "We were all at work. But Peter saw something. He's already been on Channel 2 News."

Yay for JJ.

"Where does Peter live?"

He points to the house next door, where the guy Kris Kruger called his chief elf lives. I thank them and march across the street with Roger trailing. As I push the doorbell, I aim for a look that doesn't reveal the words running through my head: "Please give me a quick interview so my videographer has time to shoot what he needs and we can write, edit, and file the story before deadline."

A voice calls out behind me. "He won't talk to you!"

I smell Sergio Magaña before I see him. An MMJ for Univision, he's famous for overindulging in cologne and showing up late to press conferences.

"Hey, Sergio. Did he not answer the door?"

"Yeah, but he's only talking to JJ."

"What the—"

Roger elbows me as the door opens. I face a man who had recently been on the receiving end of my "Hey, nothing horrible happening in your neighborhood" smile.

"Hi, I was here the other day talking with Kris for Channel 4 Eyewitness News."

"Yeah, I remember. I saw your story about the guy who died in the car accident."

"Honey, who is it?" A skinny woman with big hair edges between him and the door.

"Another reporter."

She smiles. "What station are you with?"

"Channel 4. I'm Jolene and this is Roger. We understand you found your neighbor. That must have been scary."

"I didn't see him," she says. "I only got home ten minutes ago and Peter filled me in on everything."

Behind my back, I wave a hand at Roger, a signal to get ready to roll.

"Peter, I hear you called for help. Can we talk to you for a minute?"

"Sorry, no." He doesn't look sorry.

"We can wait if you're in the middle of something."

"It's not that. I promised another reporter I wouldn't talk to anyone else." He shrugs like he had no other choice.

"You're free to talk to whoever you want."

"I'm aware of the First Amendment. But I am a man of my word."

Time for my go-to line when a must-have interview is on the verge of becoming a just-missed interview. "I really need to talk to someone who knows what's going on or I could get in trouble at work."

"Oh, honey." The woman touches Peter's shoulder. "You can't let her get into trouble."

"I'm not trying to be difficult," he says. "I hope you understand. Now, if you'll excuse me."

I'm stuck staring at a pinecone wreath on the door, mentally preparing to have my butt kicked by incompetent JJ. Then, someone mentions the Grinch. It's a woman on the sidewalk wearing a fanny pack large enough to hold a baby. I shuffle down the driveway.

"I didn't catch what you said."

"The Grinch." Her jaw moves like a cow chewing cud. "Bet he's celebrating."

"Who's the Grinch?"

"Gary's his real name but we call him Grinch." She pulls a hunk of gum out of her mouth, wraps it in a tissue, and stuffs it in the canvas pack. "He doesn't like Christmas. And he doesn't like Kris. In fact, he hates him."

"So you knew Kris Kruger? Would you mind talking with us for a minute?"

"What station are you with?"

"Channel 4."

"I'm a Channel 2 gal."

JJ scores again.

"That's okay, ma'am," Roger says with a smile. "We won't hold it against you."

Her eyes crease as she lets out a hoot. Helen Carr proceeds to tell us that she's been in the neighborhood since marrying Ernest thirty-eight years ago. She's lived alone since Ernest died from prostate cancer five years ago.

"Kris and Denise moved in I'd say, about twenty years ago." She taps a finger against her cheek. "No, that's not right. They moved in right before my grandson was born. He's eighteen now."

"What kind of neighbor was Kris?"

"A regular guy." She rests her hand on the fanny pack, the way cops do with duty belts. "At first, anyway. He'd wave hello and get your mail or watch your house when you were gone."

"Did something happen that changed him?"

"After Denise—that was his wife—left, Kris went a little Christmas crazy."

"How so?"

"You know, he went from putting up lights on his house to adding a bunch of blow-up things all over the yard. Then, he created an entrance to the neighborhood and started getting other people to add more lights. If you ask me, he was trying to outdo his wife and her new husband. They shared custody but he only had his daughter every other weekend and they rotated holidays."

"How long ago was the divorce?"

"Been quite a while." Her eyes drift to Kris's house. "I remember it was around the time we replaced our roof. Maybe twelve, thirteen years ago. Could be longer. Might've been around the time their girl started high school."

"How did he get other neighbors involved with the holiday display?"

"We love Christmas, too, and wanted to show our spirit. Our home is down that way." I follow her pointer finger, but have no clue which house she means. "We like to decorate with Winnie the Pooh and Tigger." She drops her hand. "We couldn't help but feel bad for Kris. He was a nice man and worked hard. It wasn't his fault his wife cheated on him and then tried to take all his money. I was happy to help make the season more festive for him. So was most everybody else."

The way she emphasizes "most" makes me repeat it.

"Not the Grinch. When he moved here—and before you ask that was about four years ago—Kris told him how we do Christmas. The first year Grinch didn't decorate even though Kris offered to put the decorations up and take 'em all down. Grinch didn't have to do anything. Kris has a full storage unit, plus his garage, and most neighbors store things, too. Anyway, Grinch let Kris decorate his house a couple times and then last year things got ugly."

This story is taking an intriguing turn.

"Grinch yelled at Kris: 'Stay off my lawn.' No lie—those were his exact words. I heard him." She pulls a stick of Juicy Fruit out of the fanny pack. "Grinch said he didn't want to see any Christmas decorations on his property."

"How'd that go over?"

"You can imagine how upsetting that was to Kris. This whole street is filled with lights and decorations. And my home-made caramel corn. That's a lot of work, I'm telling you. But it's worth it. The kids go nuts over it. So do their parents. If I had the resources, I'd package and sell it to visitors. That's how popular it is. We get thousands of people coming from all over."

I try to cut in but she's on a roll.

"We've even been talking about trying out for one of those TV shows where neighborhoods compete against each other for the best holiday display. Of course, we can't do it if Grinch won't play along, you know? Imagine how pathetic it would be to have one dark, sad house on the block. I mean, we'd never make it on the show, let alone win. His house would work better for a scary movie, know what I mean? Like something sinister is going on while the rest of us are being jolly."

When Helen wedges the gum into her mouth, I seize the opportunity. "Were you around today? Do you know what happened to Kris?"

She chews for a minute. "I didn't see anything, but Peter—the guy who wouldn't talk to you—said Kris was on his ladder hanging lights. I guess he knocked a bucket of water over and it spilled on the cords and he fell onto them, something like that, and he was electrocuted. Poor guy."

We take in Kris's front yard. A ladder on the ground. A hose slithering around an orange Home Depot bucket. From the roof, a string of lights hangs lifeless.

"At least he died doing what he loved. Isn't that what they

always say? Wonder what'll happen with our lights now." She looks down the block. "Maybe Peyton will lead the effort."

"That's Kris's daughter, right?"

She nods and points. "Lives over there."

"Which house?"

"The one with the ASU flag. We're not supposed to hang signs or banners, per the homeowner association, but they tend to let things slide during football season."

"Where does the Grinch—I mean, Gary—live?"

"Two doors down from Peyton, on the right. It's the house with the black shutters."

"Helen, would you be willing to talk with us on camera? Share your thoughts about Kris and his impact on your neighborhood?"

"Heavens, no. I don't have anything to say."

"Sure, you do." I present what I hope is an encouraging look. "You shared a lot."

"Too much, I suspect. That's what my husband would say. I'm going to pass on your offer."

"Thanks for nothing" is what I want to say because I desperately need an on-camera interview, but Helen was nice to provide background. "We need to get ready for our newscast. I appreciate you talking with me."

"No problem." She smacks her gum. "Maybe I'll even watch your channel tonight."

I tell Roger I want to try the Grinch. "You can stay on the sidewalk with your camera. I'll wave when it's okay to come up."

A No Soliciting sign greets me. No problem, I'm not selling anything. I press the bell, relieved it doesn't have a camera. But there is a peephole, so I add a smile.

When the door whips open, my first thought is he's no Grinch. For one, he's not green. Or covered in fur. But he does have exceptionally long fingers gripping the door.

"Yes?"

I explain I'm working on a story about Kris's death and ask if he has anything to share.

"Sure. He was an asshole who got what he deserved."

I need this interview. I can hear the station's promo: Only on Channel 4 Eyewitness News, a feud between a neighborhood Santa and the Grinch takes a deadly turn.

"What was Kris like?"

"He was a self-centered prick."

"I was told you two had a disagreement over Christmas decorations."

"That's an understatement."

"My photographer is right there." I motion to Snail. "Is it okay if he joins us so we can record a quick interview?"

Grinch shakes his head. "I'm not interested in being on TV."

Please, not another rejection.

"My neighbors think I'm evil, thanks to that attention-seeking jackass."

"Can you tell me what happened?"

His fingers claw the door. "He tried to publicly shame me because I wouldn't put decorations up last year."

"How did he do that?"

"Preached nonsense about how it's our duty as residents of Rudolph Lane to decorate, that people count on our display for holiday cheer." He's warming up, his voice getting louder, his cadence faster. "But it wasn't really about the holiday, it was about Kris's need for attention. The whole spectacle is a hassle, but neighbors play along because it's easier than dealing with his nagging."

"So what? You decided you'd had enough?"

And with that question, his anger dissipates. "Last Christmas nearly killed me. I lost my mother just before Thanksgiving after a horrible fight with cancer. She was the best person to

walk this earth. Even though I knew she was dying it was—"
His fingers fall from the door. "It was devastating."

"I'm sorry."

His jaw tightens. "The last thing on my mind was appeasing Kris. I needed to grieve. So yeah, we had words. I told him to go to hell, nobody wanted to play his stupid game anyway. Know what he did then? Went on Facebook and Nextdoor to complain about the neighborhood Grinch. Even left flyers at all the houses. Didn't use my name but everyone knew who he was talking about. I'm not going to pretend to care that he's dead. Maybe now we won't have any more forced festivities to stroke his ego and people can observe the holiday however they want." His face is as red as Rudolph's nose. "Unless that daughter and husband of hers follow in Daddy's footsteps."

If her husband is as lazy as Kris's former accountant described, the decorations will stay buried in boxes.

"I'm sorry for your loss. Thank you for explaining your perspective."

Even though I don't get an on-camera interview with the Grinch, it's more than I get from Kris's daughter. No one answers and I leave a business card at the front door with a note asking her to call. As I walk away, I change my mind. Peyton likely enters her house through the garage and, if she does, she'll miss it.

"Roger, can I get some of your duct tape?"

"Sure thing."

He rummages through a bag and I compose a message to Peyton offering condolences and asking her to email or call. Using his teeth, Snail rips off a piece.

"This is pretty small." I pull the sticky material off his fingers.

In the time it takes Snail to tear another piece, I could have driven to the store and bought a roll. I tape the yellow paper on white paint, keeping it driver's eye level, and cross my fingers.

Since there's no fire department PIO on scene, I search emails. There's one update with limited details but enough to get me through the newscast. It says paramedics were dispatched to a call about a man who had fallen off a ladder. Upon arrival, they found a male unconscious and unresponsive lying on the driveway near electrical cords and water. He was pronounced dead at the hospital.

From the passenger seat of our truck, I file my story, flip down the visor, and open my makeup bag. Sexy sends a text asking me to call.

"Check your script," he says. "I changed it a bit."

A bit? He deleted the information about the complaint Carlos filed against the city, alleging Kruger had an unfair advantage to win contracts.

"Why'd you take it out?" I ask. "We just had a meeting where watchdog journalism is supposed to be our thing. This guy is the center of my investigation."

"Questions over a city contract have nothing to do with this story," Sexy says. "This is a story about the tragic death of a neighborhood Santa."

He knows I can't argue—we're going live in six minutes. As I swipe on lipstick, a text from Gina appears telling me to check out JJ's post. I flip through her feed and smother a scream. In a ten-second video, JJ announces she's on the scene of a suspicious death and invites viewers to tune in for her exclusive interview.

Thanks to our late arrival, Roger and I are relegated to the side of Kris Kruger's yard. As I reference the driveway where he was found, Roger zooms in. JJ's walk-and-talk routine makes every other reporter want to push her off a ladder. I can tell from the way Roger's body tenses and his camera jiggles that she's ruining things. And of course, Sexy lets me know.

JJ was in your shot.

I ignore his message. Besides, I'm more concerned about my investigation. I will not let the story die with Kris. Someone killed Carlos, Kris's main competition. Someone killed Rich, the lobbyist, who helped Carlos bid on the contracts Kris won. And now, someone may have killed Kris. Maybe there's a serial killer at work. That's it. There must be. Or maybe my favorite photographer, Nate, is right and I'm forcing the dots to connect. One thing's for sure: I'm starving. The peanut butter protein bar I scarfed down on the way here isn't going to get me through the night. By the time I make it home I'm so hangry I can hardly stand to be around myself.

"Sorry, Oscar." He practically jumps out of the water to gulp the flakes. "I didn't expect to be late."

I yank open the fridge. Not much of a selection. Luckily, I'm a cereal connoisseur. Having a variety makes my lackluster culinary skills less glaring.

"What's it going to be, Oscar? Should I go healthy with Corn Flakes or drown my sorrows with magically delicious Lucky Charms?"

Oscar ignores me. "I agree. Lucky Charms."

I set the box, milk, bowl, and spoon on my Ikea table.

"Emmy, sorry to disappoint you. It doesn't look like you'll be getting a friend anytime soon."

Shoveling cereal into my mouth, I pull up JJ's story on my phone. She poses like she's on a red carpet: one knee slightly bent, shoulders back, a hand on her hip.

"I'm standing a few feet away from where the man affectionately known as Kris Kringle hung his final Christmas decoration."

Kris Kringle? No one gave me that name. She probably made it up.

Sashaying up the driveway, she maintains eye contact with the camera. "It was here that Kris Kringle met his untimely death." JJ kneels and pets the driveway like it's a kitten. "A death the victim's neighbor calls a tragedy in an exclusive interview with me."

Peter explains that after he pulled into his driveway he happened to glance over and spot Kris on the ground next to the ladder. Peter called out to him and, after getting no response, ran over, shook Kris, checked his pulse, called 911, and performed CPR.

"It's ironic that Kris's neighbor is a 911 dispatcher," JJ says.

No, JJ, it's interesting but that doesn't make it ironic.

"Right now, it appears to be an accident, but I've learned this investigation is getting extra scrutiny."

My spoon plops into the bowl, milk splashes out.

"Not everyone is quick to call it an accident. You can count on me to monitor every development and bring you the very latest in this bizarre case of deadly decorations."

I cannot be chasing other reporters like I did with Larry Lemmon's story. I eventually out-scooped them and solved the talk show host's murder but almost died in the process. Kinda hoping to avoid that. Anxiety heckles me all night, poking me out of semiconsciousness and dropping twenty-pound weights on my chest. Two business owners involved in a contract dispute die under unusual circumstances. The same two business owners worked with a lobbyist allegedly killed by a home burglar. The same lobbyist was connected to powerful politicians who are under investigation for possible corruption. And then my synapses snap. Three suspicious deaths linked by their work at city hall. That's where I should focus. If questions about Mayor Ace Logan's ethics became public, he'd lose his TV show. If

Councilwoman Zoey Patterson's bribes were exposed, she'd face jail time. Patterson's not going talk to me again and the mayor's too slick to say anything to reveal his true self. But I will find a way in.

CHAPTER

23

An insistent drone rouses me. Eyes closed, my hand reaches for the nightstand and knock my phone to the floor. Dangling over the side of my bed, I glare at the screen, as if my position is the phone's fault. A text from Jim Miranda jolts me awake.

Call me. 911.

He's never used 911 in a text. I jump out of bed and tap "Favorites" where Jim is listed as "Source." Something pulls me back. I need a minute to mull over what could be wrong. Maybe he saw JJ's story about Kris Kruger. No, his unit wouldn't be involved in a homeowner who was electrocuted while hanging Christmas lights. It must be that weasel, Ved Patel. He probably reported me for showing up at his office at city hall. Too bad, Ved, it's a public building and the public is entitled to know about your personal connection to the guy who always wins city contracts. I brush my teeth, rinse out my mouth, and prepare for a tongue-lashing from Jim about bothering people at city hall.

What I get is worse.

"Why the hell did you talk to Councilwoman Zoey Patterson? You've ruined our investigation."

"Ruined?" My voice sounds like Mickey Mouse.

"What the hell were you thinking?"

A jackhammer goes off in my chest. "Jim, I'm sorry, I forgot to tell you."

"That's not the point. You weren't supposed to talk to any council members."

I would never intentionally hurt Jim's work. I value our relationship. I got too wrapped up in reporting and didn't realize I was putting his work at risk.

"Jim, I didn't say anything about your investigation, I swear."

"You didn't have to. Showing up and asking questions was enough to scare Patterson. After she left her house this morning, my team is convinced she made them and they had to stop surveilling. Now she's being vigilant and we may never get the evidence to prove she's been trading access and votes for money."

"I'm really sorry, Jim. What can I do to make things right?"

"Stay the hell out of my way."

"Please, there must be something I can do." I wait a beat. "Jim?"

He's already hung up. It feels like a baseball is lodged in my throat. I drag myself to the kitchen, plop into a chair, and, using my cotton shirt, I rub the plaque on my statuette.

ROCKY MOUNTAIN EMMY
BREAKING NEWS
"CATCHING A KILLER"
JOLENE GARCIA

I won the Emmy for my reporting on the murder of Larry Lemmon, a controversial radio talk show host. The same reporting that earned recognition among my peers annoyed Jim, but he got over it.

THE STORY THAT WOULDN'T DIE 209
"Emmy, we'll work it out again."

The pain in my chest says otherwise.

Since I've totally pissed off Jim and tipped off the councilwoman, I consider other options. I wonder if Kris's daughter would be willing to talk about her dad's accident—if that's what it was. Maybe I can get her take on Simona Park. Since Simona was stealing from Kris and her affair with Rich Gains ended badly, it's worth exploring. I top black pants with a bold sweater and hope Gina is right about red exuding power and confidence.

At the station, I find Nate in an edit bay and pitch the idea of talking to Kris Kruger's daughter as a million times more exciting than sifting through video of politicians crammed around a podium pretending to be interested in what others are saying while counting the minutes until they get to step in front of the cameras.

"What time are they expecting us?" he says.

"They're not."

He sits down. "Jolene, I don't like showing up unannounced after someone has died. That's sleazy."

"We're not ambushing them. We'll ask politely. And I bet they'll appreciate the opportunity to talk about his legacy."

Nate doesn't respond.

"Come on, if we go now, we can grab something to eat."

His look signals I need to up my game.

"My treat and I'll even let you pick the place."

"Sold." He bounces up. "Miracle Mile Deli, here we come."

We arrive five minutes before it opens and join a dozen cars in the parking lot. The restaurant was named after McDowell Road, known as the Miracle Mile, in the 1950s. I don't know why the deli left McDowell Road, but many businesses bailed after Phoenix's first mall opened two miles away. The city's love affair with cars turned the once popular pedestrian pathway into a motor speedway. Entrepreneurs, restaurant owners, and artists are working to rekindle Miracle Mile's glamour.

"They're opening." Nate takes off like a kid on Halloween. Before I'm out the door, he's halfway across the lot.

"Go ahead," I say when he turns to check on me. "Get in line."

Inside, Nate's talking with Josh Garcia, whose grandparents opened the deli.

"How's Brayden handling his first year of high school?" Josh asks.

"Better than I did," Nate says. "We pray it stays that way. We'd really like to see our kids go to college or trade school."

After Brayden was born to teenage parents, it would be nearly ten years before Nate and his wife welcomed a baby girl. During that time, Nate worked as an Amazon driver and a technician for a production company where he learned how to shoot and edit video before landing in news.

"Hey, Jolene, it's good to see you," Josh says. "After Larry Lemmon's murder, I was afraid you'd leave us for a job with the network."

I wish.

"How's the reporting life?"

"Can't complain when we have time for lunch."

Someone waves for Josh's attention. "Duty calls," he says. "I'm glad you could squeeze us in. Enjoy."

Nate and I each order the Straw. I go with an onion roll, Nate does rye bread, and we both add fries. Neither of us talk as our teeth sink through layers of pastrami, Swiss cheese, and sauerkraut. Before I know it, the only thing on my plate is a dab of horseradish. Sometimes, my childhood instinct overpowers my rational mind that knows I'll have enough food tomorrow and the next day. Rather than stare at my empty plate while Nate works on half a sandwich, I fill him in on what I've learned.

"So, you think there's a connection between the Christmas guy's death and the car crash?" he asks.

"There's gotta be."

"That means you're pulling a bait and switch on Kris's daughter."

"How so?"

He brandishes a fry. "You told me it's a story about his neighborhood legacy."

"Of course, the story will focus on his love of Christmas— that's how he died. But I would be remiss not to ask other questions."

Nate pops a fry in his mouth, watching me as if he doesn't like what he sees.

"What?"

"Jolene, the man just died."

"I know. But just because he's dead doesn't mean he wasn't shady or cheating the system or doing bad things. I can't tell you everything right now, but trust me."

"You're the one who has to face yourself in the mirror and feel okay about what you're doing."

An employee swings by our table. "Hi there, can I get you guys anything?"

"No, thanks." Nate slides out of his seat. "We're done."

We don't talk on the drive to Kris Kruger's neighborhood. Nate overreacted and I'm in no mood to placate him. We pull onto Rudolph Lane where the neighbor who found Kris on the ground is working in Kris's yard. I ask Nate to stop.

"Why? For an ambush interview?"

"No, drama queen, I want to say hello."

I pass lights and cords coiled like rattlesnakes. "Hi, Peter, are you finishing what Kris started?"

"Guess you could say that."

"Hope the sprinkler system isn't scheduled to go off."

"No, it's turned off," he says. "You know, Kris could be careless. His obsession with having the biggest, brightest displays sometimes took precedence over safety. You have to be vigilant," Peter says. "You never know where danger lies or when it's your time."

Someone removed Kris's ladder and bucket but a string of lights droops as if in mourning.

"We're going to swing by his daughter's house to see if she's up for talking. Do you know if Peyton's home?"

"Her husband, Caleb, should be. Saw him drive by about twenty minutes ago."

"Thanks. Good luck with the lights."

Nate stays in the truck while I knock on the door. The woman who answers looks nothing like Kris. He was tall, she's short. He was chubby, she's thin. His buzz cut was gray, her auburn locks fall past her shoulders. After expressing sympathy for her loss, I explain we're working on a story about her father and ask if she has any stories or thoughts she'd like to share.

Peyton twists her hair, opens her mouth, and closes it.

"Please take your time. I know if someone showed up at my house, I'd need a minute. We can talk to Caleb first."

"Let me check with him. Hold on, okay?"

"Of course. I'll help my photographer grab his gear and we'll wait here."

I avoid Nate's eyes and say, "It's totally okay. She wants to talk to us."

He sighs and pops open the back. I grab the tripod out of the way so he can reach the light kit.

"She just needs a couple minutes. I don't know if it'll just be her or her husband, too. His name is Caleb. They work together at her father's business."

I'm talking too fast, trying to appease Nate, which irritates me. If he had met Carlos, he would understand. It's important to expose Kris Kruger's wrongdoing. Carlos's family deserves answers.

As we wait outside, I veer away from Nate. The maroon-and-gold ASU flag waves in the breeze. I have a sweatshirt from the University of Nebraska, but my closet contains no other clothes emblazoned with "Huskers," no black-and-red jewelry, and no hats featuring ears of corn. The past is behind me. And the future is beyond that door.

"We should leave," Nate says. "They're not interested."

"Yes, they are."

The silence drags for an eternity until the door opens. Caleb has a friendly smile and the palest blue eyes I've ever seen. They draw me in but also freak me out, like he could play the serial killer in a movie.

"We can talk in the dining room," Caleb says. "It's just past the great room."

Their great room is half the size of my grandma's house. A cream-colored cat stretches out on a sofa as long as a runway. Above it hangs a canvas print of Sedona's red rocks. We walk through a kitchen that smells of fresh paint and roars newly remodeled. While Nate is setting up the tripod and camera, Peyton appears wearing a long-sleeved dress the color of blueberries. She added makeup to conceal a spattering of freckles on her nose and tied her hair in a ponytail. The effect is older, more serious. Especially next to Caleb. Wearing black pants and a white button-down shirt, he could be serving never-ending breadsticks at Olive Garden.

Nate positions Caleb and Peyton next to each other with me directly across from them. He clips microphones onto their collars, flips on two lights, and announces he's rolling.

"Peyton, let's start with you."

She leans forward and nods.

"How would you describe your father?"

"He was a good provider—a great provider." She places a hand on the table, covers it with the other. "Me and my mom, we always knew we could count on him financially. It was important for my father to take care of his family, to be the breadwinner, I guess you could say. He started the company all by himself. For the first ten years, Paloma Flooring was my father doing all the work."

The cat has left the great room and jumps on a side table to observe our interview. Caleb does a "Get off" gesture, but the cat ignores him.

"Did you grow up in the business?"

Peyton smiles. "I grew up learning about the business. My dad would tell work stories over dinner, like when he hired people and took on new jobs, things like that."

"Was there a particular time when you realized you wanted to be part of the business?"

"Not really. I've always been good with numbers and when I decided to major in accounting my father hired me to work part-time while I was in school."

"That must have been a valuable experience."

"Definitely. I learned about finances and the importance of reputation. Our family name is recognized for quality work at fair prices. When I graduated, he offered me the CFO position. Couldn't turn that down."

"That would've been around the time Simona left the company?"

Her spine grows three inches. "Did you talk to her?"

"Briefly. It wasn't an interview like this."

Peyton lifts her chin and slides her hands under the table. "I don't know what Simona told you, but my father treated her like gold even though she was not a loyal employee."

Caleb rests a hand on Peyton's shoulder. "It's okay, you don't have to talk about her."

I ask Caleb how he got involved with Paloma Flooring.

He smiles. "I got involved with Peyton first."

"Did you go to ASU, too?"

"Yeah." His eyes flick to Peyton. "But I'm a few credits short."

Peyton clears her throat and says, "Twenty-four short."

"I'm going to finish."

Peyton makes a noise that's part humph and part grunt, the same sound my grandma made whenever she heard a candidate claim, "It's time to end politics as usual."

"Caleb, when did you start working for the company?"

"Right after we married. Kris hired me as a project manager. I make sure we have enough workers and materials for every job and clearly communicate before, during, and after with the homeowner or business owner."

"That's a lot of moving parts. Must be stressful."

He soaks in the acknowledgement. "It can be."

"Sounds like loads of stuff to manage. Is that where your friend at city hall comes in?"

He squints his eyes, trying to play dumb.

"Your friend, Ved. Doesn't he steer you through the bureaucratic red tape?"

"I don't know what you mean."

"Ved Patel, your best man." I point to the side table where the cat is resting next to wedding photos. "Is he in one of those?"

Peyton raises a hand, signaling Caleb to be quiet. "Excuse me, what is this about?"

"I'm just trying to understand the business."

"I thought we were talking about my father." She unclips the mic and drops it onto the table. "We need to finish planning his memorial service so you'll have to excuse us."

She pushes the chair back and stalks out of the room. Out of the corner of my eye, Nate is shaking his head.

"Caleb, I've seen photos of you and Ved. If I had a friend who could help me through a complicated process, I might ask for advice. Is that what you did?"

"Caleb!" Peyton's voice is muffled but the message is clear.

He walks us to the door without saying another word.

CHAPTER

24

As Nate pulls the truck away from Peyton and Caleb's house, I say, "See? There is something going on."

"What are you talking about?"

I pretend to knock. "Hello? Were we not in the same interview? Obviously, their friend provides inside information to Peyton's father that allows him to cash in on city contracts."

"Caleb didn't even admit he has a friend that works for the city."

"Only because Peyton cut him off. I've seen their wedding photos. They don't lie."

Nate switches lanes and turns into a convenience store.

"You thirsty?" I ask.

"No." He shifts the gear to park and looks at me. "You need to check yourself. Peyton just lost her father. She's dealing with a lot of emotions and probably couldn't care less about any contracts right now."

"But—"

"Don't 'but' me, Jolene. You know, sometimes when you play reporter you forget what it's like to be a human being."

My temper flares. "I'm not 'playing' reporter. I am a reporter."

"That doesn't mean you should ignore people's feelings."

"I'm not." I glare at him. "Not all of us are perfect like you, Nate."

"This is not about me. It's about letting your quest for a story overtake compassion and common sense."

He doesn't understand because he never met Carlos. Nate only knows him as the victim of a car crash, not the man who adopted children out of foster care. Not the man with a lifelong dream of running his own business. Not the man who was killed because he suspected Peyton's father wasn't playing fair. Before I can try to explain, our phones ping.

1070? ETA?

"I'll respond so you can start driving back."

Nate says nothing and shifts the truck into reverse.

On way. ETA is 20.
Can Nate cover bee attack?

I never imagined a bee attack would save me from Nate's venom. When I started here, I didn't understand why a swarm of bees warranted coverage. David, of all people, enlightened me. And since the story started in Brazil, it meets his definition of sexy. In the 1950s, Brazil wanted to boost honey production and imported bees from Tanzania. A beekeeper in São Paulo accidentally released twenty-six queen bees and their swarms. They made their way to the southern United States and mated with European bees. Their offspring, called Africanized bees or killer bees, are more aggressive than domestic bees because their natural environment has more predators. They nest in places you wouldn't expect, like barbecue grills, overturned flowerpots, even cracks in buildings. Pets and people who've accidentally disturbed hives have died after being stung hundreds of times.

Alex texts again.

Or u can both go.

Even if my story was a total bust, I would find a way to not keep working with Nate. He drops me off at the station without saying goodbye. Disheartened, I don't even push back on the introduction Sexy wrote for my story about Peyton's father being electrocuted. But I go to battle against his idea for a live shot. Sexy wants me on the patio with a bucket of water, a hose, and an extension cord to share tips on how to avoid electrocution. Tacky with a capital "T."

I cringe as Rachel, the anchor, reads the introduction to my story.

"It'll be a blue Christmas for a Phoenix neighborhood that's missing Santa's helper this year. Eyewitness News reporter Jolene Garcia has more on the community's devastating loss."

To get out of doing the live shot, I pitched something Sexy adores: reading live comments from our Facebook page where my story posted an hour earlier. Our other main anchor, Rick, takes the lead.

"Jolene joins me now at our social media center where our friends have been sharing their thoughts."

The camera switches from a shot of Rick and me to the monitor as Rick reads, "Here's a post from Bri in Scottsdale. She says, 'How sad. He seemed like a great person.' Sirai writes, 'I remember visiting Rudolph Lane. It was beautiful!' and Nick in Surprise writes, 'RIP Mr. Kringle.'"

We're back on a two-shot and Rick says, "Sure sounds like Kris Kruger, the neighborhood Santa, will be missed."

That's my cue to show the Facebook page the family created

to share memories. In lieu of flowers, they're asking for donations to support a holiday toy drive.

Rich wraps it up. "What a beautiful way to show appreciation for a man who gave so much to his community. Thank you, Jolene."

After getting the all-clear from the director, I retreat to my desk where Pamela, the intern, looks camera ready wearing fresh makeup.

"I didn't think you were working today," I say.

"I'm not. I'm meeting Dan for dinner."

"The sports intern?"

"Yeah," she says. "We're leaving right after the newscast."

"Where are you going?"

"I don't know. Somewhere close because he's helping with the ten o'clock show. Your story was amazing. Are you, like, doing anything more on the Santa guy?"

"Not unless the Grinch confesses to killing him."

"Huh?"

"There's a guy who's pretty jolly over Santa's death. Some neighbors call him the Grinch."

"That doesn't sound nice."

"Doesn't sound like Santa was nice to him. The Grinch says he was a bully and got what he deserved." I log on to my computer. "Are you working tomorrow?"

"Yeah, do you need help with something?"

"Don't hate me, but I haven't been collecting enough cupcakes and we have to get the samples to the lab ASAP. Can you pick up more?"

"No worries. Besides, my mom and dad are excited about seeing me on TV." She blushes. "I mean my undercover video. I told them you might use it."

"Of course we will. Without your video, we'd be in trouble."

More like I would be in trouble.

"Pamela, you'll be credited on the web story and we can include a shot of you delivering the cupcakes to the lab."

"My parents would love that."

"Let's plan on that tomorrow. But right now, I need to write a version about the dead Santa for ten o'clock."

On the nights I work late, I often recall the promise I made to my grandma because of a woman neither of us met.

"Remember Jodi," my grandma often said.

I can't remember not knowing about Jodi Huisentruit. After oversleeping for her morning news anchor shift in Mason City, Iowa, and telling a co-worker she was on the way, Jodi never made it to her TV station. My grandma said Jodi was the lead story on newscasts throughout the Midwest for weeks. In the parking lot of her apartment complex, next to her red Mazda Miata, police found a bent car key, a hair dryer, and a single high-heel shoe. Apparently, neighbors heard screams around the time Jodi would have been leaving, but no one saw anything and nobody called police. She was never found. In 2001, Jodi's family had her legally declared dead.

Keeping my promise to my grandma means living in a smaller, older complex where I can park next to my apartment and count on neighbors to call 911. Since nearly being run over at city hall, I've been on alert for silver sedans. Last night, on my way home, I thought I was being followed and drove to a fire station. The car kept going. Tonight, I triple-check the locks on my doors and windows and turn on lights in every room. Sleep will not come. I scroll through social media and flip through dozens of channels before Jessica Fletcher sucks me into a *Murder, She Wrote* marathon. I doze off sometime between Jessica living and writing in Cabot Cove and fleeing a killer in New York City.

CHAPTER
25

I wake up feeling the same way I fell asleep: like a freshly shaken snow globe. So many thoughts swirling in my head and they all connect to city contracts. Sexy is wrong if he thinks the story died with Kris Kruger's electrocution. Uncovering the truth won't bring back Carlos, but his family deserves to know who caused his deadly car crash.

I tap Emmy's wings. "You're proof that perseverance pays off."

Winning my next Emmy won't be as dangerous. Compared to facing off against a killer, investigating a cheating businessman and a politician on the take is low-risk. The anonymous text warning me to stop was so general it could've applied to any story—even a baker worried about being caught selling cupcakes with gluten. Granted, the threatening call from Darth Vader was disturbing, but I haven't heard from him again. The more I think about it, maybe the Camry driver outside city hall was distracted like me. I shouldn't have been looking at my phone while crossing the street. Not paying attention is dangerous for pedestrians and drivers.

I say goodbye to Emmy and Oscar, toss my bag in the back

of my car, and slide in the driver's seat. With a groan, I haul my sleep-deprived body out to snatch an envelope under a windshield wiper. Usually, people place postcards on our doors. Leaving a business solicitation on my car is going too far. I make a mental note to call the apartment complex manager and suggest more NO TRESPASSING signs. I rip open the envelope. Someone picked the wrong person for their sales pitch. Now I have to take time out of my day to file a complaint. I scan the paper for a phone number or email address and my hands begin to tremble.

> This is your last chance. If you do not stop investigating the deaths of Rich Gains and Carlos Rios, you will regret it. The world will find out you are a liar. Your career will be over. No one will ever believe you are telling the truth after they learn you have lied your entire life about who you are. Ignore this warning at your peril.

I open a window, hoping the air will ease the nausea clawing at my stomach. As a reporter, the only thing I can control is my reputation. Even people who claim journalists can't be trusted have called my reporting fair. My family's background is no one's business. If people find out I've been lying about my parents, they'll view my reporting in a different light. And they shouldn't. I'm not an elected official making campaign promises. I'm not a celebrity posting reels with their mom or kids. I'm a reporter. I tell other people's stories, not my own.

Ignore this warning at your peril.

I've spent my life running away from who I was to who I want to be. I've never backed down from a story and don't want to start. But I've never been this close to being exposed. I crumple the note, throw it on the floorboard, and start my car.

I hit the drive-through at Copper Star Coffee and order a doppio. I don't like strong coffee, but I don't deserve to enjoy a drink.

A perky voice says, "Can I get you anything else? Our bagels are delicious. Made right here in our kitchen."

She's disappointed when I decline. I swallow the espresso like a shot of NyQuil. The extra caffeine reduces the pounding in my head a millimeter. I should go straight to the station and work on the gluten investigation. Pamela is getting the last cupcakes today, we'll drop them off at the lab, my managers will be happy, and I can move on to another story. But Carlos's grandmother should know the man who cheated him out of business has died. I'll express my condolences and then it's case closed. I'll focus on cupcakes, just like Darth Vader wants.

I regret my choice as soon as I pull into Home Sweet Home Mobile Home Park. It's okay though, I don't have to stop. I'll just drive past the home Carlos grew up in and go to the station. Nana is sitting on the bench, next to her flower garden. She'll never know I was here. And then, she turns and looks straight at me. I hit the brakes.

"Good morning, Mrs. Rios."

"Buenos dias, Jolene." She pats the bench. "Come."

"I'm sorry for your loss." I sit next to her. "I didn't know Carlos well, but I could tell he was a special person."

"Muy especial." She sighs and pats my hand. "Do you have news for me?"

"I'm afraid the news is not helpful. There was an accident and Kris Kruger died while hanging Christmas lights at his home."

She studies my face before responding. "That is unfortunate but you are still investigating, correct?"

I cross my legs as my insides squirm. Her eyes convey expectation and faith. I avoid answering her question and ask whether she's received the autopsy report. Her nod is almost imperceptible.

"Did it show Carlos experienced a medical situation?"

"No." Her head shakes defiantly. "They say they are checking for drugs. Mijo never used drugs. He saw what happened to others who did. Mijo was an honest man who worked hard and loved his family."

We sit without speaking. Her hand brushes a pink snapdragon. "I'm grateful my husband is not here. It would break his heart to know the police think Carlos used drugs."

"Please don't think that. Requesting a toxicology report is not unusual. It doesn't mean anyone thinks badly of Carlos."

She tightens her mouth. "They need to check his truck."

"Did Carlos tell you there was a problem with it?"

"No. He always took care of it. Something happened to it. There is no other explanation." Her eyes aren't desperate. They're determined.

My mind flashes to Kris and his box of expensive tools. Maybe my instinct was right and he cut Carlos's brake lines. If so, there's no way to prove it now that Kris is dead. I doubt he left a signed confession. But I can't tell her that. She's counting on me. Carlos is, too.

"I promise I'll let you know what I find."

She squeezes my hand but it feels like my heart. "Muchas gracias." Her eyes well up. "I need to know what happened."

"I understand. I'm sorry, but I have to get to work."

She surprises me with a hug. A real hug. Her heartbeat spreads through my chest.

"Thank you, mija," she whispers.

I breathe in a sweet, floral scent before pulling away. "I'll keep you posted. Goodbye, Mrs. Rios."

"Please, call me Nana. And take care of yourself, mija."

Nana methodically walks up the three steps without Carlos guiding her and kissing her cheek. She waves before closing the door. I can still do this. I'll keep investigating, but I'll be careful and quiet. That way Nana can get the answers she needs and my secret stays safe.

At the station, I toss the wadded note left on my windshield in the trash and enter through front door to avoid walking by my news director's office. I can't deal with him hounding me about counseling. Hussein is pushing a cart stacked with packages. His steps seem lighter.

"Hello, Jolene, I looked for you yesterday."

"How are things at your other job?"

"The attorney you talked to, she helped me out. The manager got fired and my friend and me are back at work."

Turns out Whitney emailed corporate using expensive-sounding words and legal phrases lawyers love. The HR people were surprised—or acted that way—when Whitney uncovered clear images of the manager opening the petty cash box three times a week and stuffing money in his pockets. Hussein's legal victory keeps a smile on my face as I approach my desk where Pamela has set up a bakery display.

"Twenty samples ready to be tested," she says with a smile.

"Thank you, Pamela. Your work saved this assignment. Give me a half hour to check something out. Then I'll shoot video of you dropping them off."

What I find online about cutting brakes isn't particularly helpful. But it is eye-opening and not as rare as you would hope. A guy in Seattle reportedly vandalized more than thirty vehicles over a three-day period. In Missouri, a sheriff's deputy claimed a brake line on his personal truck had been cut and, in Wisconsin, surveillance video showed someone supposedly cutting brake lines at an apartment complex. Some YouTubers demonstrate how to cut and replace brake lines for do-it-yourselfers, but it's complicated and, after watching, I would be more qualified to cook a fancy meal from scratch.

Sexy interrupts my search. "We need you to cover a city council meeting."

"Ha-ha."

"Does it look like I'm joking?"

It looks like you're about to throw a wrench in my plans.

"Rick got a tip about a controversial housing project the council will vote on," he says. "Supposed to be a bunch of angry neighbors protesting."

"Let me guess. The project is in Rick's neighborhood?"

"Doesn't matter if the project is in our anchor's neighborhood," Sexy says. "He's not covering it—you are. This is right up your alley. Holding the powerful accountable. You should be thrilled."

"Not complaining about the topic." I check the time. "But, first, I need to shoot video of Pamela dropping off cupcakes. We should have results within two business days."

"I'm sure Bob will be pleased."

Maybe he'll forget about ordering me to attend counseling.

As Pamela and I head to the lab she says, "My parents are going to love seeing me in the story."

"You better prepare them for the possibility there won't be one. All depends on the test results."

"Before my internship, I didn't realize how many stories never make it on-air," she says.

Wait till you learn how many legitimate stories get ignored in pursuit of those that meet a manager's definition of "sexy."

Back at the station, I ask Alex who my photog is for the council meeting.

He makes a clicking sound and points at me. "That would be you."

"Good thing I have gear loaded and ready to go."

"We'll send a photog to shoot your live shot. And before you ask, I don't know who yet."

Normally I'd request Nate, but after our spat, I'm not feeling it. Probably he's not, either.

Alex turns back to his computer, checking emails, and says, "I emailed you info Rick found on his neighborhood's Facebook page."

"Thanks." I slide into a chair next to him and pull up the city's website. "Let me check the meeting agenda."

Council members are scheduled to vote on a zoning request to build a four-story apartment complex in an upscale neighborhood. Practically the same scenario as the last zoning story we aired. And the one before that. Residents plan to protest outside council chambers before the meeting and speak during the public comment portion of the meeting.

"You know Pamela could go with you," Alex says. "Bet she'd appreciate working on a different story."

"She did help get cupcakes."

He cuts his eyes at me.

"Okay. She got all of them."

To ease my guilt, I treat Pamela to lunch at Sticklers across from city hall. She orders a tuna salad and I get the Traffic Jam, toasted on French. We snag an outdoor table and eat in silence until I remind myself to slow down. I wipe my mouth and fingers and ask how her internship is going.

"It's awesome," Pamela says. But her tone doesn't match the words.

"You know, not every experience is great, but it can still be a great experience."

Jolene the philosopher.

"If the internship's not your thing, that's okay. Better to find out now. Know what I mean?"

Pamela nods, pushing her fork around lettuce. "I want to like it, but it's harder than I expected. Like, shooting video, editing, writing, and doing live shots. How do you get it all done in a day?"

"You have deadlines and you have to meet them. But, you're right, it can be hard and frustrating and sometimes irresponsible when we don't devote resources to do a story justice."

I finish my sandwich while she nibbles on a chip. "I might

switch majors to social media management. It's like hardly anyone watches local news." Her cheeks flush. "Sorry. No offense."

"None taken."

"My roommate's going to work in TV to grow her followers
until she can be a full-time influencer. You can make a lot more
money that way."

There's no response that's going to end with either of us feeling good, so I check my phone and say, "We better go."

Chants of "Save our homes, save our homes!" get louder as we
pass the Calvin C. Goode building. We stop so I can get a wide
shot. "I'm going to keep rolling," I tell Pamela. "Not that I expect
anything outrageous but I want to be ready. And that way I avoid
double-punching."

"What's that?"

"You know how you press the button to record and press
again to stop? I've accidentally hit it twice and didn't realize it
until I got back to the station."

"And you didn't have any video?"

"Only boring shots, none of the action."

The protestors are wearing red shirts that read SAVE OUR
NEIGHBORHOODS. A guy with aviator sunglasses clutches a bullhorn and leads chants. When he spots my camera, he lets out a
cheer and a line of people holding homemade signs whips in my
direction. Someone comes out of council chambers and talks to
Sunglasses Guy. After a few head shakes, the person goes back
inside and Mr. Sunglasses speaks into the bullhorn.

"The overzealous police won't let us take our signs inside.
Apparently, the people elected by us do not believe in freedom
of speech. But they cannot silence us! We will each have two
minutes to address the council. Let's make every second count!"

His voice sounds familiar but it's not until he takes off his
sunglasses that I recognize him. It's Fred Nimby, who called the
lobbyist, Rich Gains, an enemy of residents, posted his contact

information on social sites, and encouraged people to "give him a piece of their mind." Nimby asks if I want to interview him.

"Maybe later. For now, I need to shoot video, post to social, and get inside."

Before the controversial project in question comes up, we witness people being sworn in to serve on a youth workforce committee and listen to neighbors ask the council to reject a new liquor license application in their neighborhood.

"We are inundated with liquor stores and churches," a woman says. "We don't need more of either. We need retailers and restaurants so we don't have to drive miles to shop and eat."

Someone else says, "We welcome quality businesses that provide products and services that benefit the neighborhood by creating jobs and generating tax revenue."

"That's exactly what this business will do," says the attorney representing the liquor license applicant. "The store will have a positive impact by adding jobs and tax revenue."

Mayor Ace Logan says he understands why the neighborhood may not want another establishment selling liquor and encourages them to let the state liquor department know.

"The city is only able to make recommendations for or against a liquor license application. The state board makes the final decision," he says. "Generally speaking, unless there are concerns about an applicant's financial or criminal background, the state will allow liquor sales."

When the apartment complex proposal comes up, the developer's attorney gets to speak first. She touts open floor plans and smart home devices. "The units will have the latest and greatest technology. In fact, I would venture to guess these apartments will be more advanced than any of your homes or mine."

She wraps up by exaggerating the economic impact, suggesting a tsunami of employment and tax revenue from temporary construction jobs.

When it's their turn, residents are respectful, yet insistent that hundreds of apartments will harm their quality of life. One speaker appeals to the council's fiscal conservatives.

"It appears you may be our only hope. Please explain to your colleagues how irresponsible it is to approve a project that gives tax breaks to a private company that brought in more than twenty million dollars in revenue last year. I know the city believes we need more housing stock, but if Phoenix is such an attractive city, we should not have to pay developers to build. I respectfully request that if you are going to approve this proposal, you remove the tax breaks."

The next speaker is Fred Nimby.

"For a long time, I thought the city council represented residents, but I finally understand the truth. You are all beholden to developers. You should be ashamed of yourselves. Especially you, Mayor Ace."

"I'm going to stop you right there," Mayor Ace says. "Public comment is meant to address the agenda item, not to disparage individuals. I certainly empathize with you, but I need you to refrain from disrespecting people."

"Why? You disrespect us every time you side with out-of-state millionaires who don't care about our neighborhoods. Why don't you listen to us? Some of you aren't even listening now. Put your phones down and answer my question: Why are developers more important than the people who live here and elect you? Who will answer that? I'll wait."

Ten seconds pass on the digital timer before he speaks again.

"Since no one wants to answer, I guess I have to. Your behavior is despicable. How can you look at yourselves knowing that you are destroying neighborhoods?"

"Mr. Nimby, your time is running out," Mayor Logan says. "Please make your point without accusations."

"Okay, I'll make my point."

Fred Nimby jams a hand inside his jacket and whips out something small and dark. A police officer rushes toward Nimby as he pulls the trigger. Someone screams. Half the council ducks, the others drop to the floor. A shower of confetti hit staff who have nowhere to hide.

"Congratulations on successfully screwing taxpayers!"

One cop grabs the glitter gun, another pulls out handcuffs, and two more draw their weapons.

"Officers, please remove this man from chambers," the mayor says. "We will take a break and reconvene in five minutes."

CHAPTER
26

I grab my camera intending to interview Fred Nimby but he's surrounded by cops and I can't get close.

"Pamela, record video on your phone."

Trotting behind me, she says, "What should I get?"

"Whatever you can."

Outside council chambers, I can hear Fred but not see him. In addition to a half-dozen cops, residents have gathered around him. I climb on top of a concrete bench and he spots me.

"Did you get all that?" His face is as red as his shirt. "Can you believe the way they treat residents? We pay taxes and they are supposed to represent us. If they aren't going to listen to us, why keep up this charade?"

An officer speaks to Fred, but I can't make out his words. He's writing something. Probably citing Fred for disorderly conduct. I need to get closer, but if Fred's arrested while I'm moving, I'll miss the handcuffs going on. Jessmy Doehm, an Axios Phoenix reporter, is running our way. She must have caught the meeting's livestream.

The chambers' door bursts open and someone shouts, "We lost. Only Mayor Ace voted for us."

Boos explode like dynamite. Cops are watching and listening but no one's holding cuffs. A supervisor may have advised them to defuse the situation and not arrest Fred Nimby.

Powered by the crowd, Fred says, "One of these days, they're going to push a neighborhood too far."

"What do you mean by that?" The camera on my shoulder is as heavy as a dead body.

He turns to me and says, "Residents have had enough of being ignored and talked down to. We are going to organize and oust them. Every single one of them."

The Axios reporter pushes through the group to ask questions and Pamela follows, allowing me to set my camera down and rub my shoulder. After a few minutes, Pamela emerges and asks if I need help.

"Can you go inside, find the council PIO, and ask how they voted on item seventy?"

"That guy already said the mayor was the only one who sided with them."

"But we weren't in there and we need to confirm it ourselves."

"Oh yeah. I'll be right back."

I move to the garden area, sit, and rewind the video. The knot in my stomach unwinds. It's all there. The double-punch blunder will be with me forever. A woman approaches and asks what station I'm with. To my relief, she's not disappointed and doesn't ask about JJ.

"I want you to know that most of us are not like Fred Nimby." She's wearing the same cotton shirt as her neighbors, but it comes across as higher quality. Maybe it's her gold necklace and earrings.

"Of course, we're upset," she says. "But we don't condone violence. His behavior is appalling to most of us. It is a shame because we have to be united if we're going to make a difference."

"Has Fred ever been escorted out of a meeting before? Or done anything—verbally or physically—that's concerned you?"

"I haven't witnessed anything as bad as today. But my next-door neighbor has. She was so taken aback by his anger that she doesn't attend our meetings anymore. Maybe it's time to throw in the towel. Or move." She sighs. "Anyway, I just wanted to make sure you know we're not all Fred Nimbys."

Pamela returns with confirmation and a message from the PIO. "He said the only person willing to do an interview after the meeting is the mayor."

Mr. Unavoidable for Comment living up to his nickname.

"We don't need him," I say. "We have the mayor's sound from the meeting. If Fred Nimby had been arrested, then I would want the mayor's take on it. Were you able to get video when he was kicked out?"

Her face lights up. "Yes, I got about five seconds where you can see police directing him where to stand outside and then a bunch of people got in the shot. I'll send it now."

She checks her phone and makes a face.

"Is something wrong?"

"No," she says. "I have a class at four o'clock."

"Go. That's more important."

"But don't you need help?"

"The station is sending a photog. I'm good."

And I am—until Woman Hater shows up for the live shot.

"This blows," he says. "I was supposed to be off at five o'clock. Now I'm missing happy hour."

Since his wife left him, William has missed many happy hours and experienced endless crabby hours.

"As soon as our live shot is over, we need to break down pronto," he says. "I texted my date I'd be there by six."

A date? Woman Hater has spent months bashing pretty

much all women. I'm torn between wanting to be happy for him and wanting to warn his date.

Before I can finish saying, "Reporting live from Phoenix," he flips off the light. Woman Hater is moving faster than a dust devil. I carry the tripod to the truck and stop to read a text from David.

JJ has exclusive on Santa.

Gee, David, thanks for noticing my exclusive story about a guy who shot a glitter gun in a council meeting. I pull up the website for JJ's station and a promo automatically plays: *Did a Grinch silence a neighborhood Santa? In a Channel 2 News exclusive, JJ investigates what happened to Kris Kringle.*

I can't go there yet. First, I need to wallow in private.

I smell my grandma before I see my neighbor. The floral scent drifts into my car window. Jean Naté was the first birthday present I bought my grandma with babysitting money. She reacted the way it smelled: happy. It made me so happy I got it every year—for five more years—until she died. Grandma only wore Jean Naté during the summer, swore it made her feel cooler and cleaner. The rest of the year she smelled like Dove soap.

"Hello there!" Norma waves Tuffy's paw.

"Hi." I nod at her bored friend. "Hey, Tuffy."

"Notice anything different?"

"New perfume?"

"Oh, can you smell it?" She sniffs a wrist. "It was a free sample. It's called Jean Mae."

"You sure it's not Jean Naté?"

"Maybe. But it doesn't matter because I'm sticking with White Diamonds, Elizabeth Taylor's perfume. Do you know who she is?"

No, Norma, and I don't have time. I need to find out what JJ Jackson knows that I don't.

"Elizabeth Taylor was Hollywood royalty. Such a beautiful, talented actress. Liz—that's what we called her—was only twelve years old when she starred in *National Velvet*. She fell off a horse during filming and broke her back. The poor girl! And when she played Cleopatra, oh, it became quite the scandal. She was married at the time and so was Richard Burton—he played her love interest in the film and, it turned out, in real life. In those days, the media—"

"Norma, excuse me, I have things to do." I grab my bag out of the back seat and slam the door.

"Of course, dear. But before you go, try again. Notice anything else different?"

I perform a quick body scan. Standard track suit and sneakers. Norma's hair color hasn't changed since the station tour. I'm stumped.

"Did you get new glasses?"

"No, not me. It's Tuffy."

His brown fur is no different and his signature accessory, a bow, matches Norma's yellow hair.

"You got me."

She lifts a front paw. "Aren't they adorable?"

Tuffy's nails match the aqua hue on Norma's nails.

"I couldn't decide between blue or green. You know blue is so peaceful. But I wanted a little excitement for our TV shoot and I said to myself, 'Norma, you know green signifies growth and money.' So maybe this color will help me stay calm when Hollywood comes calling offering me big bucks!" She cackles and kisses Tuffy's head. "Anyway, we both took the plunge. Hopefully, when the station sees how coordinated we are, they'll want us both on TV. Wouldn't you just love that, Tuffy?" His ears twitch.

"What station?"

"Your station, dear. David, that darling young man, wants me to be on the air. What a sweetheart he is."

Only because you're helping him shine. He'll kick you to the curb when it suits him. Hiking my bag on my shoulder, I glance at the door. Take the hint, Norma.

"I got a call from a nice young lady named Charlotte. She said it would be for uh, what do you call that thing? She didn't say a commercial but it's like that."

"A promotion or promo for short."

Her fingers snap. "That's it! Maybe you can help me get ready for my close-up?"

"Maybe you should ask JJ since you like her station so much."

I know it's not Norma's fault JJ is beating me, but I need to be alone. I throw my bag on the kitchen floor and curse when pens, notepads, and makeup tumble out. Kicking off my shoes leaves scuff marks on the white wall. I jerk open the fridge and snatch a chocolate bar, then fling open the pantry and grab a jar of Jif. Sitting at the table, I stab the chocolate in the peanut butter and stick it in my mouth. Again and again. Five minutes later, I screw the lid back on and toss the wrapper away. I pull a half gallon of milk from the fridge and raise it to my lips, ignoring my grandmother's words.

"Jolene, we do not drink out of the carton."

It was one of her earliest lessons. Back then, I didn't know better. Tonight, I don't care. Or maybe there's a deeper meaning, something I would learn through the employee assistance program. Except I have zero intention of talking to a counselor. I wipe my mouth with the back of my hand and put the milk back on the shelf.

"I suppose you're passing judgment, too?"

Oscar ignores me. After feeding him, I schlep over to my bag, squat to pick everything up, and fall on my butt. I shove everything back in, slouch against the wall, and try to suck in a stomach full of junk. Doesn't work. I push myself up and waddle into the living room.

The remote control isn't on the glass coffee table or the couch. The only other furniture is a chair I hardly use. Still, I check under the cushion. Empty. I could hit the power button on the actual TV, but without the remote I can't pull up the newscasts I record every day. For some reason—self-punishment, I suppose—I want to watch JJ's story on a big screen. What started as needles pricking my neck when I read Sexy's text has become knives stabbing my shoulders. I pick up a couch cushion and slam it against a wall. That doesn't help, so I pound my fist into another cushion. Doesn't improve my emotional health, but it does reveal the remote hiding underneath. After flipping on JJ's station, the knives slash their way from my shoulders to my stomach.

The anchor introduces JJ's story about the suspicious death of the "Neighborhood St. Nick." That's the title above a photo of Kris wearing a Santa hat.

"JJ, I understand he loved Christmas so much that he earned the nickname Kris Kringle."

"That's right." JJ turns to the camera. "But his passion for the holiday and the joy he brought to his neighborhood was not embraced by everyone. And some fear Kris Kringle's love for Christmas couldn't protect him from the Grinch."

JJ uses a lot of "Sources say this" and "Sources say that." Enough to keep her station from getting sued and from reporting anything substantial. But most viewers won't notice. Instead, they'll get the impression there's a sinister person who hated Christmas and killed Kris Kruger because they couldn't stand his holiday cheer. Without showing the person's face, JJ interviews someone—"We'll call Joe"—who describes a neighbor that "never once said Merry Christmas" and "flat-out refused to participate in our light display." Another neighbor, "We'll call Sandy," appears on camera and says last year someone left an anonymous note on Kris's door demanding he scale back the display.

Back on camera, JJ ties a bow on her story. "On the record, police will only say they're investigating the death by electrocution, but neighbors I talked with are convinced it was no accident. They believe justice will only be served when cops arrest the Grinch who silenced Santa's helper."

In the shower, I try to scrub off the failure and nearly scald my skin. I dress in my softest sweatpants and shirt and settle in front of the TV. But not even Pat and Vanna can stop me from dwelling on JJ's story. I should have taken a closer look at Kris's neighbors. With JJ digging into Kris's death, it's just a matter of time before she discovers his connection to Carlos. I can't let her beat me. More importantly, I can't let Carlos's killer get away. Even if it turns out to be a deceased Santa's helper, people need to know.

CHAPTER

27

The next day begins on a thankful note. My personal life hasn't been publicly revealed and I've received no new threats. I need to find an expert to show me how someone would cut brake lines. Then, I can narrow down when Kris Kruger had the opportunity to tamper with Carlos's truck. Carlos probably parked outside his house overnight. I'll ask his son and, if he did, I'll check doorbell and security videos from surrounding homes. I should also get addresses for projects Carlos recently visited. Surveillance cameras at construction sites could've captured Kris following him. Then, when I have video proof, I'll offer it to Jim Miranda and let his police unit take the credit. That should make up for me interfering with the bribery investigation into Councilwoman Zoey Patterson.

"Sounds like a plan, doesn't it, Oscar?" He waves a fin.

I could try the service department at a car dealership, but as soon as I identify myself as a reporter, my call will be routed to corporate and end with nothing worthwhile. I'll have a better chance with a small repair shop or individual mechanic. Cold-calling isn't the most efficient option and I don't personally know any. Maybe Norma does.

Good morning. Do you have a good mechanic?

I don't send the text. I was rude to Norma last night and need to apologize, which will lead to a bunch of questions about why I need a mechanic.

"Oscar, do you have any ideas?" His tail waggles as he dives to the gravel.

I open the fridge with low expectations and it's worse than I imagined. Two eggs, one mushy apple, and cheddar cheese topped with white fuzz. I grab a handful of Lucky Charms and eat the frosted oats first. By the time I pop marshmallow hearts and stars in my mouth, a solution tickles my brain. But it disappears with the blue moon and rainbows. My phone slides on the counter and I snag it like the answer is there.

Sorry. My roommate told JJ about Grinch.

And how, Pamela, did your roommate find out? I could reply with a quick "It's okay" or "Don't worry about it" but that won't help her going forward.

Lesson learned. Be careful about sharing info. You don't want to help someone beat you on your story.

While getting dressed, a plan pops into my mind. I'll use my connection with Mayor Ace Logan to visit his brother. Reggie Logan has three auto repair shops: the original location near the former Metrocenter mall in Phoenix, another in south Scottsdale, and a new place in Glendale. On the staff page of the company's website, Reggie Logan is wearing a red tie, white shirt, and blue blazer. He looks like a kid who's more comfortable in jeans forced to dress up for a school photo.

"What's your take, Oscar? Would an owner remain loyal to his first shop or move to newer digs?"

I choose sentimentalism and text Alex that I'll be in late.

"Bye, Emmy. Don't get too comfy on that table all by your-self."

On the way to Reggie's repair shop, my high crashes. A lo-cal radio host is talking to JJ about her "exclusive blockbuster story."

"Tell us, JJ, who is this Grinch all the neighbors are talking about? And do you think he killed Santa?"

"As you know, Hank, police are investigating this tragic death and my sources tell me it looks suspicious."

Who are your sources? Producers angling for higher rat-ings?

"Sounds like cops are eyeing the Grinch," the host says.

"It wouldn't be right for me to identify someone who is not publicly considered a suspect—yet."

"Frankly, I find it incomprehensible that someone's devotion to Christmas could lead to murder. We'll keep Kris Kruger's family in our thoughts and prayers. And you keep us posted."

"You can count on me."

"That's JJ Jackson, Channel 2's superstar reporter. Thanks again for joining us."

"Anytime, Hank. Always a pleasure."

If I'd eaten anything more than a handful of dry cereal, it would've erupted like a volcano. I tell myself to channel the anger into justice for Carlos.

Logan's Auto Repair is located at an intersection with businesses that range from shiny to shabby. Logan's is closer to shabby. The shop has no available parking, so I pull into a fast-food lot next door. The combination of greasy fries and burnt oil comes with a side of new tire smell. Inside the shop, two men behind a counter are staring at computers, one has a phone to his ear. The man without the phone asks how he can help me.

"Hi, I'd like to talk to Reggie. Is he in?"

He eyes the man on the phone, his face half-hidden by the computer screen.

"Oh, is that Reggie?"

"Sure is."

"I know his brother, the mayor, but haven't met him yet. He looks different without a jacket and tie."

"Huh?"

"Never mind. I'll wait until he's off the phone."

I move to the wall nearest Reggie so I can listen while faking interest in a membership plaque from the Automotive Service Association, a framed pledge to be a "Green Garage," and a certificate boasting a blue seal of excellence. I'm in his face before the phone touches the counter.

"Hi, Reggie, my name is Jolene Garcia. I talked with your brother a couple days ago and wonder if you have a minute to talk."

"Sure, whatcha need?"

"It's kind of confidential. Is there someplace we can talk privately?"

He hops off a stool, slides open a barn door, and invites me to his office. Reggie is shorter than his brother with a stocky build and a gait that says, "Let's get to work." His office is the size of a single-car garage. Metal file cabinets are crammed against walls, grimy parts and cardboard boxes litter the floor. Reggie removes a stack of folders from a chair and invites me to sit on a stained cushion. He rummages around for a place to put the folders, comes up empty, and adds them to a pile on his desk. When he sits, the chair squeaks and tips back.

"What can I help you with?"

"I have sort of an unusual request. I'm with Channel 4 Eyewitness News and—"

"What?" His grease-stained hands clutch the desk. "You didn't say you were a reporter."

"I just did."

He points to the door. "You should have told me out there."

"I'm sorry, I wasn't trying to hide it. I just wanted to talk to you away from everyone else so I could explain, you know?"

"No, I don't know." Reggie's chair lets out a groan as his knee bounces. "What do you want from me?"

"Your expertise. Like I said, this may sound strange but I'm trying to understand if you can really cut someone's brakes on their car."

"Alright, what's going on?" He jabs a finger at my bag. "You got a hidden camera in there?"

"What? No. I'm working on a story and thought you could help."

"I know how you guys operate." A sheen of perspiration coats his forehead. "You're not going to trick me."

"I don't know how I could trick you because I don't understand how brake lines work."

"Trying to ambush me, huh?"

"Please, I'm just trying to understand whether you can walk up to a car and cut the brake lines without being noticed. What's involved and how long would it take?"

Reggie's shoulders collapse and he pinches a thumb and finger between eyebrows. "So, this is how it ends?"

I don't know what he's talking about, but I know enough to keep my mouth shut.

Reggie's palms push against his eyes and he whimpers. I wish I'd packed the undercover gear.

"It was just supposed to scare him."

Struggling to keep my voice calm, I say, "What happened?"

He picks at tape covering a tear in the armrest. Stuffing escapes. "I don't know." His thumb pounds the stuffing, but it pushes back.

"Something went wrong?"

Reggie scrubs a hand over his beard. "He wasn't supposed to die."

I can't believe it. Mayor Ace Logan had his brother cut Carlos's brakes. The mayor must've realized Carlos's complaint about Kris Kruger unfairly getting city contracts would lead to an investigation. The mayor could kiss the kickbacks goodbye. Not to mention his TV show. No Carlos, no worries.

"Wasn't supposed to die." Reggie rocks in the chair. I barely hear him over the squeaking. "Wasn't supposed to die."

I need his audio. Arizona is a one-party consent state, so I can record a conversation as long as I'm a party to it. Legally, I'm covered. But ethically? That's a conversation for later. Better to have and not use than regret not getting.

He stops rocking. "You gotta understand. I was behind on my mortgage and business loans . . . I mean really behind. It was a simple job. No one was supposed to die."

When he looks down, I lean to the side, dipping my hand into my bag.

"You have no idea how bad things were."

My fingers hunt for my phone.

"I needed cash fast."

And I need my damn phone.

"How much did you get?" I ask.

He shakes his head.

No way can I let him retreat.

"You know, Reggie, most people can understand what it's like to be in a tough situation. Faced with losing your livelihood, it's understandable you might consider something less than ideal, something a little questionable."

Tears swim in his eyes. "We all make mistakes."

"Yes, we do."

His back straightens at the affirmation. "I have a family to take care of."

Just like Carlos had a family.

"If I lost my business, we'd lose everything. Our cars, our house, I mean where would we live? I have a kid in college, another on the way. I had to do something."

And I have to find a way to get this on video.

"Reggie, I know someone at the police department. He's pretty high up and an honorable guy. How about I call him and explain what happened? That it was an accident."

"I don't know." He bites a lip. "Will he understand?"

He'll understand you need to be arrested.

"He can help," I say. "Let me call him, okay?"

Reggie's shrug signals he's given up. His eyes travel to a photo on his desk. He rubs a finger over the glass, leaving a smudge. I scoot my chair toward the door and pray Jim will answer.

He doesn't. I text:

911! Call me. 911!

I try to slow my breathing to counter the drum solo in my chest. As Reggie whispers an apology to his family, I hit redial.

"Jolene, I told you I'm done with you."

"Hello, Jim." My voice sounds like I'm underwater. "I need you to talk with an auto repair shop owner about a recent fatal car crash."

"What are you talking about? Where are you?"

"Logan's Auto Repair. It's at 698 Candlewood Lane."

"Are you in danger?"

"Possibly."

He repeats the address and covers the mouthpiece. Jim is sending help. I hope.

"Is someone with you?" he says.

"Yes, the owner, Reggie Logan, would like to speak with you."

"Is this about the Carlos Rios case?"

"Yes."

"Your timing stinks. Detectives are about to arrest someone for the murder of Kris Kruger."

"What?" The shock in my voice shakes Reggie out of his reverie. I offer what I hope is a reassuring smile. "Who?"

"His neighbor, Peter Gallagher."

My mind is blown. Peter lives next door to Kris. He helps with Christmas decorations. Kris called him his chief elf.

"That's nice," I say. "We'll see you soon, then?"

"Listen, get out of there if you can. I have two cars on the way."

"Thank you."

Reggie's staring at the door. He's doing the math, calculating his options. I will not let him bolt.

"My friend Jim is on the way. He's a great guy, you'll like him."

"I should call my wife."

No way, Reggie. I'm already missing one arrest. I'm not going to miss yours. I point to the photo in his hand.

"Is that your family?"

"Yeah." His eyes lock on it. "My wife, Beverly, and our daughters, Tarah and Nicole."

"They're lovely," I say even though I can't see the photo. "Tell me about your business, Reggie. Did you have the shop before you got married?"

He places the photo back on his desk and I press an app to record Reggie describing how his father started the business and ran it until the day he died.

"Ace didn't want anything to do with it," Reggie says. "He doesn't understand mechanics, not even a simple oil change. Besides, Ace always considered himself boss man material, a real go-getter who would be the face of a company, schmoozing and having people kiss his ass while his employees did the real work. Ace never saw himself like me, you know? Your basic middle-class worker."

"Is that why he hired you to cut Carlos's brake lines?"

"Ace?" His forehead wrinkles. "No. Ace wants to be in the spotlight, but he's not a bad guy."

Reggie thinks I'm a rookie reporter. Fine. I'll play along until cops arrive.

"If not your brother, then who?"

"I don't know. I got an anonymous email."

"You're saying you got an anonymous message and then you cut the brake lines?"

"No, no. At first, I didn't do anything. I thought it was a joke or something and I ignored it. But then I got a text from a number I didn't know. I told them if they didn't stop, I would report it to the police."

"Did you?"

"No. The next day I got a text that said they're using burner numbers that are untraceable." Damp rings are forming under his arms. "They told me to check my mailbox at home. There was an envelope with a thousand dollars in it."

He and the mayor must have worked on this story together.

"You don't know who sent the money?"

"Didn't know then, don't know now. But they have video of me opening the envelope." He pulls a rag out of a shirt pocket and wipes his brow, leaving a gray streak. "I can't believe I opened it outside. They were going to post the video everywhere and make it look like I was doing illegal stuff and getting cash payments."

"Did they?"

"No, because they promised they wouldn't if I cut the brake lines." He leans forward. "I didn't want to. You have to believe me. I know how to cut so the fluid leaks really slow and it's not dangerous. He should have noticed and had the brakes checked out."

"How did they know you cut the lines?"

"I sent before and after pictures. I used Snapchat so they disappeared."

"What about screenshots?"

He slaps a fist against his forehead.

"You're saying you cut Carlos's brake lines in a way they would last long enough for him to notice a problem before anything drastic happened."

"Yes, yes. I never meant for him to get hurt."

It's impossible to keep the judgement out of my voice. "Risking a life was worth a thousand dollars to you?"

His eyes dart to the family photo.

"How much more did he—did they pay you?"

Reggie shakes his head.

"It could help police track them down."

"They won't find them," he whines. "They used cryptocurrency."

"How much?"

"Nine thousand dollars."

"So, ten thousand total?"

He nods. My phone hums. I slide it next to my leg and the chair cushion so he won't notice I'm recording.

"I'd like to hear how you rescued the family business."

"Rescued, huh?" His eyes skip across cabinets and boxes. "That's right. If I hadn't stepped up, none of this would be here today." For the first time since confessing, his eyes meet mine. "I know it may not be much to some people but it's the world to me. And it was to my father."

"Some people would say it's admirable you took the initiative to carry on your father's legacy."

"See, you get it. Why can't my brother?"

Maybe because your ruthless brother only cares about himself.

"This business is about honoring the family name. I couldn't let it fail."

I ask questions about how the business grew, how it survived the Great Recession and pandemic—answers I care nothing about—while nodding and smiling and trying to breathe normally. As Reggie launches into a tale about opening Logan's third location, movement outside the office cuts him off. I grab my phone to record video. Two officers appear in the doorway. One has a hand over his holster, giving off jittery vibes. The other aced the training on approaching an agitated subject in a nonthreatening manner. Hands resting along his sides, balanced stance, relaxed voice.

"Hello, Mr. Logan. How are you doing?"

I regard my phone, torn between wanting to get exclusive video and not wanting to create a distraction that could lead to someone getting hurt.

"I'm Officer Stoots and this is Officer Mark. I understand you have information about a car accident."

Reggie nods.

"What do you say you come with us? We can take you to the station where you can talk with a detective."

"You're not going to arrest me, are you?"

"Those are not our orders, sir. We were asked to drive you downtown so you could talk about the accident. Would that be okay with you?"

"As long as we're just talking. Can I call my wife?"

"Sure, but how about we head downtown first so you can tell a detective what happened. You can call whoever you want from there."

The room is filling with uneasiness.

"Ready to go?"

I stand slowly, squeeze my body between boxes, and start recording video. Reggie's fist pounds the chair's stuffing, but it resists. It's out now and won't go back.

"What do you say, Mr. Logan?"

As Reggie heaves himself up, the chair lets out a shriek. Officer Jittery grips his gun handle. If this goes wrong, I could be collateral damage.

"Are you trying to take me to jail?"

"No, sir," Officer Calm says. "We are inviting you downtown to talk."

Reggie reaches for a drawer and Officer Jittery speaks for the first time.

"Stop. I need to see your hands."

Reggie freezes. Sweat circles his underarms. "I just want to get my phone."

Officer Calm takes a step forward. "Mr. Logan, is it okay if I take a quick look?"

My hands are trembling. My exclusive video of the mayor's brother is going to be crap.

"I don't know what the big deal is," Reggie says. "It's just my phone." He pulls at the drawer and Officer Calm is by his side before Reggie can touch anything.

"See?"

I flinch as Reggie yanks out his phone.

Officer Calm nods at his partner and says, "All good. Are you ready now, Mr. Logan?"

Reggie stares straight at my phone but doesn't speak as he shuffles by. I follow them through the lobby where employees stare open-mouthed.

"Reggie, are you okay?"

He doesn't answer and a woman at the counter yells, "What are you doing to him?"

Out the door, I run around the officers, beating them to their squad car. From the opposite side, I record Reggie ducking his head and collapsing in the back seat. He watches me through the window, tears pooling in his eyes. I would cry, too, if I was responsible for killing a man.

After they leave, I sprint to my car, hit the ignition, shift into reverse, and then back into park. I don't know whether to go to the Fourth Avenue jail where Kris's neighbor will be booked for his murder or police headquarters where Reggie Logan will be questioned and the station will send a live truck. The station! I have five unread texts, the most recent from Jim saying officers are two minutes out. The others are from Alex asking when I'm coming in. When I call, he puts me on hold. I hang up and dial the producer hotline.

"Hey, slow down," Sexy says. "We can have a photog at the jail in ten minutes to catch video of the neighbor being brought in. And you say you have video of the mayor's brother being arrested?"

"Not arrested but getting into a patrol car and heading downtown for questioning. But he confessed to me. I have the audio. No one else knows about him. And no one knows about Kris's neighbor being arrested for his murder. But I'm sure cops will have a press conference this afternoon to announce his arrest."

"You know what this means, don't you?" Sexy says.

"Yeah, I'm screwed. Everyone will get the arrest in time for their newscasts."

"Jolene, have you learned nothing from our social media meetings? Digital first! Get to posting. You own this story—the mayor's brother is suspected of cutting brakes that killed a beloved business owner. As for the neighbor being arrested, who cares if everyone else gets it in a few hours? You are first with exclusive information on a bizarre case involving the mayor's brother. That is, if you get on it now."

Charlotte from the promotions department cuts in. "If you shoot a selfie video, we'll share it on the station's social channels."

I pull the visor down and check the mirror. No makeup and no time to waste applying it.

"I'm in no shape to show my face. How about you take info from my posts and I'll send video of the mayor's brother. Run it by Bob first and make sure it's okay to use. I'll work up a short story for the web—emphasis on short—I don't want to spell everything out for other reporters."

"Jolene, stop thinking that way," Sexy says. "We're going to promote the hell out of it starting now. The more we share, the more viewers—I mean, friends—we'll attract."

"Okay. I have my laptop, but I'm not going ask Logan's Auto Repair for their Wi-Fi login. Maybe I'll hit a coffee shop. Or you know what? It'll be a couple hours before PD alerts anyone to the neighbor's arrest, so I can come back to the station and work on early newscast stories there."

"I don't care if you work from McDonald's, but I want you posting now," Sexy says. "Don't fall behind. This story's too sexy to lose our lead!"

For once, I agree with him.

CHAPTER
28

After posting video of police taking the mayor's brother in for questioning, I head to the station. I consider texting the mayor's chief of staff for a comment. Reggie Logan was adamant his brother didn't hire him, but he can't prove it. Besides, Mayor Ace Logan had a reason to silence Carlos and squash any investigation into kickbacks and city contracts. If I ask the mayor to comment about his brother being questioned about a deadly crash, at best I'll get a vague, bland statement. He doesn't deserve an easy out. The mayor should face the camera. But waiting gives other reporters time to find out the mayor's brother cut Carlos's brakes. They could get a reaction from the mayor first.

"Calm down," I whisper. "No one else knows."

But calming down is easier said than done because there's a massive piece that doesn't fit: Kris's neighbor, Peter. Why would cops think Peter killed Kris? He didn't compete for city business. And, unlike the neighbor nicknamed Grinch, Peter didn't hate Kris's holiday displays. I want to talk to my favorite former police source, but Jim has made it painfully clear he's tired of me. As I pull into the station's garage, my phone buzzes with a text from Bob.

My office ASAP.

Sexy is already in there. Probably complaining about me not posting enough to social.

"What's going on?" I ask.

"Have a seat, Jolene," Bob says.

Sexy avoids eye contact while making circles with his ankles. I sit on the edge, phone in hand, conveying I have no time for chitchat.

"I wanted to talk about your social media posts involving the mayor's brother," Bob says.

Why isn't he smiling? He should be thrilled we have exclusive audio and video.

"I'm concerned you didn't run them by a manager first," he says. "Using words like 'confession' can potentially create a problem for us later on."

"But that's what he did. I was there. Reggie Logan, the mayor's brother, confessed to cutting the brakes in Carlos's car."

"I'm not questioning what you saw or heard. I'm saying that we need to be careful. We don't know anything about Reggie. What if he's mentally unstable? What if he made it all up?"

"He didn't!"

"Take it easy."

First, they want us posting all the time, and now they say I posted too much. David, who can't get enough of social media, won't look at me. Thanks for your support, Sexy.

"I got a call from Faith Williams, the mayor's chief of staff. She says she learned about the situation from your posts. Tell me she's mistaken." Bob's tone is full of surprise and disappointment. "You must have contacted the mayor's office for comment."

"Not yet."

"Do it now," he says. "And we're going to keep the story short and simple until the police release more information. People are questioned every day and that doesn't make them a suspect."

"Did you even listen to the audio?"

"Yes, and, as I said, we don't know anything about Reggie's health or background. I appreciate what you have, Jolene. Without a doubt, your reporting is first-rate."

Here comes the "but."

"But we have to be extra cautious. At this point, we will not air any audio. David will work up a story about the mayor's brother for the early newscasts."

Bob expects Sexy to be cautious?

"I'll use your web copy for information," David says. "Please let me know when you hear back from the mayor's office."

They would be promoting the hell out of it any other time, but because there's a link to the mayor, they're playing sensitive. I want to tell them the mayor is part of the story but don't have solid proof—yet.

"We'll have you report live from police headquarters on the other big story, the murder of the neighborhood Santa."

I unclench my jaw to speak. "I'll leave now. Maybe I can get information before they hold a press conference announcing Kris Kruger's neighbor has been arrested for his murder."

On my way to the assignment desk, I text the mayor's chief of staff asking for comment.

"Alex, who's going with me to PD?"

"Nate," he says. "He's 10-17. ETA is ten minutes."

Normally, I'd be thrilled because I could vent to Nate, but I don't know what to expect. We haven't talked since we interviewed Kris's daughter and she practically threw us out when I asked about the city employee helping her dad win contracts.

"Do we know what time the presser is?"

"Negative," Alex says. "You guys can take off whenever you're ready."

Since Sexy is going to handle our story about the mayor's brother, I write an anchor intro about the neighbor's arrest in Kris Kruger's electrocution death.

"New developments in the case of a neighborhood Santa who died while hanging Christmas lights. Police now say his death was no accident. Channel 4 Eyewitness News reporter Jolene Garcia joins us live from police headquarters with the latest."

It's probably not sexy enough for David but works for me. Alex texts that Nate's in the garage. After a lukewarm hello, he turns on KEZ. The station's longtime host, Beth McDonald, is sharing a recipe for Mrs. Claus's punch. I lower the volume and face Nate.

"So, what do you think?" I ask.

"About what?"

"The mayor's brother is suspected of cutting Carlos's brake lines. Crazy stuff, huh?"

"Crazy is the right word for the situation."

I shoot him side-eye. "Listen, Nate, I don't appreciate you being so judgmental."

"No one's judging you."

"Maybe not right this minute but you did when I tried to talk to Kris's daughter."

"I thought it was tacky and I'm entitled to my opinion."

"If I hadn't talked to her, I wouldn't have pursued certain angles and we wouldn't be where we are now—way ahead of everyone else."

"Jolene, you're smart and competitive, no one's questioning that. But sometimes you push too hard."

"It all worked out, didn't it?"

He doesn't answer and jacks up the volume. Brenda Lee is rockin' around the Christmas tree as we park outside police headquarters. My station's posts promote "Jolene Garcia's exclusive reporting." A thrill runs up my spine when I see the hundreds of likes and reposts.

A text from Alex brings me back.

Presser @1600

"Thirty minutes till showtime," I tell Nate. He doesn't respond.

I check the newscast rundown and, of course, Sexy has changed my anchor intro to read: *"Shocking new developments in the death of a neighborhood St. Nick. Police say Santa's next-door neighbor was not his helper, but his killer! Channel 4 Eyewitness News reporter Jolene Garcia joins us live from police headquarters with late-breaking details on a case some are calling the Grinch who killed Santa."*

By "some," Sexy means him.

We carry gear into the lobby where an officer directs us to wait for the PIO. I'm reviewing my interview transcript with Kris's daughter when Scott Yang arrives. The sight of Phoenix's most seasoned investigative reporter makes my confidence disappear faster than candy from Elena's newsroom jar.

"Hey, Jolene, nice to see you again."

Wish I felt the same. I must have missed something major if Scott is here.

"What's the latest with the mayor's brother?" he asks.

"What are you hearing?"

"Only what you've posted. How'd you get him to confess?"

"Wait. You follow me on social?"

"Ever since Larry Lemmon's murder."

Out of the corner of my eye, I see Nate rolling his.

"If I'd known that car accident was going to lead to a confession by the mayor's brother, I never would've invited you to interview the witness with me," Scott says. "You're making me look bad."

I'm making the grandfather of Phoenix journalism look bad?

"You know, we have an opening for an investigative reporter. I can't say job security at my place is any better than TV news, but if you're on the I-team you shouldn't have to worry until you hit thirty. That's when the pencil pushers start thinking you make too much money."

I swallow hard. I'm twenty-nine.

"I think they only keep me around to teach college students the ropes. I've lost track of how many twenty-two-year-olds I've trained that ended up replacing colleagues with much more experience."

"I'm sorry."

Scott raises a shoulder like, "What can you do?"

"What's the best advice you give new reporters?"

"Don't let 'em wag the dog."

"What's that mean?"

"It's when attention is purposely diverted from something important to something less important."

"I don't get the wag the dog part."

"'The tail wags the dog' is an expression going back to the eighteen hundreds. It means something small—the tail—is controlling the bigger part—the dog."

Sounds like a confusing way to say "Question authority," but I don't want to belabor the point.

"To answer your question, Scott, I don't have any more information on the mayor's brother. Not a word from the mayor."

"His chief of staff, Faith, is smart and savvy. I thought she'd release a statement by now."

Probably trying to figure out if she's on her boss's hit list. Watch your back, Faith.

"What brings you here?" I ask.

"Short-staffed," Scott says. "I don't mind though. If I'm

going to cover a daily crime story, can't beat the murder of a neighborhood Santa."

As other stations arrive, I keep a lookout for JJ, eager to knock her down a peg. But five minutes before the press conference is to start, JJ remains a no-show. No one from her station is here. Even Sergio Magaña made it and he's late to everything.

"Good afternoon, everyone. I'm Sergeant Steve Khan. We'll begin in a couple minutes. Does anyone need a white balance?" He lifts a sheet of paper to his face so the cameras can adjust colors. "How about a mic check? Testing, one, two, three, testing. Everyone good to go?"

Behind us, a clatter signals JJ Jackson's entrance. Anyone else would apologize for the late arrival, but not JJ. Flipping her hair, she parades to the front row. Even though there are a dozen open seats, she sits next to me. I make a big production of grabbing my bag and standing up.

"This isn't school, JJ. You don't get to copy off my work."

I move two rows back and sit near Mirna Esteban from Telemundo. She leans over, bronze necklace dangling, and whispers, "What's going on?"

"Tired of her shit."

Sergeant Khan begins with the arrest in Kris Kruger's murder.

"The suspect, who is the victim's next-door neighbor, admitted to removing protective covering from the string of lights the victim held. Unbeknownst to the victim, as he arranged the lights, the suspect plugged them in and poured water on the cord section that lacked the covering. That caused the victim to experience an electrical shock, fall off the ladder, and subsequently die."

"What's the motive?" Mirna asks.

"The suspect claims he found a camera hidden in a holiday display that was positioned into a bedroom window."

"Whose window?" Scott asks.

"The window was in the suspect's master bedroom that he shared with his wife."

"What led detectives to the suspect?" I ask.

"This is where it gets complicated," he says. "Our detectives were investigating another case involving a man who died in a car crash. That man had filed a business complaint against Kris Kruger, the electrocution victim. The business complaint attracted the attention of the Arizona Attorney General's Office, which led them to examine Kruger's laptop. They found images of his neighbor's master bedroom and alerted us. Any questions about the AG's investigation should be directed to that office."

I ask if Kruger recorded video of the suspect and his wife.

"We are not going to comment any further as this is still an active investigation and we don't want to jeopardize the case." He checks his notes. "Moving on, I'm going to share limited information about a situation you may hear about from a fellow journalist."

Maybe I should've stayed next to JJ so I could rub it in.

"A local business owner is currently being questioned about a fatal car crash. We are not releasing the person's name or other information at this time. I am only sharing it because a local reporter was there as the person voluntarily agreed to talk with us."

JJ whips around and I give a little wave. That's right, he's talking about me.

"Excuse me, Sergeant," she says. "If another reporter has the information, then we should get it, too."

"Not going to happen—not right now," he says. "The person is answering questions as we speak. I have nothing else for you. If detectives make an arrest and recommend charges, I will let you know."

"This is confusing," JJ says. "Can we expect more today?"

"Check Jolene's posts," Scott says. "She has exclusive audio and video."

Maybe my station can run a promo with Scott praising my work.

"Sergeant," I say. "When it comes to the person answering questions about the fatal car crash, how are we supposed to identify them?"

"I'm not telling you how to do your job, but this person is not a suspect and not a person of interest at the moment. The person came to the station willingly to answer questions. I will say there could be another person or persons our detectives will want to speak to."

A ripple of satisfaction flows through me. I know cops mean the mayor.

As we assemble for live shots, I call out to JJ, "You know I'm the reporter the PIO was talking about?"

She fluffs her hair. "Whatever."

"Have you seen my exclusive video?"

She ignores me and swipes pink gloss over her lips.

"I got the mayor's brother being placed in a squad car."

JJ waves a jumbo-sized can of hair spray around, making me gag.

"Stand by," Nate says. "One minute out."

When the anchors toss to me, I imagine I'm reporting for a network. My live intro and tag are flawless. Nate finally drops the silent act and offers a sincere "Nice job." Gina and Elena text clapping hands and smiling emojis. JJ pulls out her phone—probably to check my story and see what she missed. As we break down our gear, she squeals with delight.

"A Mercedes! Oh, Daddy, you're the best! I promise to treat it like gold. I'll see you soon and we can hit the PCH with the top down."

The Pacific Coast Highway in a convertible paid for by Daddy. How perfectly JJ. After expressing everlasting love for her father at a volume that carries across downtown, JJ rises to full model height. I suck in my stomach and her lips curl. And just like that, I'm the dorky girl without a family.

"Jolene, you ready to go?"

Nate's timing is another reason he's earned the nickname Nate the Great.

"Thank you."

"For what?" he asks.

"Everything. I know it can be challenging to work with me sometimes."

"Sometimes?"

Nate's ahead of me on the sidewalk and I can't tell if he's joking. Before I can ask, my phone rings. The caller ID appears as "Source." The extra weight in my chest begins to melt. Jim doesn't hate me. I put more distance between myself and Nate before I answer.

"Hey, I thought you forgot about me."

"This is a courtesy call. My last one." His words sting, but his tone sears. "I only called because you alerted us to Reggie Logan, so I'm letting you know he's no longer being questioned."

"Did you arrest him?"

"No."

"But he confessed! He just gets to walk away?"

"No one said the investigation is over."

"This is a classic case for the SIU. You must have a front-row seat."

"As a matter of fact, I observed his interview with detectives."

"What did he say? Will you have anything new I can report for the ten o'clock newscast?"

"We don't solve crimes based on your deadlines."

Ah, there it is. Jim's most popular response to reporters when he was a PIO.

"You have exclusive video of Reggie leaving with officers. Can't you milk it for another newscast?"

Milk it?

"Jim, you know whatever you tell me is off the record unless we both agree otherwise."

"Let me be crystal clear. I have nothing more to tell you about Reggie Logan or anything else. Your reckless behavior has jeopardized my unit's work for the last time. Goodbye."

A familiar feeling soaks my skin and seeps into my bones. It's not the guilt I should be feeling for messing things up again. It's not the sadness I should be feeling for alienating my most valuable source. I know a better person would be reflecting on how to make amends. But I'm numb, feeling as isolated as when my only friend left our foster home to start a new life with a new family. We never talked again. Trudging to the truck, I blink back tears. When Nate asks what's wrong, I avoid his gaze and thumb my phone, mumbling frustration over police not sharing more information.

Nate is quiet for several seconds. "As you know, if the mayor's brother is arrested or charged with killing Carlos Rios, the media will be all over it. David's probably already working on a graphic for the Brake Line Killer, but no one wants a repeat of the Freeway Shooter."

"Who?"

"That was the moniker for the person behind a string of shootings on Interstate 10. Happened before you moved here."

"Was anyone hurt?"

"Not seriously, but it messed with a lot of heads. Some people stopped driving on the freeway, school buses took different routes. National media were all over the story."

"Did they catch the Freeway Shooter?"

"According to the governor, they did. Minutes after a guy was arrested, the governor posted, 'We got him.' It went viral and the guy's name and face were everywhere. He claimed he was innocent, the case fell apart, and eventually a court cleared him. Maybe that's why your source won't tie the mayor's brother to a crime."

"But I have audio of him."

"What's more important to you? One story that'll get clicks or justice for Carlos?"

"Nate, that's not fair. I'm the one who pursued the crash. I care about Carlos. I also care about not getting beat on the story."

"You're still ahead of everyone and I'm confident you'll keep it that way."

An hour later, the mayor's chief of staff emails a statement.

"I love my brother and always will. I have the utmost faith in the Phoenix Police Department and will respect the process."

Faith Williams sent the statement to all the stations. Not ideal, but I still have exclusive audio of Reggie's confession.

"We're not going to air the audio," David says.

"How can we not air it?"

"You know the media, as a whole, has a perception problem. A substantial number of people think we are biased and can't be trusted—especially when it comes to politics."

"This isn't about politics. It's about a guy who confessed to cutting brake lines that caused a crash and killed someone."

"The guy happens to be related to the mayor. That's the sexy angle. You can use the video of him leaving with officers but not his audio."

"That makes no sense. Why would I say, 'He told me this,' when we could air his actual audio for people to hear themselves?"

"I'll tell you why: AI. People may not believe your audio is real, they may suspect it's been manipulated through artificial intelligence. If you also had video of him confessing, that would be better."

"That makes no sense. If someone's not going to believe the audio, why would they believe the video?"

"Bob and I discussed it and that's our decision." He gathers his belongings. "Thank you for staying and working up a new story for the late newscast."

Unlike the legal system, there are no appeal options when the news director and executive producer are on the same side. After filing my story, I check the competition. Scott Yang didn't report anything on the mayor's brother and JJ's station only ran a thirty-second story with no video. As Nate said, I'm still ahead and plan to keep it that way.

CHAPTER
29

An unsettling feeling jolts me awake Saturday. Something important came to me during sleep. I close my eyes and order my mind to remember. When it refuses, I try coaxing. Still nothing. Falling back to sleep isn't happening, either.

"Aargh!"

I lurch out of bed, pull on running tights, and throw on a long shirt. Maybe pounding the pavement will jostle my memory. I pop in earbuds, choose a Taylor Swift mix, and bop out the door. Norma's walking Tuffy and I wave, point to my ears, and keep going. My mind needs to be free of distractions so it can call up whatever message surfaced in my sleep.

Thirty minutes later, I've got nothing but sore feet, a full-on side ache, and the beginning of a headache. The mayor's brother admitted to cutting Carlos's brakes. I wonder if he also shot Rich Gains, the lobbyist who helped Carlos bid for city contracts. My best police source has cut me off and if I show up at city hall, it's guaranteed my news director will hear about it. That's just more ammunition for him to demand I see a therapist.

I fill my biggest bowl with chips, stick it in the microwave, hit thirty seconds and embark on my version of an indoor sprint.

Open the fridge, grab a drink and the last remnants of salsa, tear off a paper towel, place them on the table, and be back at the microwave before it dings.

"Impressive, huh, Emmy?"

Between bites, I scroll through work emails I've neglected all week, automatically deleting any that are in all caps. I get enough shouting in the newsroom. An email from Alex titled "Info you requested" makes me pause. I lick salt off my fingers and open it. Well, well, well. Fred Nimby's background check turned up an arson conviction in Wyoming eighteen years ago. Getting caught might have taught him how to get away with it in the future. For example, setting a fire at the construction project he opposed. The new information moves Fred from neighborhood activist to suspect in the murder of Rich Gains. What was it he posted on Facebook about Rich and the people who work with him?

I scan Fred's posts until I find it: "The developer has hired a powerful lobbyist to ram this project through without taking into account the concerns of residents who've invested millions into their community. Anyone who works on these projects is complicit in destroying our lifestyle. It's time to take back our neighborhood!"

Alex's email contains Fred's home address. I have undercover gear and can record an interview if he's willing. If not, I can still record. Better to have audio and video. Case in point: the mayor's brother. I hop in the shower, change clothes, and run out the door.

Fred Nimby's house is in a cul-de-sac with a vibrant jacaranda tree in the front. I park my car facing out in case I need a quick getaway. Cupcake frosting has hardened on the recorder. I scrape it off and straighten the camera. Damn. Fred Nimby has a video doorbell. If he talks to me through the camera I won't know if he's here or away. Come on, I tell myself, this could be the moment you crack another case.

Before I can press the bell, a ferocious bark blows me back. Thankfully, there are no steps to fall off, but I bump into a pot, dumping flowers and soil. Hands shaking, I try to place it upright. The brute lets another one rip and the pot flies out of my hand. I flee like a bank robber. For the second time today, I'm sweating and struggling to catch my breath. I take it as a sign that I should take a break from my investigation. I head home with plans to veg out but my nosy neighbor didn't get the memo.

"Yoo-hoo, Jolene!" She gathers Tuffy into her arms. "The ladies and I are going to Organ Stop Pizza. Would you like to join us?"

"No thanks, Norma."

"Are you sure, dear? It's such a fun place. Home to the world's largest Wurlitzer pipe organ. It has thousands of pipes, percussions, even pianos. They play show tunes, Disney songs. And they take requests. It's like being in a theater."

"I can't, Norma."

"You don't have to drive. Kirti and Marcia are picking me up."

"I have plans."

Plans that include pigging out alone.

"Maybe another time then. You work so hard. You need to take a break."

No, Norma, what I need is to prove what's going on at city hall. The mayor is dirty, Councilwoman Patterson is dirty, the employee who handles bids looks dirty, too. They're collecting kickbacks and their greed led to Carlos being killed. As for Fred Nimby, his arson conviction and outburst at the city council meeting make him a prime suspect in the lobbyist's murder. He must have already been questioned by police. But I can't confirm it with my source. Make that former source.

I rip open a box of pepperoni pizza rolls, toss them in the microwave, and turn on *Wheel*.

"Welcome, everyone," Pat Sajak says. "We are celebrating families this week. All of our contestants are related and share a love for *Wheel of Fortune*. Let's welcome our first contestants: a mother and daughter team from San Antonio, Texas."

I flip it off, check my social feeds, and immediately regret it. In the driver's seat of a yellow convertible, JJ is singing, her blond locks waving at the ocean. Hashtags #newcar #californialove #daddysgirl.

I spend the rest of the day alternating between reading, channel surfing, and snacking. Before falling asleep, I encourage my mind to remember the dream that forced me awake. I end up dreaming about work. The anchors announce I have a stunning exclusive and toss to my live shot. But I'm not there.

The next morning, I have a shot at redemption because Fred Nimby agrees to meet at a coffee shop. I told him I want to follow up on the projects he's been protesting, which is true. I also want him to explain his arson arrest.

"It's great to see a reporter following issues that matter to the community," he says. "Unless it's a new restaurant opening or closing, you guys don't seem to cover it."

Preaching to the choir, Nimby.

"Are you okay with me recording our conversation?"

"With your phone?"

I pat the purse. "I have a camera and recorder in here."

"No problem."

If I have audio and video, Sexy won't have an excuse not to run this exclusive.

"What can I help you with?"

"I'm following up on the fire at the construction site."

His eyes squint. "What fire?"

I can't believe he's trying to play dumb.

"The fire at the apartment complex being built in your neighborhood. The one you've been fighting against."

"What about it? I thought a homeless person set the fire."

"Arson investigators haven't yet determined a cause. Have you talked with them?"

"Why would I?"

"Considering your prior arson conviction and opposition to the project, I thought they might interview you."

I aim for a light tone, but Fred takes it like a sledgehammer.

"What the hell is this about?"

"I'm looking into the construction site arson and Rich Gains's death. How well did you know him?"

"I knew him through his shady clients. He was their mouthpiece, parroting whatever they told him to say."

"You caught the city council off guard when you shot confetti and police escorted you out of the meeting. Would you say that's typical behavior for you?"

"Is that why you showed up at unannounced at my house?" He sits back, folds his arms. "That's right. I saw you before Louie scared you off."

"I just want to talk to you. Consider my perspective: a resident with a conviction for arson has close ties to a project that burns to the ground."

He shakes his head. "Man, you are something else. I didn't set that fire."

I'm going to need more than that. I take a sip to buy myself a minute to figure out my next question, but Fred Nimby doesn't wait.

"You wanna know about my past so bad, I'll tell you. I was nineteen when I was arrested. Sorry to disappoint you but I didn't torch a controversial development. I set fire to my own car."

My blank expression keeps him talking.

"My car was falling apart, I had a shitty job and needed money. You've heard people say they're worth more dead than alive? Well, that was my car—worth more if the insurance company paid me to replace it. You may find it hard to believe but not all of us are born into the glamorous TV life."

He yanks his phone out of a back pocket and hits the screen like a punching bag. "Here." He shoves it in my face. "Check my posts. These photos are from my cousin's wedding. In Nevada. I wasn't even here when the fire started."

I ask where he was on the day of Rich Gains's murder.

"So, now I posed as a burglar and killed a lobbyist in his house? Don't you think cops would've arrested me by now?" He bolts out of his chair, knocking it over. "This is bullshit!"

As I watch him clomp away, everyone else watches me. I pretend not to notice and check my phone. Alex sent a text asking my ETA.

On my way.

I'm trying to come up with a way to avoid Sexy when I nearly step on his face.

"Hey, look out!"

He's the one lying on the floor, legs running up the wall.

"What are you doing?"

Sexy hugs his knees to his chest, rolls to the side, and pushes himself up.

"Inversion. Improves circulation and it's great for the lower back. Part of my marathon training." He ties his shoes and says, "Let's talk about a replacement for the gluten investigation."

"You guys don't want the cupcake story?"

He mimics knocking on a door. "Hello, Jolene, there is no cupcake story. Don't you read your emails? The lab results came in this morning. Only one sample had trace amounts of gluten."

While part of me is glad, I'm also worried about its replacement.

"We had two Thanksgiving ideas. Initially, we were going to have you investigate turkeys."

Oh, the smart-ass quips I keep to myself.

"We were going to have you buy frozen turkeys and take them to a lab to compare the weight listed on the package to the weight on their scales. But, number one: time is tight. Number two: we've already gone over budget with the gluten investigation. And number three: we need a sure thing."

"What is it?"

"A preview of Thanksgiving Grandma. It's a heartwarming, local tradition that's gained national attention. Everyone loves it. Grandma thinks she texted her grandson to invite him to Thanksgiving dinner, but accidentally texted a stranger. She invites him and they've been celebrating the holiday together for years. Remind people how it started, maybe talk with Grandma in the kitchen as she's doing prep—or tag along as she shops for groceries. Interview the guy. Talk about how their lives have changed and how their relationship has grown. You'll be able to report and produce it pretty fast with no expenses."

Magic words to a news manager: quick and cheap.

"Go ahead and set that up and let Alex know when you need a photog."

The positive side of working holidays is staying busy. The negative side is the emphasis on family stories. The best way to get out of covering one story is to get a bigger one. Like the mayor resorting to the murders of a lobbyist and business owner to cover up corruption. Figuring out how he did it and how much his chief of staff is involved can only happen face-to-face. I call Faith Williams and ask for a meeting.

"One moment," she says. "Let me step out of a meeting."

The background chatter dissipates and a door closes before Faith tells me she is not in a position to discuss the mayor's brother.

"I'm more interested in the mayor."

"You have his statement."

"Yes, a statement about his brother. I want to talk to Mayor Logan about himself."

"I would advise him against that."

"That's what I would expect from his chief of staff. However, I also expect you to pass along my request so he can decide. As you know, there are numerous examples of why he's earned the moniker 'Unavoidable for Comment.'"

"What exactly is it that you want from Mayor Ace?"

"Information about the city's bid process."

"Let's not play games. The mayor is not involved in anything unethical or illegal and I don't appreciate you insinuating otherwise."

"I'm not saying he is—" I bite back "yet" and offer her a bone. "How about on background only?"

I can hear the wheels in her brain spinning.

"No attribution," she says.

"Fine. Where and when?"

"Give me a sec."

While on hold, Sexy appears and says, "We want to promote the grandma story ASAP."

I point to my phone and Sexy gives a thumbs-up. Not my fault if he assumes I'm talking to Thanksgiving Grandma.

"Jolene, I can meet you in ninety minutes."

"What about the mayor?"

"Ace can't make it. Take it or leave it."

She knows the movers and shakers and where the skeletons are hidden.

"Same place as last time?"

"Not in public. Between the investigation into Councilwoman Patterson and the situation with the mayor's brother, I can't risk being seen with a reporter." She gives an address. "It's a house."

Faith handles the mayor's calendars and social media accounts.

He trusts her with everything. She must know he hired his brother to cut Carlos's brake lines. The mayor may not know how to use cryptocurrency but Faith would. Silencing Carlos meant no one would discover how Kris Kruger used inside info to submit lower bids than his competitors and made up the difference by submitting higher bills later. The attorney general's initial investigation into Councilwoman Zoey Patterson's relationship with Rich Gains expanded to the full council. It must have been getting too hot for our cool mayor.

Before he stopped talking to me, Jim assured me no one—not even Councilwoman Patterson—knew which agency was investigating what potential crimes. Patterson called the police chief for information, but was shut down. The councilwoman, the mayor, and his chief of staff are all rotten. Now, it's a matter of determining who stinks the most.

CHAPTER
30

Faith's address leads to an area once considered far north Phoenix and home to farms. Now, most people call it central Phoenix and seasonal crops are grown in backyard gardens. Single-story houses sprawl on lots the size of football fields bordered with trees for privacy. I pass a sign promising two-story custom-made homes coming soon and wonder how the goats next door will handle construction.

The property where we're meeting is being renovated. The long, narrow driveway bows along the side of the house. Maybe Faith's planning to move in. I catch raised voices. A curse. A scream. I round the corner. Mayor Ace Logan is bent over, clawing at his face. His chief of staff is hopping from one foot to the other.

"I'm sorry," Faith says. "I didn't mean to spray it."

The mayor is howling.

"What happened?" I ask.

Faith whips around. She's clutching a canister. And my brain registers what I'm seeing—and smelling.

"Ace, hold on," she says. "Jolene, turn on the faucet behind you and grab the hose."

I fiddle with the nozzle, unsure what setting to use. Soaker, jet, shower? Faith grabs it and sticks it in the mayor's hand. He moans as water cascades off his face. I ask if it was an accident. Faith doesn't answer.

"Were you showing him how to use the pepper spray?"

Her eyes zip from the mayor to me and back to the mayor.

"Wait, why is the mayor here? I thought you said he couldn't make it."

"He followed me."

"Did he try to hurt you?" I reach for the faucet to turn it off.

"No! She hurt me." Logan drops the hose and reveals vampire eyes. "Why, Faith?"

She swipes at a tear. "You shouldn't have followed me."

"I overheard you on the phone saying I couldn't meet, but you never asked me. You haven't been yourself lately. What is going on?"

"Don't act like you care."

"Faith." As he moves toward her, Faith raises the canister, stopping him in his tracks.

"You used me. I got you elected to city council. I got you elected mayor. What do I get in return? Left in the dust as you go to Hollywood."

"Faith, you know I tried to get you a job with the show, but I'm new to all of it and don't have much influence."

"Excuse me," I say. "What does this have to do with the mayor paying his brother to cut Carlos's brakes?"

Logan's red eyes flash on me. "I did not pay my brother to hurt anyone."

"Maybe you didn't conduct the financial transaction because Faith does all your dirty work, but you're no better than your brother. You were afraid Carlos would expose the inside deals you've been getting away with and you convinced your brother to make Carlos's crash look like an accident."

"You're wrong," Logan says. "I would never do anything like that."

What an actor. No wonder he kept getting re-elected.

"Your brother said he only meant to scare Carlos, not kill him, but what about Rich Gains?" I say. "Why did you want him dead?"

The mayor looks at Faith and some kind of realization dawns on him. "No, Faith. Both of them? Why?"

"I had no choice. Rich was blackmailing me. When Carlos started complaining about losing contracts to Kris Kruger, I couldn't risk an investigation. I needed the money I got from Kris to pay Rich."

I'm stunned. Of all the people with ties to Carlos and Rich, I never considered Faith. She's the loyal, competent chief of staff.

"Faith." Logan's voice is flat, defeated. "You should've come to me."

"Yeah, right. If you'd known what Rich had on me, you would've ditched me long ago."

"Faith, we're like family. You're my confidant. You're the first person I bounce ideas off, we discuss policy proposals and talk through difficult votes. I would never discard you like trash."

She glares at him. "But you did. You tossed me aside to be a TV star. And if Rich had ever told you what I'd done, you'd never speak to me again."

"I'm speaking to you now. Tell me."

As tears run down her face, the mayor reaches for Faith and I reach for my phone.

"Stay away!" She points the canister at us. I jump back. If Logan wants more pepper spray, he can have it. "Jolene, get your hands out of your pocket."

"Faith, it's okay," the mayor says. "Tell me what's wrong. We can fix it."

She pushes a sleeve across her nose. "You can't fix it."

"I can help you. What happened?"

She sobs a response. I can't make out the words.

"Faith, did you hurt someone?" the mayor asks.

She sucks in air and says, "I . . . I killed a woman."

A swell of shock floods my chest. Faith killed Carlos. She killed Rich. And she killed another person.

Faith takes a ragged breath and says, "I was twenty years old and drove drunk."

Logan's face crumples. For years, his most trusted advisor has been lying to him. Not outright, but a lie of omission. When Logan's wife was killed by a drunk driver, Faith stood next to him as he addressed reporters. She was in the courtroom to support Logan during the suspect's sentencing. And she never told him the truth.

"My parents hired a lawyer who managed to get the records sealed." The tears have stopped, replaced by rage. "That sleazeball Rich Gains tracked down the cop on the case. He's retired but remembers it well. Rich held it over me, threatening me unless I got you to vote the way he wanted."

"Faith, that doesn't make sense. I voted against many projects, especially when developers didn't work with residents."

"Rich only needed you on the close votes."

His shoulders droop and he releases a choking sound. For the first time, Mayor Ace Logan looks frail.

"Rich got greedier," Faith says. "He wanted more than your votes. He wanted my money."

"That's when you came up with a financial arrangement with Kris Kruger," I say. "In exchange for Kris getting the contracts, he paid you."

She nods. "But Rich kept pushing for more and I couldn't come up with the money." She's still aiming the canister at us. "Rich was going to tell everyone what I'd done."

"So, you killed him," I say.

"No." She shakes her head forcefully "I didn't shoot him."

"You hired someone to do it, didn't you?"

She says nothing.

The mayor's voice is soft and weak. "Faith, that's like pulling the trigger yourself."

"You don't get it, Ace. My reputation would have been destroyed."

Better your reputation than an innocent man. My anger sizzles. I struggle to tamp it down. "Why go after Carlos? He never hurt you."

"An investigation into the contracts would've led to Rich Gains and he would've revealed my accident. My career wouldn't survive. I'd have nothing. I'd be no one. Jolene, you of all people should understand the pressure to hide your past."

My cheeks burn. Faith left the threatening note on my car. Please don't say anything more.

Logan is rebounding from Faith's bombshell and says, "I'm sorry you didn't feel like you could talk to me."

"Stop it! Stop acting like you care. If you had, you wouldn't have cut me out of the show."

"What the hell is going on?" The voice behind us belongs to Councilwoman Zoey Patterson. An armed councilwoman.

"Oh, Zoey, am I glad to see you." Faith's internal switch flips from tortured soul to political animal.

"Can it, Faith. I want answers, not bullshit. What are you doing on my property?"

"This is your house?" I ask.

"Yes," Zoey says. "The foreman called me after Faith showed up. He was confused because Faith instructed them to leave, said I wanted the crew to take the day off. You even gave them cash. How generous of you."

Faith pleads. "Listen, Zoey, I can explain."

"Explain what? How you planned to cut a deal with the cops and send me to prison for taking bribes?"

"No, you misunderstand," Faith says. "I just needed a safe place to talk to them and explain about Rich Gains."

"What about him?"

"She killed him," the mayor says.

"I didn't kill him," Faith says.

"You hired a hitman, same thing," I say.

"Impressive." Zoey shoots an admiring look at Faith. "Rich was more trouble than the kickbacks were worth anyway. So, what are you planning to do with them?"

I wish Zoey would stop waving the gun around.

"No need to act impulsively," Faith says. "Let's talk it over."

The mayor reaches into his jacket and Zoey says, "Slow down, Ace, and toss your phone on the table. You, too, Jolene."

"This is foolish," Mayor Logan says. "Let us go and you won't face kidnapping charges."

"Phones on the table. Now."

"Zoey, we can join forces," Faith says. "I can get you elected mayor. Do one term and you can move onto governor or Congress. Together, we'll be unstoppable."

Zoey keeps her eyes on Logan and says, "Jolene, I want you to go inside the shed and get the rope."

"You can't be serious," Logan says.

"Why do you want rope?"

"Jolene, you don't get to ask questions anymore." She points the gun at me. "Go! And don't try anything."

For a split second, I consider running away. She can't keep one gun on all of us. But since I can't outrun a bullet, I hustle to the shed, where I trip on a short stack of pavers. My hands save my face from slamming into a bag of cement.

"You have three seconds, Jolene."

A lawn mower and rake mock me. Nothing sharp shouts, "Grab me and I'll save your life."

"I want to see you now! Time's up!"

"Okay, okay!" I kneel to grab the rope.

Crack!

Zoey shot the shed!

"I'm coming, I'm coming!" I raise both hands over my head, the rope dragging behind me.

Zoey orders me to set the rope down. "Go back to the shed. Look to the left. Take the shears off the top shelf and walk out with your hands up."

"What are shears?"

"Don't be a smart-ass."

I'm not trying to be. Panic is messing with my brain. "On the left, right?"

"Not the right. On the left."

"Left. Got it."

Next to what looks like an enormous pair of scissors is a small tool with my name on it. Thanks to my high school job at a grocery store stocking shelves and breaking down boxes, my utility knife skills are superb. But with no pockets, I don't have an easy place to hide the knife. I pop open the storage compartment, remove the extra blade, and stick it in my sock.

"Let's go!" Zoey yells. "Hands up! Out now!"

The shears are five-hundred-pound barbells in my wobbly arms.

Zoey orders Logan to stand with his hands behind a wooden post.

"Jolene, you're going to cut the rope. Make it long enough to go around his wrists three times. Then tie his feet to the post."

With the rope bunched under my arm, I struggle with the shears. The rope falls. I pick up the shears, each hand clasping a handle. "How am I supposed to hold the rope and cut it?"

"Are you that stupid?" Zoey kicks the rope to me. "On the ground. Straighten it out. Then, cut."

As I squat, I pull the blade out of my sock. Logan clenches his hands and forearms as I wrap the rope around his wrists. I try to slide the blade into his palm but he doesn't understand my gesture—until his skin breaks. He relaxes a hand and takes the blade.

Faith says, "Zoey, why don't you give me the gun? I'm already in trouble. Me shooting them isn't going to make it any worse. We can cram them in my trunk and dump them in the desert. It'll be years before anyone finds them."

"Faith, you're not thinking clearly," I say. "If we disappear, the police are going to investigate. You'll be arrested and won't be able to buy your way out of charges again."

I want Logan to jump in. He knows her better and can make a stronger plea, but I don't want to risk drawing attention to the blade in his hand so I keep talking. "People will know you were the last person with us."

"Nice try, but Ace didn't tell anyone where he was going and, since I control his calendar, there's no record. As for you, Ms. Reporter, I know you kept your mouth shut because you sniffed another Emmy and wouldn't want to tip anyone off to your big story."

"My station knows where I am."

Zoey barks a laugh. "News flash, Jolene: you don't have a poker face, but, because I admire your ambition, I promise to make it as quick and painless as possible."

"The police will track our phones. They'll know we were all here."

Zoey says, "They'll know what we tell them: that you and the mayor ran off together. Won't be hard to believe. You crave recognition. Probably have daddy issues. What do you say, Faith? Will two bodies fit in your trunk?"

"No problem." Faith puts out a hand. "May I?"

"You are the ultimate political shark." Zoey gives her the gun. "Be my guest."

Faith's fingers clench the weapon. She takes three fast steps toward me. My eyes squeeze shut.

"Change of plans."

I open my eyes and Faith is standing next to me.

"Jolene, you're going to tie up Zoey."

"Like hell she is!"

"Zoey, the person holding the gun gets to give the orders."

"You'd never shoot," she says.

"Don't try me," Faith says. "Jolene, if you want to get out of this alive, get her."

I glance at the mayor who gives the tiniest nod. When I grab Zoey's shoulders, she knocks me down. Zoey sneers at Faith and turns away.

A popping sound comes a split second before the mayor cries out. "You shot my foot!"

Faith freezes. But not Zoey. She starts to run. I fling a step stool, knocking her feet out from under her. I jump on Zoey's back, trying to pin her arms down. She pushes up, flips me over, and bangs my head against the dirt. When I go limp, she jumps up, ready to flee. Until Faith channels a bulldozer and takes her down.

"Get the rope!" Faith yells.

As Faith grinds her knees into Zoey's shoulders, I tie her feet.

"You need to call 911," the mayor says. "My foot is bleeding bad."

Faith apologizes. "I don't know how it went off. I've never fired a gun."

"Please, I need help," he says.

"It only grazed your foot. You'll be okay." She yanks Zoey's arms. "Jolene, tie her hands."

Zoey lets loose with a string of curse words that get louder as the rope gets tighter. I wrap until the rope runs out. Faith grabs the gun and points it at me.

"Let's go."

"Zoey's not going anywhere," I say. "Now's your chance to get away."

The councilwoman is wriggling on the ground, screaming. Faith threatens to shoot her if she doesn't stop.

"You won't do it," Zoey says.

"Maybe not," Faith says. "But I'll get you to shut up."

Faith orders me to the shed for rags, paper towels, anything to stuff in Zoey's mouth. Over Zoey's cursing, she says, "Ace, can I trust you not to yell? I promise I'll call for help as soon as I'm safe."

"You can trust me," he says.

I choose a rag that looks recently washed. It smells like dirt and I apologize to Zoey. She's squirming, jerking, and twisting her body. When I get close, she bites my hand.

"Ow! This is not my fault."

"Yes, it is, you nosy-ass reporter. You should've left Faith and me alone. We weren't hurting anyone. Everything was fine until you started getting in our business."

I cram the rag in her mouth.

"Let's go, Jolene."

I'm not about to leave with someone pointing a gun at me who has nothing to lose. It's another lesson I learned from Jim Miranda during the station's "Get Out Alive" series.

"If you get in the car, you're dead," he said. "Always fight."

Then he demonstrated ways to fight off a kidnapper. Something about poking their eyes with your keys and hitting their nose with your palm. I don't have keys and don't want to get close enough to Faith's face when she's holding a gun.

"Where are we going?"

"Airport," Faith says. "First stop is Mexico. Then a country without U.S. extradition."

"What about me?"

"I hope you're not afraid of small spaces. You're going in the trunk."

"Faith, you can't—"

"Shut up! It won't be forever." She turns to the mayor with a face full of regret. "Ace. I'm sorry. I never wanted you or anyone to get hurt."

"Please let me drill air holes in the trunk," I say. "There's a tool from the shed."

"No. You won't be in there long. I'll use a burner phone to call cops once I cross the border."

Not going to happen, Faith. I bend over and plow into her torso. The gun hits the ground and we scramble for it. My arm and fingers stretch like an accordion. I'm about to reach it and Faith kicks my shoulder. She's panting. And she has the gun.

"Get the hell up!"

I can't tell if Logan is making progress with the rope, but with an injured foot, he's not going to be able to run after Faith. A bump is growing on my head and a lump in my throat cuts off my voice. Faith forces me to the other side of the house where she parked her car. A silver Camry.

"It was you! You tried to run me over at city hall."

"I tried to scare you, not kill you. It's not my fault you can't take a hint. You shouldn't ignore warnings."

"Faith, I'm sorry. You're right. We all have things we wish we could do over. People are forgiving. Don't you want to make peace instead of spending the rest of your life on the run?"

"I don't need you playing shrink. I know what I'm doing."

She pops the trunk and a breath slips through my lips. There's an emergency release latch. I should've remembered from our "Get Out Alive" series. The federal government started requiring glow-in-the-dark emergency releases after several children accidentally trapped themselves in trunks and died. I'll get in, pull the latch at a stoplight, and hop out.

"Grab the T-shirt out of my gym bag," Faith says. "Fold it so you have a nice, thick blindfold."

She wrenches off the cover to the emergency latch. Take it easy, I tell myself. You can still find the lever. With the gun aimed at my heart, Faith orders me to remove the tire iron and smash the lever.

"If you don't break it, I shoot. You've seen my aim. Do you want to risk it?"

I don't know if that means she'll shoot the lever or me, but I'm not going to find out. When she's satisfied my only escape option has been obliterated, she reaches into the trunk and tosses out a clear plastic container with a flashlight, batteries, and jumper cables.

"Set the blindfold in the trunk and put your hands behind your back."

Jim's warning from the "Get Out Alive" series blasts in my ears again: "If you get in the car, you're dead. Always fight."

But Faith's priority is getting away, not killing me. I can survive the drive to the airport. She'll park in a busy garage or a lot and, if I can't free myself, someone will hear my screams.

Faith makes me tie bungee cords around my feet before she binds my hands. She knots the blindfold so tight that colors and patterns weave in and out of the darkness.

She closes the trunk and my heart nearly explodes. I just made a mistake that will cost me my life. What's to stop her from shooting me in the trunk, abandoning her car, and taking an Uber to the airport? She's leaving the country—one more crime isn't going to matter.

The throbbing on the back of my head spreads to my eyeballs. Trying to calm myself, I focus on deep breathing. Until

I realize I'm sucking up precious oxygen. I kick up and down and on the sides. When my feet connect with a corner, relief ripples in my stomach. If I get out alive, I will owe Sexy an apology for making fun of the series. I kick the taillight. Or what I hope is the taillight. Again and again. The taillight will fall out, I'll jam my foot through the hole, and even the most distracted drivers will notice and call 911. I hope.

CHAPTER
31

The car suddenly accelerates, slamming my body. My cheek rubs against a moist patch of carpet. The sour stink of rancid milk makes me gag. What an idiot I am. I have no idea if Faith is really heading to the airport to make her getaway. She's driving fast enough to be on the freeway, but maybe it feels like freeway speed because I'm blindfolded and crammed in a trunk. Sweat coats my upper lip as I jostle and reposition my legs to kick the taillight. A faint noise makes me stop. It is the most beautiful sound in the world. Sirens. They're getting closer. I'll be free in a minute—if Faith doesn't crash and kill us. The car roars. A scream pierces my eardrums. My limbs tremble and I gulp for air. I don't want my last moments to be filled with fear, but I can't catch my breath, can't stop shaking.

"Pull over!"

The order sounds far away. Maybe it's my imagination. Hard to make out anything over my frantic heartbeat. The car shudders to a stop and my lips land on the sour milk.

"Exit the vehicle with your hands up."

The driver's door opens.

"Keep your hands up."

In an instant, hurried footsteps surround the car.

"Help! I'm in the trunk!"

"We know, ma'am. Stand by."

Before the trunk is fully open, I swing my legs out and hit something. Or someone.

"Phoenix Police. Hold still and we'll get you out, okay?"

I pull my legs back.

"Are you hurt anywhere?"

"No. Get me out. Please." My voice is raspy, begging.

"Lay still and we'll lift you by your feet and shoulders. Is that okay?"

"Yes."

I'm as wobbly as a chick.

"I'm going to remove the blindfold and then untie your hands, okay?"

The Arizona sunlight, always strong, is unbearable. Sweat stings my eyes.

"Paramedics are on the way."

Bungee cord impressions blotch my wrists. After several shakes, they start to feel normal. Can't say the same for my head. When my fingers reach the bump, I'm surprised it's only the size of a golf ball.

"Thank you," I say. "How did you get her to stop?"

"Grappler."

The officer points to a yellow nylon net wrapped around the rear tire. I've seen the Grappler in action during live coverage of local pursuits. The net is lowered from the front of a law enforcement vehicle and seizes the suspect's rear tire, forcing the car to stop.

"Where's Faith?"

He motions to a squad car. "They'll take her to jail."

"How did you know where to find me?"

"I don't have all the specifics, ma'am, but sounds like Mayor Ace called it in."

"He must have gotten free. Faith shot him. Is he okay?"

"I'm not privy to that information. I would assume he's being checked out at the hospital."

The officer escorts me to an ambulance parked in front of the squad car. Faith is slouched in the back seat and doesn't notice me.

"Jolene! What happened?"

It's Tony. I haven't seen him since he was my date for the Emmy party.

"You wouldn't believe it," I say.

As Tony checks my vitals, I keep it vague—a dispute with a source. Firefighters are notorious for circulating rumors. Even in this unimaginable situation, I'm careful not to say anything that might reach other reporters.

"Remember the arson you asked about?" he says. "At the construction site?"

I nod.

"It's not official yet, but investigators are confident it was started by an unhoused person."

I guess I owe Fred Nimby an apology.

"This bump is pretty nasty," Tony says. "How do you feel?"

"Headache, but I'll be okay."

"Swelling is isolated, so that's good," he says. "Are you sleepy?"

"No, I'm fine." But I'm clearly not on my game because I haven't called the newsroom. "Tony, I don't have my phone. Can I borrow yours for a minute?"

When Alex answers, my first words are, "Do not hang up." He sends a photog to the house where Mayor Ace Logan and Councilwoman Zoey Patterson were tied up and Nate to shoot video at my location.

"Your ride is on the way," Alex says. "If you're up for it, we'll interview you here at the station."

"10-4."

I give Tony his phone back.

"If your headache doesn't go away in twenty-four hours, you should follow up. Same if you have trouble staying awake or notice changes in smell or taste."

"Got it."

"To help with swelling, you can ice the bump for ten to twenty minutes. And you need to take it easy."

"Thanks, Tony."

"Hey." He touches my arm. "Take care of yourself."

"Always do."

Two more miles and Faith would've hopped on State Route 51 with a clear, quick path to Sky Harbor Airport. Now, everything she worked for is gone. Even the best lawyers and most lenient judges won't keep her out of prison.

Standing next to the squad car, I call out her name. I want to tell her that she should have come clean to Mayor Logan. He would have understood. But even if he had not, she could've easily found another job with her reputation. She's smart, determined, and ambitious.

Faith lifts her head and looks at me. I can't read her eyes. Keeping a secret can eat you alive, Faith.

"Jolene, what happened?" Nate's running toward me. "Are you okay?" I blink back tears as he hugs me. "You gave us all a scare."

Out of the corner of my eye, I see an officer getting in the squad car. I push Nate away.

"We need video!"

Nate fires up his camera, but the car's already moving. I can't believe I didn't borrow Tony's phone to shoot video.

"Jolene, I'm sorry. I only got a couple seconds where you can make out Faith in the back seat and then the car takes off."

"It's okay. Thanks for getting here so fast."

Nate moves on to shoot video of Faith's car, the open trunk and my blindfold on the ground. A light tap on a horn gets my attention. I want to shake my head in case I'm seeing things but it hurts too bad.

Sexy parks and jogs over to me. "Jolene, you gave us quite a scare. Are you sure you don't want to go to the hospital?"

"No. The paramedic said I'm okay."

"I'll take you back to the station," he says. "But we want you to take it easy. If you're not up for an interview, that's okay. We don't want to pressure you."

I'm afraid my injury affected my hearing because it sounds like Sexy is expressing compassion. On the way to the station, he offers to get me food or something to drink. Future me will regret not ordering an expensive meal but present me wants to get back to reporting.

Bob refuses to let me report on the showdown with the mayor, his chief of staff, and the councilwoman. I'm starting to think the bump on my head may be more serious because I don't put up a fight. I record an interview with our anchor Rick in studio. Elena will report live from the Fourth Avenue jail where Faith was booked, and Gina will be live from the hospital where the mayor and councilwoman were taken.

Sexy sidles up to my desk. "Do you prefer Uber, Lyft, or Waymo?"

"For what?"

"To go home," he says.

"I have my car."

"You are not driving. You've been through an ordeal and need to rest."

"I can get a ride from someone after the newscasts."

"Jolene, you are going home now. Bob's orders."

I pick driverless Waymo so I can be alone with my thoughts.

When it stops outside my apartment, I manage to run inside before my nosy neighbor notices. I should have negotiated a free dinner because my fridge is as bare as a tree during an Omaha winter. Lucky Charms fits the mood and I take the box and milk into the living room to watch the news.

According to a statement from the police department, Faith is being held on assault and kidnapping charges, with more charges expected. For once, Mayor Logan, aka Mr. Unavoidable for Comment, is not talking. But Councilwoman Zoey Patterson is. Unfortunately, not to my station. Of all people, JJ gets an exclusive with her. The councilwoman does a lot of blustering about a political witch hunt and implies the mayor is out to get her without providing proof or details. JJ, not knowing anything about what happened at the house or the attorney general's corruption investigation, asks nothing substantive and her story is a confusing mess. Still, it includes several shots of JJ listening and nodding intently as if she has a clue.

A knock at the door interrupts my channel surfing.

"Oh, my goodness, Jolene, how are you?"

"I'm okay, Norma."

"I saw your station's post on Facebook and was so worried. When you didn't answer your door, I called the station and that nice young man David told me you were on your way home. So, I got to work and made this for you." She presents a rectangular dish. "It's Tater Tot casserole. I hope you like it."

"Thank you, Norma."

The creamy, cheesy concoction warms my hands.

"Oh, you poor thing, your wrists must hurt."

"They're okay. The marks will be gone by morning."

"I'm in shock over everything. I voted for Mayor Ace. I thought he was a decent man."

"Don't draw any conclusions yet. Police have a lot to sort out."

"You're right, dear. But his chief of staff?" She shakes her head. "What a bad seed. She could've killed you."

Tell me something I don't know.

"David said you'll be taking time off to rest. Do you need groceries? I can run to the store tomorrow."

"I'm good, Norma. Your casserole will last several days."

"You let me know if you need anything."

"I will. Thanks again."

I'm tempted to eat straight from the dish but GRANDMA'S RECEIPES reminds me to use a plate. Norma adds bacon to her casserole. And extra cheese. Delicious. After washing my fork and plate, I feed Oscar and wipe off the counter. My hand hovers in the corner. I open Grandma's box and flip to "M." I pull out a photo and sit at the kitchen table.

"This is Emmy. I won her for reporting. It was a huge story. I was even on CNN."

The woman in the photo is holding me on her hip and smiling. I'm three years old.

"I wish I remembered where this was taken. We look happy."

I leave the photo on the table and head to my room. I open the top dresser drawer and reach in the back, under socks. It's the same spot my grandma used in her home. I remove the folder and skim documents I've memorized. Child found outside in the rain wearing only a diaper. Mother tested positive for amphetamines and methamphetamine. Child removed and placed in foster home. Child returned to mother. Child removed and placed in foster home. Child moved to Omaha to live with maternal grandma. The last line in my file from the Illinois Department of Children and Family Services reads, "Whereabouts of biological parents are unknown."

At the table, I prop the photo against Emmy, place the folder next to my laptop, take a deep breath, and begin searching. A cry shatters the silence. I grab a glass, and guzzle water.

Squeezing my eyes, I take a deeper breath. When the shaking subsides, I play my grandma's favorite music. Crystal Gayle is singing about it making her brown eyes blue.

There she is. My laptop reveals my mother's name, age, current and past addresses, even a cell phone number. The tears come when I see the list of relatives. I'm not there. I click on three names connected to my mom but no one sounds familiar and their locations don't overlap with any of her addresses. Not surprising since it's a free search.

I use an app to call the cell number so it will go straight to voice mail. I'm not ready to talk to the woman who abandoned me more than twenty years ago, but I want to hear her voice. Instead, I listen to a computer tell me the number is no longer in service.

I strike out on Instagram, Threads, and X.

"Come on, Facebook."

The results are overwhelming using only her name and I add her last known city. Wiping away tears, I scan the profile pics. No one stands out because I have no idea what she looks like now. If my heart controlled my hands, I would've logged off long ago. It can't handle more cracks. And then my heart stops.

Her profile photo is from her high school graduation. She looks like me. Or I look like her. Lynn Anderson is singing now, about how she never promised me a rose garden.

My mom's account doesn't allow me to access her photos, friends, or personal details. Her last public post was two years ago. A sunrise photo with the caption: "Every day is a second chance."

I wrap ice cubes in paper towels and press it against my bump. The cold jolt to my head is a welcome contrast to the heavy ache in my chest. I turn off the music, blow my nose, and come up with a plan. Based on the people search site, her last address was a shelter for women. It's past office hours, but shelters don't operate like banks. Someone will answer the phone.

"I'm sorry, we are unable to share any personal information about our guests."

"I understand, but it's my mother. I don't need to talk to her. Can you just tell me if she's there?"

I'm on hold long enough to dig through my work tote, find two mini bags of M&M's from Elena's jar, and eat every piece.

"Thanks for your patience. I'm new and had to check with someone. Based on our records, it does not appear that your mother is a current guest here."

"Current? So, she's been a guest in the past?"

"We are duty bound to protect everyone's privacy." It sounds like she's reading a document. "Some guests have fled domestic violence situations, some are avoiding bad actors in their recovery, and some are starting a new life. I'm sure you can appreciate our desire to support our guests so they can regain their independence."

My mom was there. No idea how long ago. I find three other women's shelters in the area and the responses are the same. But one person hesitates. She's my last chance.

"Sherese, I appreciate you taking time with me and I respect your position. What if I mail a letter? Can you make sure she gets it?"

"Our location is confidential," Sherese says. "And to be clear, I never said your mother is here."

"I understand the need for confidentiality. I have no desire to create drama or disrupt my mother's recovery. This is the closest I've ever—"

My voice breaks. And clarity comes. It's not meant to be.

"I'm sorry," I say. "Forget it. Thank you for your help."

The photo goes back inside the box and my case file goes back—way back—in the drawer. I'm about to jump in the shower when my phone rings. I recognize the 212 area code, but not the number.

"Hello again, it's Sherese."

"You caught me off guard with the New York area code."

"I'm using my cell," she says. "And you never got this call. Okay?"

I rub my stomach and try to breathe. I'm not ready.

"I looked you up," Sherese says. "Your reporting is impressive. You could probably find your mother on your own if you kept searching."

If that's what you called to tell me, I'm not interested.

"She could probably contact you, too, if she wanted. Do you understand?"

Sherese has given my number to my mom.

"I understand. It's her choice whether to contact me. I'm glad she has my information."

"Yes, she does," Sherese says. "But no promises."

No problem. I'm used to it.

CHAPTER
32

Two weeks later

It's my final visit to the Home Sweet Home Mobile Home Park. A crowd has gathered at the entrance, united for a cause, separated by their jobs. Residents and people who worked with Carlos stand on one side, while lawyers and architects representing the developer assemble on the other. In the middle, a handful of city employees are listening to Mayor Ace Logan.

"Thank you all for coming," he says. "This is a special day for our city."

He announces the developer has agreed to designate twenty percent of the luxury apartments for low-income residents.

"These homes will be the same quality as the others," he says. "And that's not all. The development will honor the legacy of Carlos Rios by building a garden in his name. It will replace the unsafe pool and be the first thing residents see when they arrive home. Carlos's garden will be a beautiful amenity and daily reminder of a man who devoted his life to his community and family, including his grandmother, who has lived here for fifty years. I invited Mrs. Rios to share a few words and she graciously agreed."

Logan leads the applause and steps away from the podium. Nana moves with a calm authority. She's the main attraction. Her words will be the ones people remember. Even the suits have put away their phones.

"Muchas gracias. Thank you, Mayor." Nana takes in the cameras.

Carlos's story is no longer mine alone. When the mayor's brother was arrested for cutting Carlos's brakes, every local station jumped on it. Some national outlets, too. While Nana told me she has been unable to forgive Reggie Logan for causing Carlos's crash, she places no blame on Mayor Logan. "No family is perfect," she said. But her grandson, Carlos, came closer to perfection than most people.

Nana releases a long breath and begins. "I would give anything to have Carlos with us. We all would." She fingers a crucifix necklace. "He knows how much we love and miss him. Our loss is your loss. Carlos was the kind of man you wanted to be your friend." She smiles at Carlos's wife and children. "He was the kind of man you wanted to be your father and your husband. Carlos was the kind of man we need more of. He overcame a troubled childhood and started his own business. Carlos worked very, very hard to take care of his family. But he always made time for us. Some of my favorite memories are Sundays after church." She closes her eyes and parts her lips, as if traveling back in time. "Carlos would play soccer with the children and help with their homework. He always set the table for our family dinners." She opens her eyes and beams. "Carlos loved my pozole almost as much as I loved him." She makes the sign of the cross. "I appreciate Carlos being honored in the neighborhood where he grew up. Mijo never really left, because he visited me almost every day. Thank you for remembering Carlos. It is very important to me and our family."

After taking photos with Nana's family by a sign that

reads FUTURE SITE OF CARLOS'S GARDEN, Mayor Logan pulls me aside.

"You're moving good for someone who was shot in the foot," I say.

"Grazed," he says. "I was blessed with a fast recovery. How are you doing?"

"I'd be better if you'd given me the garden information to report first. I earned it, don't you think?"

"Isn't it better to share Carlos's legacy as widely as possible?" He flashes the smile that clinched five consecutive elections.

"I heard your TV show may have fallen through." I'm being kind. The production company and network dropped Logan at the first whiff of controversy.

"My agent said we could fight it. After all, I've been cleared of any wrongdoing. But I have no desire to be dragged into the underbelly of Hollywood. I'm going to keep doing what I do best: bring people together." He spreads his arms, taking in the surroundings. "Like this. Here's an exclusive for you: mayor retires to form a coalition that will work with neighborhoods and developers to improve the process and build strong communities that respect the past and embrace the future."

"Doesn't sound like retirement."

"It's my calling." His expression morphs from campaigner to contemplator. "The days ahead will be challenging. Knowing what my brother did has been . . . testing my faith, to say the least. I will always love him. And forever wonder why he did not come to me for help. I feel the same about Faith. How could she hire my brother for such a despicable act? And to hire a hitman to kill Rich Gains."

"Faith was your chief of staff for many years. I can't imagine what you're feeling."

"In a way, I failed her. I wish she'd trusted me enough to talk about her past. I like to think I would've shown compassion. We all have fumbles and missteps. In her case, it was tragic and altered lives forever." He gives a little headshake. "And then there are other misjudgments, like mentoring a council member who disappoints you in the most horrible way."

"It sounds like Zoey Patterson is trying to portray herself as the victim, like she was being set up to take bribes."

It's information I get from other people's reporting because my longtime source, Jim Miranda, still won't talk to me. It's been two weeks and I've left three voice mails. I want Jim to know I thought about him when I didn't know if I would make it out alive. I miss his scoops and friendship.

"The courts will certainly be busy and so will I," Logan says. "As I told CNN, I was shocked by my brother's actions. He must face the consequences. At the same time, I will not abandon my family. I'll support him—and Carlos's family—any way I can." He offers a handshake. "Jolene, I want to congratulate you on a job well done. The people of Phoenix deserve an open, transparent government and your reporting is making a difference."

You shouldn't go into journalism for praise and awards—although verbal recognition and winning an Emmy are appreciated. Journalism is meant to shine a light on wrongdoing, share information about issues that impact the community, give voice to people who don't have political clout, economic power, or a celebrity platform. I am grateful to have shared Carlos's story.

"Jolene, I'm happy to see you again." Nana squeezes my hands and kisses my cheek.

Half the residents of Home Sweet Home Mobile Home Park have left, and those remaining have two months to find housing. Nana tells me she's moving next week.

"How do you feel about leaving your home?"

"Mijo was right. Home is not a building. Home is where your family is. I will take the flower garden I built with my husband to my new home."

A young man approaches and says, "Nana, excuse me for interrupting. I want to remind you about our meeting with the architect to review the garden designs. Please let me know when you are ready."

Nana waves him closer. "Mijo, come. Meet Jolene Garcia. She is the reporter who would not give up on your father. Jolene, this is Carlos, Jr."

"It's nice to meet in person," I say. "We spoke on the phone and you sent a photo and family statement after your father passed. It was an honor to meet him."

"He was one of a kind," Carlos, Jr. says. "I know everyone thinks their dad is special, but my dad really was."

My eyes burn, and before I can put on my sunglasses, Nana pulls me in and hugs me tight. "Thank you, mija."

Carlos, Jr. guides Nana to the old swimming pool where a man is smoothing blueprints on a table. A young girl runs over, curious about what the grown-ups are planning. She plants her elbows on the table and rests her face in her hands.

"Lola!" A woman hurries to the table, offering an apology. Nana smiles, shakes her head, nothing to be sorry about. The girl giggles as the woman lifts her up for a closer look. As I snap photos to post to social media, my phone rings.

It's area code 212. Sherese is calling from the women's shelter. Or maybe she's letting my mom use her phone. After a lifetime of uncertainty, I could finally get answers. Nerves jitter in my chest. Do I want the answers? Surrounded by cameras is not how I pictured a reunion call. Shaky legs lead me to a gravel patch. I've made it this far not knowing why she abandoned me. Will she plead for forgiveness? I'll let it go to voice mail. She doesn't deserve my response on her first try. After all,

I've gone my entire life without her. She can wait until I'm in a better place. But my mom may never call again. I close my eyes and say, "Hello?"

"Hi, is this Jolene?"

I fall against a car to keep from buckling. My mom's voice is crisp and clear. She must finally have her shit together. This is actually happening.

"Yes, this is Jolene."

"I'm Kate Taylor with the network news."

A stew of disappointment and relief sloshes in my stomach. The network must want video of the mayor's announcement so they can run an update.

"We've been following your work," Kate says.

"Do you want the same story I file locally or something different?"

"My apologies for the misunderstanding. I handle talent acquisition for the network. We'd like to fly you to New York to discuss a correspondent position, if you're interested."

For a moment, I can't speak. The girl who worried where her next meal would come from, who grew up not knowing if her parents were dead or alive, who never knew if her grandma truly loved her, is getting a once-in-a-lifetime opportunity to fulfill her dream.

"Yes," I say. "I would love to come to New York."

ACKNOWLEDGMENTS

Although this book is a work of fiction, the stuck elevator really happened. Credit to Dustin Gardiner for reporting it first. But the mayor in my story is made up. So are all the other characters. Throughout my reporting career, I worked with a variety of dedicated public servants. Some of their names are blended on these pages. Same with reporters, photographers, anchors, producers, and news directors. For everyone along my journalism path—whether we connected, clashed, or both—thank you for experiences that have influenced my writing.

Thank you to my agent Jill Marsal and my editor Madeline Houpt for guiding me in the right direction. I'm fortunate to have an incredible team at Minotaur Books/St. Martin's Publishing Group, including Kelley Ragland, David Rotstein, Meryl Levavi, Alisa Trager, Laurie Henderson, Lena Shekhter, NaNá Stoelzle, Jennifer Rohrbach, Hector DeJean, and Sara Beth Haring. Thank you all for making my childhood dream come true. Dreamscape Media, it's been a treat.

Always and forever on my preorder list are Kellye Garrett and Mia P. Manansala. Thank you for the early encouragement that kept me writing. J.A. Jance, Hank Phillippi Ryan, Linda Castillo, and Lee Goldberg, your generosity means the world.

Sending Arizona love to Allison Brennan, Jenn McKinlay, Paige Shelton, and Jen Johans.

Barbara Peters, I've expressed gratitude countless times and I mean it every single time. The Poisoned Pen Bookstore feels like my second home thanks to you, Patrick Millikin, Patrick King, John Charles, Bill Smith, Karen Shaver, and the rest of the gang.

A special thanks to Changing Hands Bookstore, The Mysterious Bookshop, Newnan Book Company, Wordsmith Bookshoppe, and other independent bookstores that embraced my debut.

Many thanks to Michelle Beaver, Jessica Boehm, Cynthia Chow, Whitney Clark, Oline Cogdill, Mariana Dale, Nancy Dudenhoefer, Tim Eigo, Olivia Fierro, Abbigail Glen, Tyler Gorton, Laura Hahnefeld, Lesa Holstine, Terik King, Casey Kuhn, Leah LeMoine, Dru Ann Love, Daryl Maxwell, Robin McClain, Neil Nyren, Rachele Pang, Rebekah Sanders, Patty Talahongva, Stephanie Utkin, Henrietta Verma, Vanessa Weber, Phelicity Wiese, Lawan Williams, and Kristopher Zgorski.

To the booksellers, librarians, reviewers, bloggers, Bookstagrammers, and book clubs who support my writing, I can't thank you enough. I wish I could list every person, but please know my gratitude runs deep.

Thank you to my grand-staircase step-counters, Stephanie Bracken, Dan Wilson, and Nick Valenzuela. We all came up with the same number!

I'm grateful to the Tucson Festival of Books, especially Bill Finley, along with One Book Yuma and Julieta Calderón. Groups that have inspired and supported me include Sisters in Crime, Mystery Writers of America, International Thriller Writers, Left Coast Crime, Malice Domestic, PEN Arizona, and the Society of Professional Journalists Valley of the Sun Chapter.

Phillip Estes, I can never repay you for responding to my panicked texts every time I hit the wrong key, convinced I'd deleted my manuscript. Ellys Cortez, you're a great cheerleader. Mark and Brixton, thank you for reminding me to play. Bentley, you were the best writing partner ever. I miss you.

Books have been my friends my entire life. To be a reader who writes is an honor and a privilege. When someone shares a scene or a line that made them think or smile, it moves me to tears. Whether you've been with me from the beginning or this is your first time reading one of my books, I offer a heartfelt thank you.

ABOUT THE AUTHOR

Lauren Gilger

Christina Estes is an award-winning reporter who spent more than twenty years covering crime, public policy, and business for TV and radio stations in Phoenix, Arizona. Her reporting has appeared on CBS and National Public Radio. Christina's career inspired her mystery series featuring reporter Jolene Garcia, which began with *Off the Air,* winner of the Tony Hillerman Prize for Best First Mystery Set in the Southwest.

Visit her at www.christinaestes.com.